War's Last Dance

by

Julia Underwood

For Emma
with best wishes
Julia Underwood

Published in 2013 by FeedARead.com Publishing – Arts Council funded

First published 2013 by Endeavour Press Ltd.

A CIP catalogue record for this title is available from the British Library.

Dedicated to Paul

Contra mundum

Chapter One

London, August 1945

Isabel stood immobile in the middle of the street. A flimsy airmail letter fluttered in her hand. Only the chirrup of the bell on the postman's bike broke the silence of the airless street. Wheels wobbling, it rounded the corner to disappear into the suburban maze. The perfume of roses, over-ripe vegetation and backyard chickens scented the sultry atmosphere. The dazzling sun baked the dusty gardens, crimping the edges of leaves and petals into crisp frills.

Isabel's sandals stuck to the molten tarmac; treacly residue clung to the heels. Her shriek pierced the air. She rushed from the road and in through the gate of her little rented house, hardly aware of what she was doing. It felt as if someone had punched her in the chest, knocking the air from her lungs.

'Penny, Penny! Daddy's coming home!' Isabel waved the letter, with the familiar BFPO sign on the envelope, around her head like a flag. Her eyes swam with tears of relief; the pupils wide as a cat's at dusk. Her hand shook as she read the contents again. She tried to absorb the message, to register its meaning, as she stumbled into the house. For once the censor had not defaced the letter with the heavy black lines that gave earlier communications the look of a school essay corrected by a stern teacher. A letter at last! They hadn't heard from Bill for months, even after the War ended in May amidst universal jubilation.

Throughout the war news from abroad had arrived belated and haphazard. Anticipated with foreboding or eagerness, it had broken the spirit with despair or filled the recipient with hope. Now, finally, it brought joy; this could mean an end to loneliness, to drudgery and a meaningless grey existence.

'He'll be back from Italy next week!'

Isabel slumped onto the shabby sofa, teasing her fingers through her dark curls as she read the letter again. The drab uncut-moquette rubbed like sandpaper against the bare skin of her legs; she wore no stockings during the day. Her head span with giddiness. Could happiness make you giddy?

She panicked for a moment. Oh God, what will it be like? When you haven't seen someone for ... two years since his last home leave? He might seem like a stranger. Trepidation and delight tumbled through her head. She drew her knees up and hugged them close to stop her fears from overwhelming her.

The need for Bill that she had suppressed for so long came flooding back in a great warm tide. A shiver of desire ran through her as she imagined his arms around her, his warm, strong body pressed against hers, his kisses on her face. A soft breeze of a sigh escaped her lips. I can't believe it! He'll be home in just a week; the wait will seem like an eternity.

Penny had followed her mother from the front door, where she had been watching. She advanced shyly, clearly not comprehending. A straight bob framed her heart-shaped face and, as usual, a thumb was stuck in her mouth. She watched Isabel dubiously and came close to her knees.

'We're to meet him off the train in Town,' Isabel said, grabbing the perplexed Penny onto her lap and giving her taut little body a huge hug. 'Oh, darling, isn't it exciting?' She rubbed their cheeks together, realising Penny could have no concept of what this news might mean.

Four-year-old Penny regarded her mother in silence; a worried frown creased her porcelain-smooth brow. Something unusual was happening. Trying to capture Isabel's mood, she wriggled off her lap.

'Daddy's coming home!' she repeated, turning a ragged circle around the settee, waving her arms above her head as she attempted to generate some excitement. Fondly Isabel watched the child run off through the open French door into the garden, aware that she couldn't be expected to join wholeheartedly in her own joy. The poor mite was a baby; she'd never known her father. She must be thinking – who is this Daddy person of whom I have heard so much yet seen so little? Isabel knew she had to reassure the child that her world would be unchanged, but now she would have two parents to dote on her; even to spoil her a little.

As soon as she had recovered from the surprise, Isabel dashed round to her sister's house. Doris lived only a couple of streets away with George, her husband, and their two lively boys.

'Doris!' she called from the path at the side of the house. Not waiting for a reply, she rushed straight into the kitchen through the back door. 'Bill's coming home. Next week. The postman just brought the letter.'

'Ah, that's wonderful! You'll be wanting some help then, to get ready for him,' Doris said, observing the grin on her sister's face and wiping her flour-covered hands on her apron. 'Come and sit down, let's have a cup of tea and talk about it.'

Isabel meekly did as she was told and sat at the kitchen table, pushing aside the pastry-making paraphernalia. 'Do you think Grace will be able to help too?'

'Of course, she's not too busy at the Post Office at the moment,' Doris replied, ruthlessly disregarding the fact that the third sister frequently worked double shifts due to the shortage of qualified staff.

A frantic week of preparations followed the news of Bill's imminent arrival. The modest little house where she lived with Penny needed a thorough spring clean to satisfy Isabel. She wanted everything to be perfect. She needn't have worried, her two sisters eagerly mucked in. Their merriment filled the house with laughter. Always a garrulous trio, they accompanied their work with nonstop chatter.

'Let's get on with it then! There's no point just sitting around talking about it.'

'No slacking, you. Give it some more elbow grease!'

'I'm so grateful – you're a couple of godsends!'

'Don't be daft, Bella! We don't mind. We've got to make the place spotless for Bill. Lots of spit and polish, he'll be used to that.' The sisters laughed with a hint of irony, for they viewed with some mirth their elder sister's view that Bill was a superior being worthy only of the best in all things.

'Stop hanging around like a wet week – go and make another cup of tea, we're gasping.'

They cheerfully tied floral pinafores over their frocks, round slim waists; figures kept trim by the deprivations of war. They arranged scarves about their permed curls - Doris's blonde and Grace's as ginger as the marigolds in the garden - turban-like with a bow at the front. Behind the semi-detached cottage – two up, two down with a tiny kitchen and inadequate bathroom – stood a pocket-sized garden given over almost entirely to growing vegetables to supplement the rations. The neat rows of stately leeks, feathery carrot tops, purple beetroot leaves and chubby dowager cabbages elbowing out the rest, represented a tribute to hard work. Established by George and rigorously maintained; everyone shared in the crop. The sisters weeded and hoed and harvested whatever produce was available.

'There's enough cabbages here for a small army!' said Doris.

George normally put his strong back and arms into the gardening. In a restricted occupation, he hadn't been in the fighting War. He worked as an unpaid air-raid warden and on the railway, Southern Region. 'Someone's got to run it,' he said with a note of pride. But they all knew he still felt a sense of guilt at being relatively safe at home whilst his contemporaries lost their lives all over the world. His guilt was particularly unjustified as he suffered from chronic asthma and would have been rejected for service in any case. He came to help the women with the heavy work whenever he could.

The girls vigorously polished the windows with vinegar and old Daily Mirrors until they gleamed. They recoated the doorstep with the red tile paint their Dad had found in his shed. They collected as many clothes-ration coupons as could be mustered and piled them on the oilcloth surface of Isabel's kitchen table.

'I was saving some coupons for new shoes for Jimmy,' said Doris, 'He'll have to wait till next month. His sandals still fit him. You have 'em, love. Go up to town and get something nice. No need to go to Smartwear for this, it's a special occasion!'

You could buy an outfit and pay on credit, one and six a week until it was yours, at Smartwear, a clothing store in Watford, near the hospital. This innovative shop supplied many an emergency outfit.

During the bleakly frugal years of the War their needs had been basic. "Make do and Mend" became their watchword. They seldom used all the clothes coupons issued but shared garments amongst each other and passed the older children's cast-offs down to the younger ones. Luckily Penny was too young to mind wearing boy's shorts and sandals. So now they could scrape together surprisingly quickly enough clothes coupons for an outfit and food ration points for a feast for the homecoming. The little buff books with "Ministry of Food" written on the cover were well-thumbed and full of retailer's stamps where they had been cancelled.

'We'll make a cake with the sugar and butter from the last Australian food parcel. Is there any dried fruit left?' Doris asked.

These welcome gifts from Bill's relatives in Australia arrived at irregular intervals. After months at sea they often arrived battered and dented and sometimes crushed beyond usefulness. But the family fell on the contents with delight. Packets of dried fruit, tins of butter and boiled sweets for the children - often crystallised through long exposure to the air but delicious nonetheless - all contained in these life-enhancing packages. Tinned hams and tongue, dried egg – riches to those used to a measly ration of one egg per week, and those usually went to the children, and treasure for those preparing a welcome-home banquet.

A dry August; true to the season. Brilliant sunshine blazed on the little house and raised their spirits. The air and the neglected shrubs buzzed, thick with bees. The fragrance of roses and honeysuckle mingled with the sooty aroma from the nearby railway line and the less pleasant odour of the canal at the end of the garden. George spotted a rat or two and contemplated getting a dog to keep them at bay. But what would they feed it on?

Their own meagre rations wouldn't stretch to the nourishment of even the smallest dog.

'Well, at least we've got a bit of summer for once.' The sisters basked in the unaccustomed rays when they took a moment to rest.

Isabel set an old galvanised bathtub on the tiny patch of grass not dug up for vegetables and filled it with water. Penny and Doris's two boys splashed around in it for hours shrieking with laughter.

'Mummy! Jimmy's going to put worms down my neck!'

'She splashed me!' her tormentor justified. Their shouting and squabbling split the viscous air of the heat wave. The children's skin tanned to a golden brown.

Grace, a prodigious knitter, constructed a new cardigan for Penny from one of her own, unravelled and knitted up again in an intricate Fair Isle pattern with coloured scraps left in her bulging knitting bag.

'You're so clever,' Isabel said, holding it up to the light, 'you've got such patience. I'd never be able to do that. Penny will love it!' She gently folded it away for Penny to wear when they went to meet Bill.

Bill sent a parcel for Penny with some special dresses from Italy, where he was serving at the War's end, beautifully sewn with smocking and frills in delicate fabrics. Florals and gauzes, checks and stripes adorned with intricate embroidery. Penny greeted them with suspicion as she stroked their fragility with careful fingers.

'I won't have to wear them every day will I, Mummy?

'No, darling, just for best.'

Elaborately embellished underwear, French knickers, slips, camisoles and nightgowns, light as spider's webs, accompanied Penny's frocks. Made by Italian nuns out of parachute silk, Bill explained in his letter. Isabel marvelled at the sheer delicate luxury of them. Twirling in front of her mirror in the diaphanous, cloud-soft fabric she treasured in anticipation the time when she would be able to wear them for him. Touched by his thoughtfulness she still felt a little guilty about possessing such luxury in these days of austerity. So much to treasure. Lovingly she packed everything away in tissue paper to await his return.

'Soon, my love,' she whispered to herself, 'you'll be here again.'

She gazed out of her bedroom window into the bright summer sky, imagining the joy of their reunion. Surely, before too long, life would be back to normal and they could be happy again.

Chapter Two

London, September 1945

An ancient alleyway two doors away from the house led to the bridge across the foetid canal and to the station. They'd made their way here early, not wishing to be late. From the platform, holding Penny's hand close beside her, Isabel could see into the back garden of her home. From that angle it appeared eerily alien; a place where a stranger lived. But this had been her home for most of the war.

They had been evacuated for a few months in 1941, with Penny still a baby. They'd been billeted in the country somewhere in Yorkshire, but Isabel, a city girl at heart, hated it. Homesickness struck her and she missed her family. Her dour hosts had considered their guest flighty and much too concerned with her appearance even though she made herself useful around the farm; milking and mucking out the cows, and looking after the hens. A minor dispute ended in bitter recriminations and after a mere six weeks in the country Isabel returned to London. She would rather take her chances against the bombs than stay where she was not appreciated.

'A couple of old skinflints,' she told Doris. 'Wouldn't let us have any butter, insisted we used that horrible marge, even though I was milking the bloody cows for them!'

The housing shortage, due to the bombing, meant that there was little choice of homes for a mother of one. Bill was outraged at the ordinariness of the little house she ended up with; not at all what he was accustomed to.

'I can't have a wife of mine living in a place like this!' he'd said when he first saw it, during his brief leave shortly after Penny's first birthday.

'A wife of mine,' mimicked Isabel. 'How many wives have you got? Anyway, don't be silly; we were lucky to get it. And that was only because George knows someone on the housing committee. I'm very lucky that I didn't have to go back to live with Mum. It's perfect for us, near the family. I'll soon make it nicer. I think we're lucky, we could have ended up in a Bump-your-Head.'

Many homeless families were billeted in these pre-fabricated buildings – constructed mainly of asbestos sheeting and corrugated iron, whose curved ceilings seemed so low that they were given this descriptive name. They were only supposed to be a temporary measure until better accommodation became available, but Isabel knew people who had already lived in one for years. Some people ended up in converted railway carriages, marooned in sidings, like long caravans, and they seemed to enjoy this bizarre way of life.

'You can make them quite cosy,' someone assured her.

Isabel and Penny had survived, which was more than could be said of many people. Isabel shuddered at the memory of the relentless bombing, the lives that had been lost. A neighbour, Mrs Stephens, and all four of her children died one night in a devastating, random act of violence that had hardly affected anyone else in the street except for a few broken windows and cracked plaster. It seemed completely arbitrary; it could have been any one of the houses in the road. How sorry they felt for her husband, still serving somewhere on the Eastern Front and not aware of the tragedy.

For Isabel it was just a matter of waiting; waiting for the War to end and for Bill to come home. At least she had known that he was safe. As an intelligence officer he never served at the front line, in the way of indiscriminate death. She had never been forced to experience that paralysing fear, like an intractable pain, that she witnessed afflicting other wives terrified that their husbands would never return, that the telegram changing their lives forever would one day be thrust into their hands by the embarrassed telegraph boy.

She travelled up to Kensington on the train to do her shopping, leaving Penny with Doris for the day. She visited Barkers, the genteel department store patronised by her mother-in-law when she wasn't in Harrods. Not without a pang of remorse at the expense, four guineas altogether, as well as over two hundred clothes coupons, Isabel bought a suit, in lovely cornflower-blue wool; skirt and jacket and a saucy hat, fine black straw with a pretty curved brim and a red ostrich feather that curved vivaciously over one eyebrow. How lucky to have such a generous family, thought Isabel as she stroked the fabric of the skirt down over her slim hips.

'Give over, Bella,' they said before she went, 'we're not going anywhere in particular. No need for us to dress up. You buy yourself something nice. You deserve it. '

The preparations for Bill's return nearly wore them out. But the little rented house sparkled, the larder bulged with festive food and Isabel knew she looked as well turned out as she could in the circumstances. I don't want him to think I've been letting myself go whilst he's been away, she thought.

All ready; at last the day arrived. Isabel and Penny bathed and preened, preparing themselves for the reunion. Anticipation and euphoria almost took their breath away. Penny was caught up in the whirlwind of her mother's energy, her small frame so taut with excitement that she tended to burst into fits of giggles for no reason at all and dance around in circles with her waving arms outstretched like a frenzied bird.

'You're daft as a brush, you are,' Isabel laughed.

In a flurry they caught the sooty train to Victoria. They had a compartment to themselves, insulated from the world. Isabel chatted to Penny all the way, happier and more vital than she had been in ages. Her eyes sparkled and her fair, clear skin glowed under a thin layer of Coty powder.

'You're looking lovely, Bella,' shouted Jim, the stationmaster, an old friend. 'Going to meet the old man?'

'Yes,' Isabel called back. 'He's coming into Victoria.'

The wooden doors of the train carriage banged closed behind them and they attempted to relax on the itchy seats. The compartment had a door at each end from which you could step directly onto the platform at your destination; no corridor ran from end to end of the carriage. Black and white photographs of English seaside resorts in earlier times decorated the walls of the compartment, between the seats and the luggage racks, whose twine mesh hung down resembling an abandoned collection of string bags. The ladies in the photos wore long dresses with bustles and large feathered hats. On the beaches stood wooden wheeled bathing machines to protect the modesty of the lady bathers.

The feather on her own hat bobbed and waved as Isabel told Penny all about the times before the War. How she had met her father; their life together. Penny had heard it all before but never tired of listening to the stories.

'London was such a thrilling place then, Penny, beautiful, before the bombs. Glamorous and gay. Nightclubs, restaurants, dancing. We'd go to the theatre and out to dinner with friends. The Trocadero, Quaglinos, Simpsons, even the Savoy sometimes if we were feeling flush. Daddy and I had some wonderful times.'

Her face glowed with the memory of their unforeseen happiness. A bubble of elation built in her stomach, almost making her feel nauseated. She could hardly contain her excitement. Soon she would be reunited with Bill, after all this time. Everything would be all right again. The journey flew by and they soon reached Victoria station.

The smoky terminus swarmed with humanity. Demobilisation from Europe began sluggishly in July and soldiers in the first groups were arriving home; those who had been in the forces for the longest; often those who volunteered in the early days of the War. Bill was not one of those being demobbed, however; he had to return to his new posting after this leave.

How on earth are we going to find Bill in this crush? Isabel thought. Crowds of soldiers began to alight from trains, bent with tiredness and burdened with heavy kit like punch bags balanced on their shoulders as well as back-packs and other baggage. They all looked very similar in their uniforms, how could you pick out an individual in this crowd? The waiting families surged forward in a great wave. Many of them quickly found their loved ones and drew them into their embraces.

Cries of joy, kisses and hugs; laughter and tears. Safe home from the War! Men, relief and joy written on their features, jumped onto the platforms and swarmed around the station, searching for familiar faces. When they found their families they swung the pretty ladies in their new clothes off their feet; clasped the children in their arms; greeted their siblings with embarrassed kisses. They kept coming in joyous waves. But Bill wasn't amongst them.

At one point Isabel saw a man in a Captain's uniform that resembled him and she ran up.

'Bill, Bill…' she called, her hand outstretched to touch him, but when the man turned around it was a stranger, smiling apologetically. She dropped her arm and moved away, disappointment a deadening weight on her heart.

They waited until the last wooden doors slammed, the heavy latches clicked into place and the trains began to shunt away. They were not the only disappointed ones, the ones who slowly and reluctantly turned to go home without their sweethearts and husbands, not quite believing that there was no-one there for them to greet.

The journey home seemed longer and much, much slower. Isabel sat in a dejected huddle gazing blindly out of the sooty window. Penny found nothing to say but huddled up against her mother on the seat whose rough surface irritated her bare legs. Isabel stared out of the window, her face drawn. The ugly rear walls of the suburban houses, stained with railway soot, stared back. Occasionally there yawned a great gap where a bomb had demolished a few, the edges of torn wallpaper poignant against the shattered brick. Broken shards of abandoned furniture, banisters wrenched from their moorings, staircases hanging precariously in open space. Empty gaping fireplaces that would never see a comforting blaze again; the remnants of a human tragedy.

Gazing at this scene, Isabel remembered how it had ended. The killing and terrifying bombing had continued almost to the end of the war. Towards the end 'doodle-bugs', as they called them, the dreaded V2 rockets, terrified them more than anything. They whizzed silently out of the skies until they emitted a high-pitched whistle before they hit their target. It all finished in

March when a rocket hit a block of flats in the East End. About nine hours later another burst harmlessly in Kent. That was the end of them, to everyone's extreme relief.

For four more days Isabel and Penny dressed up and travelled to Victoria to meet the troop trains. Disappointment met them every time. No sign of Bill. No one could help them. They could get no news, no information. It was impossible to contact anyone still abroad. The co-ordinator always said the same thing after the futile scanning of his list.

'Come again tomorrow, ducks. Maybe he'll be with the next lot,' he dismissed them gently.

But amongst the thousands of men returning from the War, Bill never arrived. Isabel began to despair, frantically trying to think why this was happening. Oh, God, perhaps he's not coming back after all. Perhaps he had to stay on in Italy. Maybe he wanted to. Perhaps he doesn't want us anymore. Her worries became more and more irrational.

He's found another woman; those Italian women are so glamorous. But then why did he write to say he was coming home? Her thoughts went round and round in an agonising loop. She hardly slept and as a consequence she felt exhausted, her limbs weak and trembling, her eyes dry and prickling, with dark rings beneath them.

The next day they decided not to go up to London.

'I couldn't bear that awful journey again; all that way for nothing. Come on, Pen, let's treat ourselves. We'll go to the pictures in Wembley and then have tea at Fullers.'

They had grown weary of the futile pilgrimage into town; the sad trek home. Isabel knew Penny loved the cinema and especially relished the thought of the tea shop's iced coffee cake, which, if you were lucky with your slice, might have a walnut on top. That seemed a much more interesting proposition.

'Oh yes, let's, Mummy.'

They left a key with their neighbour, 'just in case,' and set out.

They saw "Lassie Come Home" at the Odeon. Tears streamed down their faces in the sad bits. Penny loved the dog and the poignancy of the story.

'Couldn't we have a dog Mummy, please?' she wheedled.

She was chattering, full of the film and coffee cake, when they arrived home. Isabel put her key in the front door, preparing a negative reply – a dog, oh horror!

'Wasn't it awful, Mummy, when they thought Lassie was lost?'

Penny's dark eyes popped wide open - for a man sat on the bottom step - a man with no shoes on and his shirt unbuttoned. She glared at him disapprovingly from behind her mother's skirt, shyness, disgust and burning curiosity battling within her. Penny had hardly ever seen a man up close before, except for Granddad, and he was old and sick, and Uncle George. This man wasn't old and bent, but tall and strong, tanned and healthy. Penny shrank further behind Isabel's skirt.

Isabel flew forward, dropping Penny's hand, her handbag and the Evening News bought at the station.

'Oh, my God!' she shrieked. Her cheeks glowed and she felt as if her heart would explode. At last!

'Darling,' the man stood up, grinning, stretching out his arms, wide and alive.

'Bill, oh, Bill!' she cried as they kissed and hugged and laughed. Isabel's hat veered to a silly angle on her head, threatening to fall.

'My God, you look beautiful,' he breathed between embraces. 'How I've longed for this moment.'

Penny loitered, shocked and bemused on the doormat, overcome by embarrassment. Isabel released the man and turned towards her.

'Penny - this is your Daddy.' At last Isabel had remembered her. Still breathless from Bill's welcome, she pulled Penny forward and crouched down to where Bill sat once more on the bottom step. She introduced her gently to the father she was really meeting for the first time. Penny couldn't be expected to remember him, as she had only been a baby when he had last seen her. He was as strange to her as a passer-by in the street. Penny approached him doubtfully, not sure how to react to this male phenomenon. She glanced over her shoulder at Isabel and registered the reassuring smile on her mother's face as she pushed her forward.

'Penny! What a big girl! Come here, darling.'

He leaned forward and swept her up into his arms and kissed her, but his chin bristled and she didn't like the way he smelled. She pushed him away without a word; dropped to the floor and rushed past him. Ran up to her room. Horrid man, she thought.

Penny's prime position in her mother's time and affection was abruptly usurped. During the air raids she and Isabel slept in a nest of eiderdowns and pillows in the sturdy steel cage built under the oak dining table, the Morrison shelter, until eventually, bored with the discomfort of that, they recklessly snuggled together in the big bed upstairs. Now he slept in that bed - every night. Penny could hear them in there late, before she fell asleep. They talked a lot and often they giggled. She could hear the old bedsprings creaking. They seemed to be having fun. Penny felt left out and jealous.

'When's That Man going away, Mummy?' she asked indignantly. A question greeted with much mirth by the grown-ups and repeated to anyone who would listen. Only Nanny, Isabel's mother, understood.

'She's only four - of course the poor little blighter's going to 'ave her nose put out of joint. She's always 'ad your undivided attention. She don't know the man,' she said. Nanny had her reasons for sounding bitter; she didn't much like her daughter's choice of husband.

'Thinks 'e's too good for us. No good'll come of it, mark my words,' she'd prophesied. 'He won't like that poxy little house after what he's used too. Servants, too I wouldn't wonder.' She illustrated her disapproval with a dramatic sniff.

Isabel admitted that sometimes Bill's presence was irksome. It was lovely to have him back, of course. But she had got so used to being alone with Penny, their routines; doing just what she wanted. Bill's presence frequently intruded and he seemed to have changed. He was no longer as relaxed and assured as before and unaccustomed to taking other people into consideration, especially when one of them was only four. Sometimes he spoke to them sharply, as if he were giving orders.

As Doris said when Isabel complained to her about his encroaching presence, 'Men do clutter up the place so.'

Isabel often found it necessary to chide him.

'For goodness sake sit down and relax, Bill. Your pacing is giving me the pip! You'll wear a groove in the carpet – it's thin enough as it is!'

'Sorry, love – can't help it. This place seems so small,' He stretched his arms out, 'I feel as if I want to push the walls out with my hands. It's all that pacing in the Italian *palazzos* – interrogating prisoners of war.'

In the last months of the war Bill's duties took him to Milan to question prisoners about their part in the War before the fall of Mussolini. The work proved stressful as he constantly asked the same questions of hostile captives.

'Were you a member of the *Fascisti?* Who were your officers? Where are your leaders now?'

Searching out the worst Fascists proved a thankless and remorseless task. Every morsel of information was stored and utilised and, occasionally, led to the capture of a war criminal.

It seemed a long time to Penny, but the reunion anticipated with such joy, ended quickly. After two weeks Bill's leave finished. His orders were to take up a new posting in Berlin, as a member of the Allied Control Commission set up to govern the defeated Germans. His job would again be to interview prisoners of war, and civilians, to try to root out those people who had been members of the Nazi party during the War as well as to help administer the resettlement of the displaced populations of Europe.

An enormous amount of work waited. Huge migrations of people surged around Europe, from the East, to escape the Russians, and from the West, those people displaced by the War and Nazi occupation of so many countries; many of them released from slave labour camps in Germany and other occupied territories.

During his leave Bill struggled to make friends with Penny but the child displayed a stubborn streak, she refused to accept 'That Man' into her life. She adamantly spurned his embraces and only took his gifts – delightful little trinkets and toys from Italy – with reluctance. But she stashed them away in her room in secret places and studied them covertly. Bill and Isabel took the little to the cinema and out for meals; they tried to make it fun.

'I wish she liked me,' he said to Isabel, 'I need more time with her.'

'Don't worry, darling, she's confused. Later, when we're living together again she'll have a chance to get to know you better.'

Soon the leave ended and Bill dressed in his uniform again and waved farewell as they watched from the newly painted step. How smart he looks with his khaki tunic and those belts and buckles all gleaming and his cap under his arm, thought Isabel.

Earlier Bill had taken Isabel into his arms. She tried hard not to cry but the treacherous tears burned her eyelids; bereft at the thought of him going away again.

'Don't worry, darling, we'll be together again soon. They'll be letting families come out. Soon, I promise. Please – don't cry.'

Kissing her tenderly he soothed her fears.

She endured his leaving with a leaden heart. She stood on the step with Penny as he hopped into the taxi patiently ticking at the kerb. Isabel didn't think twice about the expense, even if it was taking him all the way up to town; it would cost a small fortune. She couldn't imagine him using the train. Isabel shivered as they turned back into the house. How cold and empty it seemed.

Chapter Three

Hook of Holland, 1946

'Mummy!' Penny's eyes rounded with fear as the weight of the crowd behind sluiced them through the narrow doors from the congested dockside. They were ejected into the station like pills from the neck of a bottle. The chill wind on the dockside was replaced by an airlessness unexpectedly sliced with icy draughts.

'Hold on to my hand, Penny. You mustn't get lost, darling.'

Penny clung on harder with a hand already cramped from the effort of keeping firmly attached to her mother. Isabel's other hand carried the heavy suitcase as well as their smaller luggage. Her pale face creased with anxiety as she searched hopelessly for a porter. The crowds milled about as if some giant hand were stirring them from above. Some looked aimless and lost, some purposeful and urgent. So many people; impossible to attract anyone's attention. For a moment Isabel felt bewildered and abandoned.

Despite her tiredness after the gruelling voyage across the Channel from Harwich, five hours in an overcrowded boat, Isabel still displayed an insouciant air of elegance. She wore the stylish blue suit bought at Barkers for Bill's homecoming. The smart black hat topped her dark waves, the jaunty red ostrich feather trembling around the brim. The hat perched at an impossibly precarious angle over one finely arched brow. Penny loved that hat. Her constant stroking of the soft fronds had almost ruined the feather.

The throng pushing and shoving from behind forced them to move forward. Isabel stumbled and her ankle pivoted unnaturally – the last thing she needed was a sprain.

'Hold on a mo, can't you? I'm trying to hold everything at once.'

Adjusting her grip on the bags Isabel abandoned the search for a porter and staggered on. She felt the all too familiar beginnings of a headache tightening around her temples. They must find their train. Everything seemed so alien – nothing like a station at home, it sounded wrong, smelt wrong. Unfamiliar, foreign features surrounded them. Advertising hoardings promised goods that surely hadn't been available since before the War. Newspaper and magazine vendors displayed strange, incomprehensible headlines. What a peculiar language Dutch was!

Unexpectedly the apprehension she felt on disembarking the packed ship evaporated and Isabel realised that she was on her way to Bill at last. The journey was begun! No turning back now. She felt exhilarated with a surge of new energy. Taking a deep breath, she straightened her shoulders and strode on. I can manage this on my own.

Blackboards bore hastily scribbled notices that should have helped Isabel but the script was foreign and illegible. She stood bewildered in the huge, confusing station hall; turned this way and that looking for clues. Look on the bright side, she thought; at least neither of us was sick on the boat. It's not going to be so bad after all. Just got to find the right train…

Penny jumped at the penetrating shriek of a whistle; a train letting off steam.

'It's so big in here, Mummy.'

Isabel gripped her hand more tightly. 'Isn't it, darling? Even bigger than Victoria.'

'And there are so many people.'

The glassed roof seemed so high above them, as if part of the sky itself. They could see birds flying up there, roosting on the heavy iron girders. Little illumination filtered through the grimy glass panels. Even the ponderous lights hanging on massive chains did little to relieve the gloom. The odours of burnt-out coal, soot and dirty steam hung thick and heavy in the air. Isabel could hear strange hissing and shunting noises above the more familiar racket of the multitude, which seemed to be moving in every direction at once.

'What's wrong with them, Mummy?'

Penny pointed to a group of British soldiers marching raggedly behind their Sergeant. One leaned on crutches, several carried an arm in a sling, and some had a patch over an eye or a bandage round their head. Shambling slowly to the dock, a cloud of weariness hung over them. Although the Sergeant turned every now and then to check his flock he made no effort to hurry them. His patient concern led him to adjust a kit bag, to straighten a crutch, to pat a faltering man on the back with a word of encouragement.

'Walking wounded,' explained Isabel, pulling Penny closer to her, 'still not home, poor souls.'

The War had ended over a year ago, but it was taking a long time for all the men to be repatriated. Perhaps these had languished in hospital all this time. What rotten luck to be wounded right at the end of the fighting.

At last the journey to join Bill in Berlin had begun. Penny's fifth birthday had passed and she grew daily, almost visibly. Isabel felt a shudder of fear as if a passing ghost had touched her hand. A long time had passed since they had lived together. She could barely remember the happiness they had shared at the delirious start of their marriage. This almost felt like going to meet a stranger. But she rejoiced to get away from the drab shabbiness of England; the tawdry, joyless house she and Penny had occupied alone for so long, but for that brief leave at the end of the war.

She stood in the middle of the vast station hall; worry lines gathering on her forehead and that threatening headache throbbing in the background.

'Can I help you, ma'am?'

Isabel and her daughter turned and gazed up at the figure in uniform towering over them. He must be well over six foot, Isabel thought, and he looks very young.

'Carry your bags, ma'am?' he offered.

He bent closer to them and smiled with perfect teeth, speaking in an accent that Isabel recognised immediately. Grace dated a man who spoke like that; several, in fact. GIs, they called them. As usual, Mum disapproved, 'Bloody Yanks,' she'd muttered, 'all money and no morals.'

'Give over, Mum,' Grace countered, 'they're great fun. And look, they bring me nylons.' She pulled up her skirt to demonstrate this most precious commodity sheathing her shapely legs. 'Better than the old gravy browning and pencilled-in seams aren't they?'

The GIs also helped out with the rations, bringing gifts of oranges, eggs and steaks from their PX, the American forces store. Mum, suspicious as ever, delivered dire warnings.

'You'll need to give more than a kiss and a cuddle for them things, my girl, mark my words.'

Back in the present Isabel assumed her haughty face and pulled herself up.

'No, thank you very much. We can manage,' she discouraged the boy in her poshest voice, warier than usual of talking to a stranger in this foreign place. She struggled to lift the suitcase from where she had dropped it. The American grinned and ignored her. He swung the case up effortlessly even though his kit bag encumbered his other shoulder.

'If you'll forgive me, lady, you need my help. You look after the kid; she looks half scared to death. Where to?'

In no time, with their helper at their side, using his athletic body as a battering ram through the crowds, they found the right platform for the train to Berlin and were settled safely in their seats. Isabel felt she should apologise for her earlier rudeness. She held out her hand to him.

'Thank you so much. I'm sorry…'

'You're welcome, ma'am.' He tipped his cap in a mock salute. 'It was the feather that did it.' Isabel touched the hat, now on her lap. 'Great hat! Good luck.' And he was gone, striding away through the crowds to find his own berth.

In the narrow compartment every inch of seat was occupied, like sardines compressed into a tin. The air, thick with stuffiness, tasted of warm wool and mothballs; too many people breathing in a confined space. Penny sat beside a very fat Dutchman in a musty-smelling suit, who grumbled whenever she stirred. She curled up with her head on Isabel's lap, but soon she fidgeted with discomfort, cramped in that small space. She accidentally kicked the man with her dusty shoes.

'Can't you keep the wretched child still?' the man complained in a thick accent. Penny opened her wide button eyes and suddenly, quite out of the blue, feeling very peculiar, in a spectacular multicoloured fountain, she vomited all over his lap.

Chapter Four

Holland, 1946

'*Rotkind* ...!' The Dutchman's face flushed; apoplectic with rage. He stormed to his feet and surged out of the compartment in a flurry of newspaper, briefcase and fury. He never came back. A wave of relief swept through the carriage as everyone spread out along the seats. Isabel blushed with embarrassment and Penny, poor scrap, began to cry; her little body shaking with sobs and her face red and hot, buckled with grief.

'I'm so sorry,' Isabel apologised. Their fellow passengers murmured with sympathy. Cloths and handkerchiefs were offered to help mop up. A lady took Penny onto her lap and staunched her tears whilst Isabel cleaned up.

'It doesn't matter, little one. The nasty man frightened you I think,' she crooned.

Luckily most of the damage had been done to the Dutchman's trousers. Someone slid open the window and a rush of clean air soon filled the compartment.

'Thank you so much.' Isabel settled Penny beside her, wrapping comforting arms around the child; murmuring soothing words. Now that the fat man had gone they could all settle comfortably. Penny looked much better; the tears drying on her cheeks.

'I'm tired, Mummy,' she whispered.

'Poor old Sweetie, there's been too much excitement for one day. Try to sleep, darling, and we'll be there in no time.'

God, I wish that were true, she thought. It'll be hours

and hours on the train before it reaches Berlin. She stretched her neck, trying to release the tension and gazed out of the window. Dusk was painting the landscape with sooty brush strokes under vast, empty, pewter skies. The outlines of a few sparse trees losing their summer leaves swayed in the gently moving air. Where were the famous Dutch flowers? The colour? The horizon seemed a million miles away because the landscape, once they escaped the suburbs of the Hook, stretched into the morbidly grey distance, almost featureless and flat, flat, flat.

Occasionally the skeleton of a ruined building punctuated the scene, its remaining bones pointing accusingly into the dismal sky, probably the result of shelling or bombing early in the War or during the destructive retreat of the Germans from occupation; driven back by the Americans and the British. Motionless windmills, some with sails damaged and hanging like broken limbs, were outlined starkly against the clouds.

As night crept slowly across the land Isabel could no longer see the countryside through the train's window, but her own face gradually appeared in the dark glass. She saw her dark hair permed into neat waves around a thin, pale face. Not too bad looking even though her makeup had all worn off. Mouth a bit too wide and thin, not exactly a fashionable Cupid's bow. Still, her lashes were thick and dark around her eyes, her best feature, Bill said. Her breath clouded the window and she turned away from her scrutiny. I should try to sleep, she thought, allowing her eyes to close; I'll need the energy later, it's such a long journey.

The train trundled slowly across the Dutch countryside. She remembered the familiar sound the wheels made on the tracks back home - rackety clack, rackety clack. The unfamiliar foreign rhythm of these wheels lulled her into a stupor. Clickety clickety rack, clickety clickety rack. Images of London floated into her head…

Chapter Five

London, 1938

'Aw, go on, Bell, come with us. Hilda's dropped out - I promised,' Aggie wheedled.

They were removing their makeup in the tacky converted corridor that served as a dressing room for the chorus behind the scenes at the Apollo Theatre. Aggie begged with agonised persuasion shining from her false-eyelashed eyes. She gave Isabel a tiny caress on the shoulder, now swathed in an exotically patterned silk kimono - all magentas and peacock blues, after removing her costume.

'Gawn! You'll love it!' She grinned pertly at Isabel, nudging her arm playfully.

Everything about Agnes Dawson was pert, as her many admirers often told her. Pert blonde curls, pert nose, pert breasts, especially when lifted by the saucy costume the management compelled them to wear for the finale of the colourful, brash revue in which the girls performed.

Isabel and Agnes stood at opposite ends of the chorus line - Isabel tall and gracefully elegant; Aggie small and compact. Standing together they could have seemed comic were they not both so very pretty. All this despite the cheap tattiness of their costumes and the straggling ostrich feathers, tired from overuse, attached to their rear ends. 'Like a lot of frazzled bloody chickens,' someone had joked.

'They'll take us somewhere smashing to eat, Bella, probably the Troc. You'll love it. Jamie's friends are lovely; we'll have a great time.'

'I can't, Aggie, Mum's expecting me home.' Isabel dragged her fingers through the outsize tub of Ponds Cold Cream they used to remove their stage makeup. She spread the cream thickly across her face and, after some energetic rubbing, removed the resulting mess with a large bundle of cotton wool. She dabbed carefully around her eyes to take off the garish coating of Midnight Blue eye shadow and thick mascara.

'Besides, how on earth could I get home to Wembley after dinner?'

'Don't be silly, love, they'll get us a taxi.'

'A taxi?' Isabel exclaimed, in a Pygmalion moment. The extravagance! These young men might be worth meeting if they'd pay for a taxi to take her all the way home. A bit of luxury for once couldn't hurt. She'd always avoided going out with the so-called "stage door Johnnies", considering them to be foolish young toadies.

As Mum warned, 'They're only after one thing, my girl. Go out with one of them and you're in trouble. Why can't they find girls of their own kind?' Mum's predictions always seemed to have a negative theme.

Isabel would be breaking several of her mother's many rules if she agreed to go with Agnes. She struggled with her conscience for a few seconds. In the end temptation got the better of her. I'm 20, for goodness sake; I can do what I like. The prospect of a good meal certainly had its appeal. There'd just be warmed up mutton stew and potatoes when she got home. She found herself wavering.

'Look, Hilda can't come; she's got to get home for her Dad. I promised I'd bring a girl for Jamie's friend. Please, Bella,' Aggie's wheedling continued.

Isabel weakened. 'Oh, well, if you insist. But he'd better be handsome!'

Agnes hugged her. "Urry up then, stop dawdling. Get dressed. They're waiting, you know.'

'Mum'll be hopping mad. I wish I could let her know I'm going to be late.' Being able to telephone and warn her strict mother would have been useful, but hardly anyone had a telephone at home – certainly no-one Isabel knew. They used the phone box at the end of the road in an emergency and Mum grudged that too.

'For Gawd's sake, ducky, you're not a kid anymore.' Aggie echoed Isabel's own thoughts. 'Explain to her when you get in. She'll be thrilled you're mixing with the toffs.'

Isabel doubted that. Mum was a stickler for good behaviour and didn't have much time for toffs, except in their place, of course. It was bad enough that she performed in the chorus of this show. Mum hadn't been too bad about her being in the ballet – for some reason she seemed to think that more respectable, classier. But it hadn't lasted. Isabel cracked her jaw when dropped by a male dancer during a lift in a pas de deux. The ballet company had dispensed with her services - not least for the stream of invective she managed to utter through her broken mouth.

'We're surprised at your lack of breeding,' they'd said.

'Sod that!' She'd stormed as best she could. 'Stupid clumsy bastard's broken my jaw!'

With classical training, beauty and poise, there had been little difficulty in finding work in one of the many reviews in the West End. The theatre was booming in the late 1930s, with musical revues one of the most popular forms of entertainment and people sang the more memorable songs all over town. The depression finally seemed to be over and people had begun to spend money again.

Things were still not easy for people working in the theatre. The chorus was very poorly paid; the girls were lucky to see two quid a week and had to supply their own makeup and tights.

'Come on Bella! Get a move on.'

Soon they emerged; stage makeup off, street makeup on. Fox fur-collared long coats over faux silk dresses; high-heeled shoes on their tired feet. Silly little scraps of tulle and flowers perched on their heads, 'cocktail hats'.

'Aggie, I'm not sure about this,' Isabel suffered an attack of nerves on her way along the dingy corridor that led to the stage door. Her mother's warnings resounded in her ears. Perhaps she was doing the wrong thing; inwardly she cringed with nervous dread.

Agnes hugged her arm to her side. 'Come on, kid, we'll have a wonderful time!'

''Night, Malc', they cried in unison as they passed the doorkeeper, 'see ya tomorrow.'

''Night, girls,' Malcolm acknowledged, pushing open the doors and holding them aside. They stepped out into the open air.

Isabel paused on the step. Although she saw it every evening after the show this scene never failed to astonish her. It seemed that a small crowd of penguins had gathered on the pavement. The young men all wore dinner jackets, or white ties and tailcoats; some even had cloaks over their shoulders. Top hats adorned many heads and most were removed as the girls emerged. Cheerful smiles lit the open faces.

Two of these visions detached themselves from the throng. Isabel recognised Jamie's boyish features; he often took Agnes out. Behind him stood a taller man, a look of disinterest, even arrogance, in his eyes. The faint smile on his handsome face could almost have been interpreted as a sneer. He hovered in the background like a reluctant suitor waiting for the slimmest excuse to make his escape.

'Agnes, my dear!' cried Jamie, beaming. He swept off his hat and kissed Agnes's hand fleetingly. 'And this is your friend - Hilda isn't it?' Isabel thought he seemed very friendly as he stretched out his hand with a broad grin creasing his homely face.

'No, Hilda couldn't make it - this is Bel ... Isabel.'

'Delighted to meet you, Isabel, James Carter at your service. May I introduce my friend William Barton? We call him Bill.' James pulled his friend forward by the elbow. 'You'll have to excuse him, he's a bit shy.'

Bill bowed awkwardly over their hands and muttered a greeting. Isabel thought he looked as if someone had starched his underwear. But he shook hands properly and didn't bolt.

Perhaps he's not so arrogant, thought Isabel, just shy as Jamie says. He's jolly good-looking. Maybe it won't be such a bad evening after all. I like the sound of his voice and look - he's managed a proper smile!

'Pleased to meet you,' said Agnes grandly, extending her

manicured hand. But she then spoiled it by giving a little bob like a lady's maid.

'How do you do?' Isabel used her best voice, cool and cultured. She hoped those expensive elocution lessons proved worthwhile.

'Delighted,' said Bill, regarding her with eyes as bright and intelligent as any she had seen and that elusive smile hovering on his full lips.

James took charge. 'Come on, girls. Where'd you like to go? Dancing? Dinner first, I think. The Trocadero's not far. We could walk.'

'Told you so,' Agnes whispered in Isabel's ear and gave her a nudge in the ribs.

The little group swept along. Bill had tucked Isabel's hand into his arm and stood on her right so that she walked away from the kerb. Quite the gent, she thought. Soon they reached Piccadilly Circus. The elegant Art Nouveau frontage of the Trocadero hid an even more fashionable, brightly-lit interior. Lavish flower arrangements filled the foyer, scenting the air, and glass chandeliers supplied glittering illumination.

They left their coats with a smiling woman in the cloakroom just inside the door, crossed the hallway with its imposing stairway leading to the upper floors and stepped down three steps into the dining area.

Carpets sank beneath their feet; thick and lush. Seats softly upholstered and buttoned in thick red plush formed booths around the tables at the periphery of the room under over-sized mirrors. In the centre, tables were circular and set for two, four or six people. Since the tables around the edges of the room were already occupied, they were led to one of those tables set for four.

The silverware gleamed; the glasses sparkled. Each table bore a fragrant posy of flowers at the centre and the table napkins, by some mysterious craft, were fashioned into swans. Isabel was reluctant to demolish hers when she sat down, but their waiter, with a flourish that loosened the folds, deposited it on her lap. Isabel could find no words at the opulence of it all and gazed around her, dazzled. Blimey, this was classy!

'Isn't it lovely?' breathed Agnes into her ear.

'A top-hole restaurant,' agreed Jamie. 'Have anything you want.' He waved at the menus magnanimously. 'We'll start with a bottle of champagne,' he instructed the waiter.

Lavish dinners in 1938 London were commonplace and the presence of two generous hosts made it even better. They ate soup and a fish course followed by even more expertly crafted dishes. Isabel's *paté de foie gras* tasted ambrosial, the delicate rosemary perfume of her tiny chicken, divine. What luxury, a whole little chicken to herself!

They ate and drank royally, taking their time. A four-piece band discreetly played popular tunes beside a tiny polished dance floor. The diners danced between courses to "Night and Day", "You're the Top", "Cheek to Cheek"...

'I'm in Heaven'...

'I could climb the highest mountain,
And reach the highest peak,
I wouldn't like it half as much,
As dancing cheek to cheek.'

'Enough! I've been dancing all evening!' protested Isabel.

'But not with me,' grinned Bill and twirled her around the floor again. He really seemed to be relaxed and enjoying himself now.

'You're a very good dancer! I'm impressed,' said Isabel.

'Boarding school. Saturday mornings; mandatory ballroom dancing classes. Very hot on the social skills, my school!'

Public school, Isabel guessed. His manner and bearing proved it. She gave herself up to the pleasure of being whisked around the dance floor by a handsome man who could dance.

Eventually Bill allowed her to sit and rest her aching feet. She wished she could take her shoes off; the soles burned as if she had thrust them into a fire.

'Tell me all about yourself. I want to know what you do when you're not at the theatre. Where do you live? Where did you go to school? Everything,' Bill said, leaning towards her with an engrossed expression. He topped up her wine glass and took a sip from his own.

'Oh, Bill. It's not very interesting. I'm just an ordinary

girl. I live with my Mum and Dad and younger sister in a house in Wembley. I have another sister who's married and has a baby. She lives nearby. Nothing unusual about us.'

'What does Dad do?'

'He's a Guard.'

'Scots or Grenadiers?'

'No, silly, on the railway. He's the one that waves the green flag to say it's safe for the train to move off.'

Bill laughed, but not sneeringly, just at his mistake. 'Sorry, I must have sounded a terrible snob.'

'Not at all. You're nearly right. He was in the Scots Guards in the War; a Sergeant Major. Everyone calls him Jock, he really is Scottish. But he was invalided out in 1917. Gassed in the trenches.'

'Horrible. How is he now?'

'Not good. He still coughs a lot.' Even twenty years later Isabel's Dad suffered from the damage done in that terrible war.

'Poor man. A friend of my father's was gassed too - lungs practically destroyed.' Bill's tone clearly expressed his regret.

Sadly, Isabel pictured her father choking on his ruined lungs each morning as he struggled to get to work. But he claimed he was lucky to be alive at all.

'At least Dad's mostly in the open air with his job; that helps. He shouldn't have to work at all but we can't manage on his War Pension. Grace and I do what we can.'

'And your mother?'

'Mum doesn't work anymore. She looks after us all. She used to be…' Isabel paused shyly, she wasn't sure that she wanted to impart this information. But Bill seemed so sympathetic. 'Well, she used to be in service. She worked in the house of one of Queen Mary's Ladies in Waiting. We thought that was very grand.' She laughed to cover her embarrassment.

'My word, moving in exalted circles!' he exclaimed.

Isabel couldn't detect any irony in his voice. He really seemed genuinely interested. She couldn't quite make out what he did for a living; some sort of work in the City, it seemed, in the same company as Jamie. But she didn't like to question him.

They chatted for a while and then Bill excused himself to dance with Aggie. Isabel watched as they sailed around the floor.

Aggie seemed to still have plenty of bubbly energy. Bill made her giggle and Isabel felt a pang of jealousy. How silly, she thought, I've only just met the man. I'm nothing special to him; he's obviously attentive and charming to all the girls. But she couldn't deny that she found Bill incredibly attractive.

The tender way he showed Agnes to her seat impressed Isabel. He pulled the chair out for her and saw her comfortably settled before he sat down himself. He has beautiful manners, she thought as she watched him listening with apparent fascination to Aggie's prattling. He looks as if he's really interested in her. I suppose that's how it was with me, just good manners. She jumped at the touch of Jamie's hand on her shoulder, startled out of her reverie.

'Would you care to dance?' he asked mock-formally, bowing low. 'Trip the light fantastic? Fandango across the floor?' He wriggled his eyebrows at her in a way that reminded her of the Marx brothers.

Isabel laughed. 'How could I refuse, kind sir? But please, Jamie, just one, I'm exhausted and my feet have had it.'

The evening drifted away like a puff of lazy smoke. The band began to pack up their instruments. The restaurant had almost emptied and the lights dimmed still lower. The little group had drunk their fill of champagne and at three o'clock in the morning they emerged into Piccadilly, tired, slightly tight and happy. Jamie hailed a taxi for the girls and whilst he gave directions and handed over money to the driver, Bill said goodnight. He held Isabel's hand in both of his and gazed directly into her eyes, his voice quiet and serious.

'I've had a wonderful evening, Isabel. I hope we can do it again soon. Just the two of us next time, eh?'

'That would be lovely,' she breathed, meeting his gaze evenly. As he bent close to her a lock of brown hair fell over his forehead and Isabel only just managed to stop herself from tenderly stroking it back into place.

The girls hopped into the cab and settled in the back seat. As the taxi moved away Isabel peeped out of the back. If they turn away immediately I'll know they aren't really interested, she thought. Why would someone like that care about a girl like me?

What have I got to offer? Bill must know lots of elegant, classy girls, debs probably. Those privileged few who were presented to the King each year and then had a London 'Season' to find themselves suitable husbands.

She kept her head turned to the little oval window in the back of the cab. She had to rub some greasy dust off the glass with her hanky to see out. Jamie was striding towards the Haymarket, but Bill had paused and gazed after the taxi, a strangely rapt expression on his face. As Isabel sank down into the seat pulling her fur collar round her burning face she realised that something momentous had happened.

Chapter Six

Holland, 1946

The monotonous rhythm of the train changed. With a great screeching of brakes and carriages juddering backwards and forwards, it ground to a noisy halt. Isabel could hear shouting close by; the slamming of doors up and down the train. She sat up and looked out of the dark window, her face pressed against the glass. They seemed to have stopped in the middle of nowhere. From her side she could see only featureless countryside and some industrial-looking buildings. Penny whimpered on the seat beside her as Isabel shifted round to look the other way.

She still couldn't see much. She got up carefully so as not to disturb the child and slid out of the compartment into the corridor. The air struck mercifully fresher here as the upper parts of the windows had been opened. At each end of the corridor stood a soldier with a gun, blocking the way. The uniform resembled that of the American they had met at the Hook. Isabel leaned against the brass rail, set at shoulder height, and peered through the grimy glass. She could see a makeshift station. More soldiers marched up and down the wooden platform waving their arms or rifles, shouting at anyone trying to get off.

'Stay on the train! No disembarking here. Wait for border control. Have your passports and papers ready.'

Grenze – a notice said in gothic script. Written below, in large red-painted letters, appeared the word BORDER. The German border, she surmised; the beginning of the American Zone. At last we're making some progress. Before leaving home she'd perused the old atlas at Mum's and despaired at the length of the journey across Holland and Germany. They were only about halfway to Berlin.

'Out the way, lady.' A soldier pushed her roughly. 'Sit down in your seat till we complete border formalities.'

His uncouthness made Isabel's hackles rise; he wasn't nearly as polite as the American who'd helped them at the Hook. She shrugged off his hand and returned to the compartment where the other occupants stirred at the sounds of activity. Wearily they searched for passports and other travel papers. Penny woke, rubbing her eyes and stretching her arms.

'Where are we, Mummy?'

'At the border with Germany, darling. We'll be moving again soon.'

This, unfortunately, proved a vain promise. Two weary hours later the train wheezed and rattled into life. Meanwhile the soldiers and border guards patrolled the corridors, minutely inspecting papers and questioning travellers. Isabel's case was straightforward and they spent only a short time with her.

'I'm travelling to Berlin with my daughter to join my husband, who's working with the Allied Control Commission.' She thought it sounded quite impressive but the soldier's eyes showed no interest and he simply handed back her documents without comment before moving on to the next person.

The soldiers forcibly ejected some passengers from the train with rough handling and harsh words. Wrong travel papers I suppose, thought Isabel. Why anyone would want to travel illegally to Berlin I can't imagine. Conditions there were supposed to be appalling. Starvation and disease prowled amongst the ruins; violent crime and black marketeering were rife. Who'd want to go there unless they had to? Or really wanted to and had a good reason to go - like me?

The released brakes sighed and the doors slammed closed behind the American border guards. The remaining passengers echoed the sound, sighing with relief when the carriages finally shunted off. At least if you travelled along you felt as if you were getting somewhere. The passengers took a while to settle down and most gave up the struggle to sleep. A trio of men started a card game, which appeared to be a sort of Rummy, and played quietly in the corner opposite Isabel, using the little shelf table under the window for their cards.

'Join us,' they suggested.

'No, thanks, I'm hopeless at cards. Don't worry about me; I'm not going to sleep again now.'

The train accelerated, like a horse that senses it is nearing its destination, eager to arrive. Several hours had to pass before they approached their goal, but it seemed no more than a couple of hours later that the train once again slowed to a cacophonous halt, grinding wheels sending up sparks along the track.

The soldiers that boarded the train this time were even less gentle than the Americans. This was the beginning of the Russian zone. So these patched, sullen bullies were examples of the Great Russian Army. Dirty, scruffy and surly, they pushed and shoved up and down the corridors yelling at the passengers, using words no one understood and delivered in the crudest way possible.

'All stand up! Stand up now! *Aufstanden!*' Someone managed a few words in something other than Russian.

A female soldier, whose foul breath in Isabel's face made her turn her head, roughly pulled her to her feet. The woman grabbed her chin and stared at Isabel's face. With a contemptuous guffaw she made some ribald comment to her male companion. They sniggered lewdly. As they grabbed her passport Isabel suppressed a smile when she noticed that they held it upside down and didn't notice until they came to her photograph, which they scrutinised with unnecessary pantomime, comparing it to her face and laughing. Satisfied at last, they moved on.

The border formalities took even longer this time. More passengers were summarily expelled onto the line with their few possessions. They gesticulated at the oblivious Russians, begging to be allowed to stay on the train. The Russians, when they became bored with the remonstrations, brutally pushed the people aside with rifle butts, sometimes striking someone.

Where on earth could those poor people go? They were in the middle of nowhere. Was there another train that could return them to Holland? Could they stay in the American Zone? Isabel felt shocked at the callousness. She did not realise then that as time went on she would become immune to the sight of the human flotsam of war that washed at the shores of what civilisation remained in post-war Europe and the thoughtless brutality directed towards them. Millions of displaced persons strove to reach some sort of haven, forming a seething population of the dispossessed moving in any direction that seemed to promise new hope.

Abruptly the train jerked and, stumbling, Isabel brought her head in from the window where she had been hanging out to observe the activity outside. She returned to her seat and hugged Penny to her side. The child's eyes drooped, still groggy with sleep, but she snuggled warm and pliant against her. The train trundled on through the countryside of Russian-occupied Germany, towards Berlin, a city ruled by four conquering powers, marooned in the centre of this alien hinterland.

'We're nearly in Berlin, Pen! Only a very short while now and we'll be seeing Daddy!'

She began to fuss with their belongings, collecting their luggage together, her heart pounding. How could she bear the excitement? She would burst with it before they even got there. Calm down, she told herself, or you won't be able to speak when we arrive. She glanced out of the window. With brutal shock she registered that the tottering canyons of ruined buildings beside the track were the beginnings of the devastation that was Berlin.

Chapter Seven

Berlin, 1946

The unforgiving concrete of the platform began to register on Bill's feet; they burned and pulsed within the expensive leather. He felt as if he had been pacing back and forth for hours. Trying to contain his nervousness, he tapped his glossy swagger stick against the seam of his khaki uniform trousers. In common with many other officers, he had found a tailor near the *Ku'damm* who had remodelled the tunic to fit his muscular frame more closely. He held his cap slotted under his arm. His batman, Charlie, had polished his few surviving brass badges and buttons to a regulation sparkle. The rest were replaced with wartime black plastic. CCG, read the shoulder flashes, Control Commission in Germany, the military arm of the Allied Control Council, the government in effect, set to replace post-war chaos with some sort of order.

He turned to his friend, brought along for moral support and in the hope that his cheerful banter would cover any awkwardness in his reunion with Isabel.

'For God's sake, John, where's this bloody train?'

Captain John Marriott, slouched on a *Bahnhof* bench smoking one of his interminable cigarettes, had projected his feet far out onto the platform due to the length of his legs. He puffed and relaxed into the seat.

'Be here soon, old boy. Got to be patient. No Fascists around to make them run on time any more. You seem nervous.'

'Nervous? No. Apprehensive - maybe.'

'Don't split hairs. The memsahib will be thrilled to bits to see you; you can bet on it.'

'This may not be quite the welcome she was expecting. The flat's still a mess.'

'She'll hardly notice. Believe me, Bill; unless she's the house-proud type, she's not going to mind a few bullet holes in the plasterwork. From what you've told me she won't give a hoot.'

'You may be right. I still wish she could have waited a bit longer - till I could get it properly done up; slapped on a bit of paint. We only got running water last week.'

He slumped down beside John and picked up the silver cigarette case lying there.

'Why do you smoke these things? I thought you were hard up. You can buy anything with them. I bought that huge double bed with a couple of hundred cigarettes the other day.'

'Got to get your priorities right, Bill. Me, I've got no little wife to keep warm at night - I may as well smoke the things.'

Bill grinned, spotting an inaccuracy in this statement. 'That's not what I heard.'

'OK. I'm getting my share, but not with the kind of girl you could take home to mother,' John winked.

Certainly not *my* mother Bill thought, she didn't even approve of Isabel. He grunted and tried to relax on the hard wooden seat, some of whose slats were missing. He had tried to persuade Isabel to delay her arrival. Their letters had become argumentative and their occasional telephone calls, anticipated with great longing, difficult. He was ambivalent – he looked forward to see Isabel again, and Penny, funny little thing with her plain face and straight, fine hair. She wasn't a bit like her mother, maybe she would blossom when she was older. But he didn't like the way things were in Berlin. It was ugly. The defeated Germans' attitude was, not surprisingly, morose often to the point of violence. On top of that Bill's living quarters were far from ideal. Windows cracked, taps corroded and leaking and yes, bullet holes in the plaster.

'Can't you leave it for a few months, darling, until I have a home ready for you? This place is still a mess.'

'Bill,' she'd replied firmly. 'We've been apart for five years. Now the Army is at last letting us wives join our husbands. There is nothing on earth that will keep me from you for a moment longer than necessary. Penny needs a father - she hardly knows you. She never will if you don't spend some time together. Besides, it doesn't matter what the flat is like, this place is hardly a palace. I can't wait to get away from it.'

Bill remembered with a shudder the paltry little house in Wembley, but he had looked around the sparsely furnished apartment, until recently occupied by several young officers, and despaired. He tried another tack.

'You know how much you'll miss your family. And Penny will miss the boys, won't she? I work very long hours you know. I won't be home much. You'll be lonely.'

'Oh Bill! It sounds as if you don't want me to come. Of course I'll stay here if you really don't want me.'

He could picture her sad, troubled face and knew he was lost.

'I love you; I long to have you here all the time. I don't think this is the best time, that's all. But if you're determined, you must come. Don't say I didn't warn you - conditions are awful.'

Now Isabel was on her way with the mutely sullen daughter he hardly knew. Penny had certainly made her antagonism felt when he'd seen her on that last leave. Bill remembered her tight, stubborn face. Peculiar little mite, she must have been jealous. She'd had her mother to herself all those years; his presence must have seemed an intolerable intrusion.

At least conditions here were better than they had been. The remembered horror of his first arrival in Berlin nearly a year ago still stirred him. The Russians had arrived in the defeated city ahead of the other armies, taking it for their own. In spite of the agreements beaten out at the post-war conference at Yalta, they showed reluctance to give any part of the city over to the other Allies. For months the Allied Control Council argued over the division of Germany in general and Berlin in particular.

When the British and Americans finally arrived it would have been hard to imagine that things could have been worse. Apart from the more obvious visual evidence of corruption the most noticeable thing on landing in Berlin, at Templehof Airport, was the smell, the heavy sweet smell of decay. The stench of putrefying flesh, toppled buildings and recent fires. Many dead bodies still lay beneath the rubble.

Stretching away into the hazy distance they could see the ruins of the city laid out in a panorama of destruction. A fog of residual smoke from extinguished flames hung in the air. Once in their transport they weaved through the barely cleared streets between cliffs of ruined buildings, their empty facades holding nothing behind them. Bill was wryly reminded of the faces of debutantes he had known.

'God, it's worse than I imagined. How can they repair this?'

Those words, a mantra repeated over and over again in stunned whispers, echoed as they slowly advanced through the chaos. Dead bodies littered the streets, a danger to everyone, spreading disease and encouraging vermin. The Russians just left the bodies where they fell and the civilians could summon neither the energy nor the will to bury them.

Bill had seen the results of bombing in the East End of London and around Wembley. Terrible indeed, but not as bad as this. Here devastation was more complete than in any other city in Europe as Berlin spread so widely and had been subjected to bombardment from the air, by artillery attack and then to intense street fighting when the unrelenting Russians arrived. Berlin was seen as the root of evil, the seat of Nazism, and was to be utterly destroyed. Hitler refused to surrender, so the fighting continued for much longer than necessary.

'Berlin will fight to the last man,' the Nazi leader insisted. So the defeated Berliners endured months of unnecessary suffering and death. Those who wanted to surrender and put out white flags were summarily executed by the SS and their bodies displayed outside their homes; hung from the lampposts as traitors. The Nazis finally turned on their own people.

The ruins seemed to stretch forever in dunes and mountains of rubble between towers eviscerated by fire. The borders of the cleared main roads had been crudely embanked with walls of salvaged bricks holding at bay the once grand facades of buildings. An occasional mass of girders like a parody of warped climbing frames in a children's playground pointed starkly into the sky.

The young British officers watched dusty lines of pale, thin and poorly dressed women, passing broken bricks hand to hand - those hands encased in rags or cardboard to protect them - they tapped off the broken mortar as best they could and stacked the intact masonry into embankments that held back the piles of rubble. These less damaged bricks would be used again when reconstruction began.

Bill couldn't help feeling sympathy for these poor women, known as the *trümmerfrauen*, who were paid a pittance, but could not get a ration card unless they did it.

'They shouldn't have to do that. Aren't there any men to do it?' he asked. But there weren't. The only males in the city were too old, too young or too sick or wounded or even war-shocked for manual work.

'Don't feel too sorry for them, old boy,' John had said, rolling a cigarette from a tin of Old Holborn, part of a consignment newly arrived from England. 'They're probably the wives and girl friends of *Gauleiters* and Gestapo murderers and torturers – they may even have taken a hand themselves. Don't waste your pity on them. They didn't have to follow Hitler.'

But all the same they struck Bill's heart with sorrow. He thought of what it would have been like if the British had been similarly brought low and Isabel had been forced to wear out her hands on such tasks.

Thousands of shambling refugees, displaced persons - or DPs as they were known - their few possessions carried however they could, had started to arrive from the Eastern provinces now occupied by the Russians. They arrived on impossibly overcrowded trains, dead or dying from starvation, many of them orphaned children.

Their influx began as soon as the Western zones were opened to them. Some of the luckier ones had handcarts and old prams to carry their goods. Others had their backs bent beneath their burdens, heads down like scavengers vainly searching for treasures at their feet. Propaganda told them that Berlin was barely touched by War. They were deeply shocked when they arrived to see the grim reality and cried bitter tears. This was the ultimate symbol of the end of the Third Reich. Where was the glory now?

'What on earth are we going to do with all the D.Ps?' Was the question asked by everyone– at least two million had arrived and there were not sufficient facilities to deal with them. Not enough shelter and certainly not enough food. The question was partly answered when the extent of Nazi atrocities was unearthed. Eighty one Belsen-type camps were found in the British zone alone. Many DPs were housed in these ex-slave-labour camps, concentration camps and empty barracks, as well as in bombed-out schools and hospitals. They found shelter in those cellars and attics not already occupied by Berlin residents and fashioned makeshift caves in the mountains of rubble with whatever materials they could find. But conditions were terrible and many starved or died of disease.

Bill and a party of other young officers were sent to find themselves billets.

'Things are better in the suburbs, go and look there,' the Quartermaster said.

In a borrowed jeep a party drove to the wooded outskirts with less marked devastation. They selected a villa in an area known as the Grunewald.

'Take any one you want,' their commander said. 'If there are Germans still in it, turf them out. Don't forget who's in charge now. There's no need to be polite about it. If they make a fuss, tell them you'll shoot them.'

Bill discovered later that the more wealthy Berliners and Nazi party dignitaries had decamped when the Russians were pounding at the gates of the city from the East and the other Allies, the Americans and British, had halted at the Elbe, waiting for the Russians to take the city. They piled their valuables, their children and their luggage into the last functioning private cars in Berlin and, whilst at the same time urging Berliners to fight to their last breath, fled to Switzerland or Austria, not realising that the latter would fall to the Allies in short order.

The building the officers selected was empty; much to their relief, as threatening residents at gunpoint had little appeal. The villa's generous proportions spoke of prosperity and opulence. Unfortunately, earlier occupation by Russian soldiers had rendered the interior extremely unpleasant. The squatters did not seem to have understood the function of the toilet facilities, possibly because there had been no mains water for a long time. But they had used any convenient corner they could find for their natural functions.

Much of the ostentatious furniture had survived, though often damaged with gouges carved out of the wood or glass doors smashed, perhaps because it was too heavy to move. The glass was still intact in most of the window frames, but many of the walls seemed to have been used for target practice. A crude drawing of Hitler, etched in charcoal on a wall in the hallway, was covered and surrounded by violently excised pockmarks. It appeared that they weren't very good shots.

'There's a pile of logs out the back,' John noticed, 'I'll start a fire. It'll get rid of some of the damp smell.'

'But will it help with the stink of shit?' someone yelled. 'Filthy buggers, those Russkies.'

They lit a fire in the handsome tiled stove that stood in the corner of the hall, towering to about eight feet, almost to ceiling height. Even in its neglected state the brownish tiles gleamed and the chimney seemed clear enough to light a fire. Once the smoke died away it warmed the house from top to bottom.

What must have once been a beautiful garden now tangled with overgrown bramble and weeds. Some of the larger trees had been felled for firewood and the remnants left littering the shaggy lawns. The greatest shock came when they found two bloated corpses floating in the fountain. As both were naked it had not been possible to identify their nationality.

'The fat bastard must be Russian,' someone hazarded. 'No German could look like that after what Berlin's been through.'

'Come on! Get the corporal to arrange a grave digging party. We can't leave them there.' Bill turned away in disgust, hoping he didn't look as sick as he felt. He went inside and chose a bedroom from the eight in the house. It was bigger than any room he'd occupied in his life. The camp bed and single chair looked pathetically inadequate on its wide wooden floor. All he had to add was his trunk of kit. He'd have to find more furniture to make it seem more like a home from home.

'There's a whole stash of wine in the cellar,' John called in to tell him. 'Come on, we might as well get plastered.'

'We'd better not drink it all. With no water we'll probably be cleaning our teeth in it. I'm surprised the Russians haven't had it all.'

'Mostly hock, old boy. Not the Russian's tipple, they prefer vodka.'

Before long a REME unit drove a water tanker into the street every day to supply the requisitioned houses. Eventually some kind of mains water was restored, although at first it was only from a standpipe in the street. They still had to boil every drop, for disease was sweeping the city. Typhus, typhoid, diphtheria and dysentery were rife. Happily the hock was only called on to wash down their rations, when they got around to cooking any.

Now, nearly a year later, the house had been roughly divided into two apartments. The other original occupants had moved away, some awaiting their wives and some secretly living with friendly *fräuleins.* And some had been posted to other cities, Hamlin, Hanover and Luneburg. Bill occupied the ground floor, using some of the reception rooms as bedrooms, and a colleague from the Control Commission, a civilian conscript, Dennis Masters, lived upstairs. They shared the hallway and Bill used the bathroom just at the top of the stairs. It wasn't a bad arrangement. As they waited for their families to join them they rattled around in the huge house.

'Quite a nice little nest we've got here, Bill,' Dennis said, 'almost as good as Cheltenham. I just wish someone would open a decent golf course.'

Bill looked at his apartment doubtfully. Though partly furnished in fine Teutonic style, anything of real value had gone and the walls and floors were vast bare acres. Naked light bulbs hung from the ceilings and where ornate sconces had once adorned the walls. Since bulbs were scarce and unreliable, the flat was often pitched in gloom. Bill scrounged as many candles as he could so that at least he could try to make the rooms more cheerful for Isabel. It might even look romantic, he hoped optimistically.

The glass in the double doors between the rooms, engraved with graceful Art Nouveau motifs, had been broken or cracked. Bill regretfully and carefully removed the remaining shards, mindful of Isabel and Penny's safety.

'When your family arrives you can get yourself a maid,' Bill was told. Until then Bill had relied on his batman, Corporal Charlie Pierce, to look after his needs. A batman was to look after an officer or group of officers during battle, to see that their designated officers' kit and uniform were in order and that they got food and sleep as. They acted as waiters in the Mess sometimes and some could even turn their hand to minor repairs of kit and vehicles. Charlie was certainly one of these. He had been a car mechanic in civvy Street and, after following Bill around Europe, was his staunch ally. But now, as his family was coming, Bill was entitled to a maid and Charlie, to his disgust, was relegated to more work at the Mess. He still took care of Bill's uniform, polishing the brass and making sure all was in good trim.

Bill needed to find a maid. By asking amongst other officers, relatively old hands at living in Berlin, Bill found Irma. She arrived on the doorstep one morning as he was towelling the remnants of shaving soap from his chin.

The girl standing on the doorstep seemed impossibly young and thin, so thin. He had been told she was eighteen, but she looked younger. Her emaciated face peeped out between blonde plaits neatly coiled around her ears.

'*Entshuldigen, Herr Kapitän, ich bin* Irma.' She informed him with a little bob.

'Ah, Irma, please come in.' Bill said in his perfect German. He had difficulty in persuading her to sit down whilst he interviewed her briefly. Even then she perched uneasily on the edge of the armchair. She eyes stared wide in her gaunt young face as she scanned the living room. The festoons of cobwebs weighed down with dust in great swags, the heaps of rubble, the piles of loose plaster inexpertly gathered by Bill and his friends were all rapidly taken in by her domestic glance.

'Yes, Herr Barton I can do this. It will take time, but I can make it nice for your wife. Do not worry.'

Bill stood up, extending his hand to help her up; relief written on his face. How fragile she is, he thought with a tremor of pity.

'Bless you Irma, you're hired. There are cleaning materials in the kitchen. If you need anything else I'll see what I can do - I think they've got mops and things down at the NAAFI, just let me know.'

In the few weeks since he'd hired her, Irma had wrought miracles. For one so slight and undernourished she appeared to have boundless energy. She lived in, sleeping in a bare little room next to the kitchen, but she seemed happy with the arrangement and was already putting on weight and looking healthier. Bill had been afraid that she would not be strong enough for the work., but she seemed to thrive on it.

After a few days he could hear her singing in the kitchen as she prepared his breakfast, meagre though it was. She brought it to him in the dining room where he sat in solitary splendour at the magnificent dining table, which had survived the Russians' occupation with only one deep scar.

'Thank you, Irma. It's lovely to hear you singing – I hope you're happy here.'

'*Danke sehr*, I am happy to work with you.' She bobbed with downcast eyes.

'You don't have to curtsey, Irma.'

'I think I should, sir,' she stammered, 'you are my master.'

'No, really, there's no need.'

'I fetch more toast.' She scurried away, blushing fiercely.

A few days later he told her the news, received the day before in an air letter from home.

'My wife and daughter will be arriving next week, Irma. Try and make the place as cheerful as possible. We'll have a decent dinner when they get here. I'll see what I can get at the NAAFI - I've got hold of some extra ration points. I couldn't bear to give her rissoles.'

These hard grey little meatballs made from minced meat of dubious origin became a staple part of their diet as the meat in their rations was hardly fit for any other purpose. *Pissoles*, John called them.

'Frau Barton and the little one!' Thrilled, Irma bustled around tidying and polishing with new energy. She made the beds with blankets and linen supplied by the Army. Some of the blankets were so thickly felted and heavy that they would hardly bend over a bed. One was spread on the floor of Irma's room to act as a carpet. But Isabel would be sending some of their own things from England, good sheets, soft wool blankets, towels and feather pillows, all of which were a welcome gift from Bill's mother; purchased, naturally at her favourite emporium, Harrods. They would arrive in a week or two; Carter Paterson arranged this transport for the Forces.

From somewhere in the neglected garden Irma gleaned an armful of flowers and leaves, some dusted with bright coloured berries, which she arranged in mugs and jam jars around the flat.

'Well done, Irma! It looks almost like home. Mrs Barton will be pleased.' Bill surveyed the flat, already transformed into a passable imitation of a home.

Now here he stood, at the *Bahnhof,* chilled, bored and kicking his heels alongside other husbands waiting for their families. He was glad John had joined him. They had met in the early days of the War at a training course at Bletchley Park and become good friends.

'Delighted to come along, old chap,' said John. 'You've told me such a lot about the lovely Mrs Barton. Wild horses couldn't keep me away!'

Finally, two hours late, the sinister gunmetal grey engine's blunt nose slowly steamed between the platforms. Crashes resonated through the station as doors were flung open before the train ultimately came to a dignified halt. Heads hung from the open windows, people pushed frantically up and down the corridors. Weary passengers, stretching their legs after the long journey, began to climb down onto the platform. Bill's heart started to beat faster and foolish tears started to his eyes, reminding him how much he had been looking forward to this day.

Bill recognised the hat immediately, even before he saw Isabel's face. The red feather rippled playfully in the draught. He stepped forward and called.

'Isabel!' Involuntarily he stretched out his arms, his swagger stick and cap forgotten on the bench as he stumbled towards her.

A blast of steam was released from under the train and Isabel disappeared into the mist.

John had caught his first glimpse of her though.

'By George, Bill,' he breathed, 'you're quite right, she's a corker!'

Chapter Eight

Berlin, 1946

Bill clasped Isabel and Penny together in a hug, his arms wide to cover them. He murmured words of welcome. Finally he released Penny; put her onto the ground and drew Isabel close into his arms. After a few moments of watching their passionate embraces, kisses that tilted Isabel's hat and ruffled her hair, John intervened.

'Come on, you two. That's enough of that. I'm going to show Mrs Barton to the car. Madame, your chariot awaits!'

He grasped Isabel's hand briskly and ceremoniously tucked it into his elbow, addressing Bill casually over his departing shoulder.

'You, Major Barton, take care of the child and the luggage. I am going to look after your lovely wife.'

Isabel turned back to laugh at Bill. 'Help, I'm captured!'

'No,' John whispered breathily into her ear, making her giggle, 'I'm the one who's captured. Come, let us away. The rest of the party will follow.' And with a theatrical flourish he strode towards the exit.

Isabel laughed up at him. What a nice man. A few inches taller than Bill and thinner, he had almost blue-black hair and the most amazing sapphire blue eyes. His uniform looked as if it had been poured onto him. He's incredibly good looking, she thought, almost like a film star. If she wasn't so besotted with her husband she might have fancied him already. She let John lead her off the platform into the forecourt.

John swept her with an imperious swagger from the smoky station and into the back of the waiting car, helping her in with solicitous hands. She managed the manoeuvre with as much dignity as she could muster. Climbing around the tipped-up front seat required considerable flexibility.

'I'm going to have to part from you for a moment, my darling. Your husband will want to sit in the back with you. We don't want him getting jealous, do we?' He patted her hand before releasing it.

The army driver swung the cases into the boot at the front of. Bill carried Penny in his arms and soon caught up. The child had relaxed her head onto his shoulder, her thumb tucked in her mouth and clutching her precious Teddy in her other hand.

'Look, Daddy, there's no engine. He's putting the cases in the front.'

'That's right. It's a *Volkswagen*. The engine's in the back.'

'That's very funny,' said Penny as Bill put her on the ground and he climbed into the back of the car next to Isabel.

John took his seat in the front and stretched his arms out towards the child.

'Come, Penny, sit on my knee. I want to hear all about your journey.'

Penny looked at him doubtfully from under frowning brows, but couldn't resist his grin and the questioning angle of his head and jumped in. Soon she was chatting with unaccustomed volubility, clearly besotted.

'We've been on a big boat and a train. It was ever such a long way,' she prattled.

John laughed when Penny told him about being sick all over the Dutchman.

'It was horrid, but it made him go away.'

'You know, I've often felt tempted to do that to a fellow traveller. But I don't think I'd get away with it. It helps being a pretty little girl with big brown eyes.'

Isabel forgot her weariness as she snuggled up against Bill in the back of the car. Her bones ached and her muscles were weak and she felt as if she hadn't eaten in a week, but with his solid strength beside her she felt as if she could tackle the whole ghastly journey again.

Her heart still pounded from the joy of their reunion. As she became calmer she clung to his hand, never wanting to let go, and gazed out of the car's small windows. She had no words as she looked at the horrors beyond those windows. How awful it was!

'Steady on, love, you'll be breaking my fingers in a moment.'

The driver skillfully navigated the narrow channel between the walls of rubble. Isabel knew that the car, Hitler's famous '*Volkswagen*', a car for the people, had been embraced by the allies as a suitable vehicle to get them about. It resembled a crouching scarab from the outside, a beetle without the antennae. This one was painted a matt khaki. Army insignia and CCG shields were painted on the rounded wings. The utilitarian interior showed no concession to luxury. The engine rattled noisily, but it had a bustling business-like efficiency as it propelled them through the ruined streets.

'Air-cooled,' explained John later, 'much better in winter. You don't get frozen radiators and breakdowns. Believe me; it gets very cold in Berlin.'

Isabel acknowledged this information politely. She knew nothing of cars as her family had never owned one; nor did she know anyone else who had. Even Bill's wealthy mother didn't possess a car of her own and hired a chauffeur-driven vehicle or used taxis when necessary to take her to Knightsbridge or bridge parties with her cronies. She would never dream of getting on a bus or Tube.

Isabel watched Penny fondly; she seemed to be happy with John. The child was recovering rapidly from the journey and her good humour filled the car with giggling at his absurdities.

'Look, Penny,' John pointed, 'there's the *Tiergarten* - that's what the Germans call the Zoo. It means "animal garden".'

'I've been to the Zoo in London; I liked it. I rode on a camel. Will you take me to the Zoo here - please?'

'Sorry, there aren't any animals there now. Not even any camels.'

'Did they all run away?'

'Well, some did. But I think a lot of them just died; there

was no food for them, you see. And some were eaten.' replied John.

'Eaten? From the Zoo?'

'Yes, even the penguins. Taste like fish, you know.'

'Urgh! I couldn't eat a penguin.'

John kept to himself the true, grim reality of the conditions they had found in the Zoo. He remembered the solitary emaciated elephant, trumpeting forlornly in his pen and the hippo swimming round and round the bloated corpse of his mate in his fetid pool. They were dependent on desperate German volunteers risking their lives to feed them on whatever they could scrounge. Elephants were very partial to rose petals, it seemed. The antelopes, goats and camels had been eaten and the carnivores had died from starvation or escaped into the forests, to be shot eventually by hunters.

John pointed out what interesting features of the city remained, whilst Isabel and Bill whispered together on the back seat like a pair of teenagers.

Soon more trees stood at the sides of the roads and less rubble strewed the surface. The houses grew larger and more architecturally commanding, set back from the roadway by carriage drives and shrubbery. Here damage was less terrible than in more central parts of the city; they had reached the Grunewald, a residential suburb set amongst woods.

'Well, this is it,' said Bill as the driver deposited them at the kerb and started to unload the luggage.

Isabel tried not to shudder as she saw the outside of the house. The stonework showed evidence of artillery fire where chunks had been blown out by shells and shrapnel. Four wide steps led to solid wood double doors from which gouges of timber had been wrenched by gunfire, with holes right through in places. A piece of plywood nailed on the inside covered these breaches. Chicken wire was stretched and tacked across the dangerously cracked glass panels in the upper part of the doors. They opened onto the echoing vastness of the hallway. As she stepped in Isabel found that she couldn't restrain herself.

'My God, Bill! You could hold a football match in here!' she exclaimed, gazing about in awe.

'I know, it's ridiculous, isn't it?'

'My Mum's house would fit in here twice, no, three times.'

'Well, we have to share the hall with Dennis, you know. He lives upstairs. His wife Emma's coming over soon. I expect she'll be company for you.'

Isabel continued to look at the hall and the wide staircase, holding tight onto Penny's hand. Was this where they were going to live? In this battered palace that looked like somewhere that a giant had decided to demolish with his bare hands.

Irma crept from her room at the back and stood; stiff and huge- eyed, by the tiled stove, which later Isabel learned was called a *Kachelofen* after the Dutch tiles from which they were made. Bill held out his hand.

'Irma, come and meet Mrs. Barton.'

Irma stepped forward and bobbed, too shy to speak. Isabel felt embarrassed too. She had never dreamt of having a maid of her own. She smiled gently and extended a hand towards the girl. How thin she looked, but very pretty with her big blue eyes and that thick flaxen hair wound in plaits around her ears.

'Hello, Irma, I'm very pleased to meet you. And this is Penny.' She ushered the child forward.

Irma's face broke into a brilliant smile; shyness forgotten. 'Ah, the little one, *wie hübsche*!' She bent down and began to help Penny out of her coat. 'You and I will become great friends I think. Come…' she glanced at Isabel, 'if I may, I will take her to the kitchen and make her a drink and she can have some of the biscuits I have made. Would that be good, *kleine*?'

Penny followed Irma into the kitchen, buoyed up with the prospect of food.

Bill guided Isabel on a tour of the apartment. They walked into a room with a wide window that overlooked the garden, around which someone had draped quantities of white muslin. A stuffed rabbit leaned against the pillows on the bed.

'It's lovely, Bill. And so bright.'

'That's Penny's room. Irma found the toy at the market.' He stepped out and opened another door. 'And this is ours, I hope you like it.'

Bill led Isabel into the room next to Penny's. The furnishings were sparse, but imposing; a wide double bed stood centrally on one wall, a wardrobe of intimidating proportions loomed against another. A pair of unmatched small tables stood at each side of the bed. A threadbare rug, the colours faded to a muted patina, lay on the bare, polished boards. Muslin also festooned this large window.

'He bought the bed with cigarettes,' John informed her, leaning against the doorframe.

'As well as some of the other stuff,' said Bill. 'The wardrobe was here, marvellous isn't it? The Russians probably couldn't move it, it weighs a ton.'

Isabel gazed longingly at the huge bed piled high with pillows and a thick feather eiderdown; a welcoming nest. How wonderful it would be to throw herself on to it and give in to her exhaustion. But that wouldn't be fair to Bill and John. She bounced on the edge of the wonderfully comfortable mattress and scrutinised the massive, elaborately carved wardrobe, monument to some Bavarian artisan.

'Well, I should just about be able to fit my pathetic collection of clothes in there! Where's the bathroom?'

'Top of the stairs. There are two bathrooms up there. The other is Dennis's. Too complicated to get one put in down here, I'm afraid. The budget wouldn't run to all that plumbing.'

Moving across the wide hallway, Bill opened double doors to the drawing room. The late afternoon sun still shone outside so Isabel's first view was encouraging. Green and golden light flooded through the French windows onto the parquet floor polished to a sparkling sheen by Irma. She hardly noticed the scratches in the wood, the inexpertly patched plaster and the lack of paint.

Each end of the room, which stretched from front to back of the house, had a window. A rounded bay overlooked the street at one end and French doors opened into the garden at the other. An oak fireplace, carved with bunches of fruits and flowers, was built into the wall opposite the door to the hall. Logs and coal were laid in it, ready to be lighted. An ornate side table stood on the same wall as the door, with bottles and glasses on it. Two sagging armchairs, wide and comfortable-looking, were upholstered in faded blue velvet. A large sofa faced the fireplace its upholstery a frayed tapestry weave. Several small tables had been arranged haphazardly amongst the furniture.

'What a lovely room! So light.' Isabel sank onto a sagging old chair, laughing as her weight displaced the soft cushions. 'Whatever happened to the springs? I may never get up again!'

She picked up a roughly hewn piece of pinkish marble from the low table in front of the chair.

'What's this? It looks like a slice of petrified steak.'

'Ah, that,' said John, 'that's a lump of Hitler's desk, liberated from the Chancellery. Everybody grabbed a chunk as a souvenir. The Russians had smashed it up when they looted the place, just left the bits lying around. It'll make a good paperweight.'

Isabel dropped it hurriedly onto the table where it came to rest with a resounding clunk. 'Hitler's desk! God, how horrible.' She shuddered to think that the monster may have touched that same piece of stone.

John produced a bottle of French champagne from somewhere, a vintage *Veuve Cliquot.* He popped it open expertly and poured it into mismatched glasses waiting on the ornately inlaid table etched with scratches and gouges by the previous tenants.

'A toast, I think. To Mrs. B. Welcome, and may you be very happy in Berlin.' John grinned at her cheerfully.

'To Mrs. B.' echoed Bill. He whispered in her ear, 'I love you - it's wonderful to have you here.' Isabel stroked his face tenderly.

'This is lovely, John. I don't think I've had champagne since before the war. Where on earth did you get it?'

'No questions, no pack drill, my love,' answered John, tapping his nose meaningfully. 'But anything you need and can't find at the NAAFI, come to me, I can get almost anything, even in Berlin.'

Bill looked at him sharply. 'You'll get yourself into trouble, John, messing about with those black market *wallahs*. Steer clear of them - really, I mean it.'

'Come on, Bill. Don't give me a lecture today. A man's got to do what he can to survive in this hellhole. Besides, I'm putting away a nice little nest-egg for the future Mrs. Marriott, whoever she may be.'

'Just be careful, John. You hear of some nasty 'accidents' happening to people who interfere with the system. There are some real thugs in that racket. All the gangster dross of Europe has jumped on that particular bandwagon. Half of them are living on our hospitality in the DP camps. '

John shrugged and sipped his champagne.

They had become quite merry by the time John rose to leave and Isabel remembered Penny.

'Where's Pen? I haven't seen her for hours.'

'Irma will be looking after her. She adores kids.' Bill said.

They found Penny fast asleep and tucked up in her bed, the thick feather cover forming a mound over her and the new rabbit tucked in beside her teddy. Irma sat by the bedside gently crooning a song in German. The tune sounded familiar to Isabel.

'What's that?' she asked Bill. 'Such a pretty song.'

'Brahms Lullaby - everyone knows that one.'

'Guten Abend,
Gute Nacht
Mit die Rosen bedacht ...'

Chapter Nine

Berlin, September 1946

The first weeks in Berlin filled Isabel with a mixture of horror, awe and surprise. Horror at the scale of the devastation in the city; awe at how the inhabitants managed to survive their personal hell and surprise at how the occupiers were coping and managing to sustain some sort of order.

During the day the streets and railway stations thronged with people. Refugees still poured into Berlin at the rate of hundreds a day, by rail and on foot or by any sort of transport they could find. Sometimes an Army vehicle would hoist an exhausted refugee on to the back, risking a bollocking from the Sergeant. They were not supposed to show compassion to or aid the enemy, but many of the DPs were not Germans, but came from countries all over Europe. Often they had been used as forced labour in the factory camps or were escaping the Soviet occupation in Eastern provinces.

The influx put enormous pressure on the infrastructure of the city. Although some kind of water supply and sewerage had been restored, they frequently broke down and the electricity supply remained unreliable. As candles and lamp oil were hard to come by, at night the city was often plunged into silent darkness. A strict curfew was enforced and armed Allied soldiers in pairs patrolled the streets at night. They were frequently ambushed, their weapons and boots stolen, and left for dead amongst the cliffs of rubble.

On moonlit nights the outlines of the ruins were lit in eerie stark relief against a silver backdrop. At these times, after curfew, there pertained the stillness and silence of a world abandoned by man and God.

People wandered the streets, searching for food; a constant preoccupation. Isabel learnt that at the War's end the ration was insufficient to sustain life, even less than that supplied to internees of Nazi concentration camps. But American aid increased and by the time Isabel arrived, the ration rose. Supplemented by foraging, hunting (even for squirrels and wild birds) and the black market, people survived.

In an impromptu market set up near the ruined *Reichstag* and other sites, people sold the possessions they had no use for to Allied soldiers for tinned food and supplies from the PX, the American army's store, or the NAAFI, the British equivalent. Many desperate women turned to prostitution to feed their children.

The best jobs were in catering; rich pickings could be gleaned from the slop buckets and dustbins of the occupiers clubs, hotels and messes. Back in England there was no sympathy for the Germans' plight; bread had been added to the list of rationed foods. But conditions were much worse in Germany and Isabel wrote to tell the family, though they refused to believe all of her stories.

'Why should we give them anything when bread is rationed? That didn't happen even during the War. They lost the war didn't they?'

'But we can't just let them starve, they're not all evil. Babies and children are dying,' Isabel wrote. 'There's a lot of sickness, thank goodness we had all those inoculations before we left home.' She remembered their painful, swollen arms after the injections; Penny had been quite ill.

Bill worked with the Control Commission, trying to sort out former Nazis from the 'good' Germans and interrogating DPs. Once having filled out a questionnaire, a *fragebogen*, about their wartime activities, those passed as non-Nazis were given a certificate, nicknamed a '*Persilschein*', which entitled them to a ration card and work.

'Why's it called a '*Persilschein*'?' asked Isabel.

'It's a joke - because Persil washes whiter than white.

So they're clean as a whistle. To be honest, it's ironic because according to the people we're talking to hardly anyone was a member of the Party at all. No one actually owns up to it,' Bill explained.

'But that's ridiculous.'

'Yes, it is. We know that you couldn't get a job unless you joined the party – as a postman and certainly not as a teacher or policeman or anything in authority. They call them the *Muss-Nazis.* '

'But what happens if you don't get a *Persilschein*?'

'The proven Nazis go to prison. They'll be tried eventually. The others get their *Persilschein,* and then they can get a job and a ration card. Anyone who can't prove they didn't work hand in hand with the Nazis goes directly to jail. Of course we've got plenty of evidence against them. The Nazis kept the most amazing records of absolutely everything, and didn't manage to destroy them at the end, and many witnesses have come forward. It's a pity they didn't stand up to the Nazis earlier; it would have saved a lot of suffering.

'The huge camp at Sachsenhausen is one of the prisons. It was a slave labour camp – holds about 60,000 people. We released hundreds of starving survivors from there, many of them Jews. We're still finding these horrible places.'

'You've put these people all together in one place?'

'Yes. And to other camps.'

'God, it must be horrible.'

'Well, it's no holiday camp – that's for sure. Gives the Nazis a taste of their own medicine.'

'But you are making some progress, aren't you Bill?'

'There are so many of them, Isabel. It would take years to talk to them all. I'm sure that in the end we'll just give up and let them get on with it. But for now this is our job. Actually, the Yanks have stopped doing it; not enough man-power, they say. They've handed over to German civilian investigators.'

Bill worked with several colleagues, Army staff and some British civilians, in a requisitioned school building relatively unscathed by bombing. The gym, still with climbing bars on the walls and climbing ropes tied up to the beams, was used as the interrogation centre with tables and chairs laid out in ranks down its length. Most of the wired glass in the high windows had survived. It was an ideal place for crowds of people to be processed because they could wait in nearby classrooms and banks of toilets were available to them; the water supply allowing.

The people sat in stoical patience; they didn't mind waiting as they were warm and there was the chance of a hot drink. Members of the Catering Corps or the Red Cross were on hand with the tea urn and, sometimes, a biscuit or two. Medical personnel made the rounds to make sure that the 'clients' weren't carrying infectious diseases or vermin and treating them. The air was often filled with clouds of DDT as they dusted people for infection-carrying lice.

Dennis Masters from the upstairs flat worked with Bill. A civilian assigned to help with the mountain of paperwork generated by the operation, he had been recruited at the end of the war to help out the Military Government in Berlin. Many other civilians had been conscripted to help the tottering administration in the British Zone now that so many Forces personnel had gone home. Dennis expected his wife, Emma, to arrive any day now.

'I thought I'd got away with it,' said Dennis to anyone who took an interest. He cornered Bill one day and forced him to listen to his diatribe. 'I was too old for conscription while the War was on. Now they've decided they need people to help you lot out and don't care how old we are. I'm bloody furious; I had to leave a good job to come here. I doubt if it will still be there when I get back; then what am I going to do?' Dennis couldn't disguise his deep resentment.

'What are any of us going to do?' replied Bill, with marked lack of sympathy. 'Most of us have no jobs to go back to. But I expect there'll be plenty to do to get Blighty back on its feet. We've just got to get this lot sorted out first. How many are there today?'

'About a hundred,' replied Dennis. 'Stinking out the waiting rooms. I'll get the Corporal to send in the first ones.'

Every day the grinding monotony of the work of the work oppressed them. The interviewees waited with their scant possessions, fearful of leaving them in their miserable digs. Many were German civilians, many foreign workers, desperate to return to their countries but without the means. Some were POWs from liberated camps; some Russian army deserters or White Russians reluctant to return to the Motherland where they knew their welcome was likely to be death or a one-way trip to the Siberian gulags.

'Why do they keep coming to Berlin?' Isabel wondered.

'They seem to think conditions are better here and there's work for them. They have no homes. About 25 million people are homeless in Europe, you know.'

'Wouldn't it be better to stay in the countryside?'

'Yes, it would. There's food and it's safer – not so much crime and disease. Anyway, half the Berlin population takes the train into the countryside every day to find food. They exchange their valuables for potatoes and cabbages. There are going to be lot of rich farmers when this is over.'

Isabel had witnessed the influx of refugees; their possessions piled high on any transport they could find or bundled on their shoulders as they staggered into the city. Bewildered old men gazed in suppressed horror at the sights they encountered; women with children wailed in despair.

'We're worried about the winter.' Bill carried on. 'We were bloody lucky last year; expected it to be bitter. It could have been a disaster with coal production so low - but by a miracle it was mild. I don't expect we'll be as lucky this time. We did a lot of the preparation last year, dug a load of graves before the ground froze and we've got warehouses full of coffins.'

'Does it really get that cold here? Would so many people die?' Isabel asked.

'Oh, yes. There's such a shortage of food and Berlin gets colder than the coldest parts of Britain. We're in the middle of a land mass; there's no benefit from the Gulf Stream. Starvation is the main worry – many people to feed and more arriving each day. But we muddled through last year, or were very fortunate, depending on your point of view. People were hungry, and still are, but there was no famine. I don't know if we'll be as lucky this winter, with no reserves to speak of.' Worry furrowed his brow.

Isabel gazed at him, her eyes full of concern. He worked too hard. All the suffering he was seeing must be getting to him even though he didn't always tell her about it. He had become very tight-lipped. This was probably the longest conversation they'd had for ages. He normally came home exhausted and fell into bed after the briefest of meals. He never saw Penny, leaving the house before Irma got her up in the mornings and too late to do more than drop a cursory kiss when he got home. He'd changed, Isabel thought; not so willing to chat, quieter and more in-turned than when she first knew him. They seemed to have lost their openness and trust.

'I hardly see you, Bill. I never get to talk to you. Couldn't you spend a little time at home? When are we going to get back to normal?'

A brief look of scorn crossed his face. 'How can we get back to normal in the face of so much human misery? We need to work round the clock to get it straight, let alone 'back to normal'. I told you it would be like this.' Disdain and annoyance caused his voice to sound harsh and bitter.

'You shouldn't take it so personally. I thought you'd have a little time for us. You must get some time off.'

'There's the weekends, I see you then.'

'You always work on Saturday mornings and then you're in the Mess the rest of the day, chatting with your cronies. There's Church parade on Sunday and kowtowing to the Colonel and his clique. We're not exactly together, are we?'

'I warned you it would be like this,' Bill reiterated. 'You could have stayed in London, close to your family. You'll have to make the best of it now you're here.' He spoke with finality and a marked lack of feeling for her plight.

His words shocked Isabel. He spoke coldly, offhandedly, as if he didn't care how she felt. She wanted to reach out and explain how loneliness was engulfing her, how much she needed his company; some of his time just to herself. The thought had crossed her mind that they should try for another baby; she didn't want Penny to be an only child. She would have liked to discuss it with him; the possibility at least. But he'd set his features. He obviously didn't want to discuss anything and he looked so tired.

'All right, darling,' she sighed. 'I'm sure I'll be able to find something to keep me busy.'

But with Irma doing the housework and caring for Penny, Isabel found little to occupy her in the flat, although she had pottered in the garden. But she didn't want to get too engrossed with that, having spent the war in hard labour on her scrap of suburban garden, scratching at her vegetable patch to give them provisions to supplement the rations. Although the garden at the back of the Grunewald mansion could have been beautiful there was still a long way to go since the deprivations of the war had turned it into a jungle, exacerbated by the vandalism of the Russians. It sometimes made her think of the thickets of briars surrounding the sleeping Princess Beauty in the fairy story, impenetrable and constantly catching at her clothes.

Tidying up alone would take months and with autumn approaching there was little more she could do than tug away at the tangled brambles and cut back the overgrown shrubs with the secateurs that John had foraged for her. There always seemed to be a bonfire burning up the pruning and fallen leaves.

Although Bill working for long hours, Isabel was not always alone; John seemed to have much more free time.

'What does he do, Bill?' Isabel asked. 'He never seems to be very busy, nothing like you.'

Bill became reticent and, uncharacteristically, he stammered. 'Um, some sort of hush-hush work, I believe. He's always disappearing on some secret mission or another. You wouldn't have taken him for a man of action would you?'

'No, I wouldn't.' Isabel couldn't imagine John in the role of secret agent. He looked as if he would be more at home in a diplomatic salon, charming visiting dignitaries over glasses of champagne.

'Can't keep track of him half the time. I think he's too closely involved with those black-market people. I've no real idea what he's up to. I don't even know if it's official – he never tells me anything. But I suppose he's able to look after himself.'

Well, at the moment John seemed to have plenty of time for Isabel, something she felt nothing but gratitude for. His visits were not only a distraction from her loneliness but a pleasant diversion. She certainly enjoyed the presence of a charming companion.

'I've come to show you the sights, darling, such as they are.' John stood on the doorstep one sunny morning soon after her arrival in Berlin, his cap in his hand. 'Get your coat; I've got a car waiting.'

'A car! How did you manage that?'

'I've got a bit of official business to do later. I'll fit it in when we've finished.'

Isabel marvelled at his casual attitude. But she went inside and put on her coat and hat and kissed Penny goodbye. The child was happily making cakes with Irma. She barely looked up from her vigorous stirring, her hair and cheeks dusted with flour and flushed with the heat from the stove.

'We're making *Kuchen*. Irma's showing me how. See you later, Mummy. *Auf wiedersehn*.' She waved the wooden spoon in Isabel's direction, dropping dollops of cake mixture on the floor.

Isabel waved goodbye from the doorway. Penny would be enrolling at the Army school soon. She was already behind with her education, but Isabel wanted her to settle down and get to know her father better before sending her off to her first school.

'Bye, baby.' Isabel was happy that Penny was beginning to learn German. She seemed to be making much more progress than herself. Soon her daughter would be translating for her.

John bounced down the steps and gallantly opened the door of the VW. Isabel liked John. He made her laugh and she felt safe with him. He was very like Bill in many ways, but he had a harder edge than Bill, accompanied by an original, sharp sense of humour. John was more like a real soldier, tough both physically and mentally and of course he had the looks of a matinee idol. Bill was softer somehow, more thoughtful – he had a difficult war but very different from many serving officers. After all, he had never seen a shot fired in anger, spending most of his time behind the lines, interrogating prisoners; the consequence of speaking several languages fluently. It could not have failed to change him psychologically, even damaged him a little.

'Where first?' asked John 'Let me think, there's so much choice – I know, the NAAFI. You'll need to know about that, God help you.'

The *Volkswagen* rattled over the loose rubble that littered the streets as the walls of debris at the sides constantly avalanched down onto the roads. Isabel wanted to ask John to go more slowly but didn't, mainly because she couldn't get a word into his constant flow of chatter. He gave a non-stop commentary on their route, identifying all the old streets and sights; all completely meaningless to Isabel. It would be months before she could recognise the ruined buildings as the famous churches and palaces from before the war. Frustration and anxiety was nearly driving her mad when they finally squealed into the forecourt of the Forces' store and parked perilously close to the windows, in a neat straight line beside the wall.

'You'll get us killed, driving like that!' she managed to protest.

'Don't worry, darling, you're safe with me. Anyway, there's not much traffic is there? No-one's going to bump into us.'

Isabel chose to ignore this remark, merely raising an eyebrow at him. There were many things to crash into other than vehicles. John grinned, grabbed her arm and led her into the store.

A large requisitioned building near the centre of the British zone housed the NAAFI. It had probably been a department store in a previous life. It stood next to a requisitioned cinema, the Kino, frequented by the allied forces and families, showing films sent from England and America.

A canteen served strong tea and bitter coffee and simple meals for the occupying soldiers. Fish and chips, eggs and beans on toast, apples and custard and other typical delicacies; British cuisine at its most basic. It smelled of steam, frying fat and old food; all somehow comfortingly familiar and English.

The place reminded Isabel of similar self-service places at home, Lyons Corner Houses or the ABC cafes, but with poorer quality. At least the staff smiled and welcomed the Forces clientele. The staff consisted mainly of WAAFs with occasional male members of the Catering Corps to supervise. The rest of the space beyond the cafeteria was given over to the sale of essential household items.

John and Isabel sat down at one of many round metal

tables after queuing at the self-service counter to buy their drinks. At least it was cheap.

'Good God, what's this?' complained John after the first sip from his cup, 'Tastes like that *ersatz* rubbish they make from acorns.'

They tried gamely to enjoy their coffee, which Isabel thought was more likely to be Camp coffee essence from a bottle - the taste of chicory really strong, and the few stale shortcake biscuits. How she longed for a nice chocolate biscuit, something she hadn't seen for a long time.

'We don't use real money here,' John explained, 'we use these things called BAFFS. They're supposed to be worth the same as money in England but look different.'

Indeed, the pound notes resembled Monopoly money and the coins consisted of hexagonal plastic pieces, the red ones pennies and the yellow ones halfpennies. Isabel couldn't take it seriously as real money.

'It's so that they can't be stolen and used on the German economy which is fragile enough as it is; we're trying to get the Mark back on track. You can only use Baffs in here or in the *Kino*, or at the Mess or our other places.'

The NAAFI also supplied other goods to the British families. Every week a truck delivered food rations. These consisted of a box of staples; salt, flour, tea, coffee, cocoa, margarine and cooking fat; whatever meat was currently available, potatoes, vegetables (usually cabbage) and tinned goods. Also, tins of evaporated milk, no fresh being available, and leaky bags of powdered milk. This last arrived mostly in large hard lumps, almost impossible to dissolve smoothly, and it tasted horrible when put in tea or on cornflakes. But Penny enjoyed eating the lumps whole, like sweets, and it could be used in cooking where other flavours disguised the taste.

Tinned evaporated milk, watered down, enhanced tea and coffee. At first Isabel couldn't bear the taste, but she was used to it now. Very little sugar turned up and they used saccharine tablets, with a bitter aftertaste – Isabel avoided them.

Exploring the shelves, Isabel found that the NAAFI sold many of the essential non-food items. Toiletries and haberdashery, make-up and stationery were all available intermittently. The light bulbs and candles always disappeared almost as soon as they arrived, as everyone needed those and toilet paper was always in short supply.

'Don't worry, Isabel, I'll get hold of some for you,' John said when she couldn't see what she wanted. And, invariably, he would turn up next day with a grin and a parcel in exchange for their unused cigarette ration, which they didn't need as neither smoked.

'A very valuable commodity, cigarettes,' said John, 'You can get anything with them – they pass for currency now and also chocolate, or cocoa and real coffee, if you can get any,' he smiled hopefully, his head on one side like a puppy.

'Sorry, John. We've used our ration this week.'

Sometimes John couldn't borrow the car and they took public transport for their outing. He escorted her to Potsdam and the lakes; not really lakes but wide extensions of the river, and to the *Tiergarten*, no longer inhabited by animals, as he had explained to Penny. Not a single bird sang in the amputated trees which had struggled into leaf in the Spring and now reluctantly dropped them again as Autumn approached.

They also ventured into the centre of Berlin to the Hotel Moser, the once-grand hotel now serving as the Officer's Mess. The staff mostly consisted of elderly German staff, bent over with despondency and ailments but still as efficient and deferential as Isabel remembered from the opulent hotels in London. An A-board stood on the pavement outside with the optimistically normal message, "Afternoon Tea is Now Being Served", just as Isabel had seen outside similar establishments in the West End of London. It made her smile.

'I expect there'll be a party soon. They're always arranging something, a dance or a cocktail bash. Any excuse will do,' said John. 'We invite officers from the other zones so it gives you a chance to meet the French and Americans, and occasionally some Russians. At least it breaks the monotony.'

Isabel shuddered – Russians! She had heard some terrible stories about the behaviour of the Russians in defeated

Berlin. Poor Irma, still heart-broken since a Russian soldier had shot her adored Alsatian. But stories of rapes and thieving abounded. Irma and her mother knew many women who had been violated. They were lucky to escape them, hiding in their ruined eyrie. The Germans Bill and Isabel encountered hated all Russians with a passion.

'*Gott zei dank* we ended up in the British zone,' they'd say.

'I'm not sure I want to meet any Russians,' Isabel said to John.

'Don't worry, darling, some of them are quite civilised,' he reassured her.

Sometimes Isabel wondered if John's casual affection was a little too demonstrative. He flirted with too much enthusiasm, like someone courting a new lover. Should she keep him at a distance? But she soon realised that his breezy camaraderie and genial affection were part of his natural charm and did not mask any deeper feeling. He really seemed to enjoy her company. She certainly looked forward to seeing him, her only friend in this alien city now that Bill practically ignored her.

'Can't see you tomorrow, darling. I've got to take out the girlfriend. She's getting a bit restive.'

Isabel hadn't met John's girl, but had heard about her from Bill. He was vague about her origins.

'She's a lovely girl, very lively. French, I think, or Russian. She doesn't actually tell you much. But she's very pretty and seems to be devoted to John. Hope he's good to her.'

Isabel hoped so too. John deserved someone to make him happy.

Chapter Ten

Berlin, Autumn 1946

She had been living in Berlin for three weeks when Isabel received an invitation. It came from the colonel's wife, Mrs Stewart-Jones. Obviously a summons and delivered in the form of a proper stiff printed card, it spoke of tea, at her residence. 'Bring your children,' it demanded.

The feel of the card in her hand alone filled Isabel with apprehension. So far she had managed to avoid meeting the wives of senior officers, but knew she must eventually. The hierarchy of class imposed on British officers meant that the wives took on the rank of their husbands and were treated accordingly. But it also meant that she could not make friends among the wives of the so-called Other Ranks, who would be her natural choice. To appear in the Sergeant's Mess on a social evening would have been unthinkable and anyway, Bill would never dream of going. But she longed for a good old knees-up or sing-song round a piano, surrounded by people with whom she could have a laugh.

The usual mode of transport for army wives and families on semi-official business, or into the NAAFI or to take the children to the Forces' school, was an army vehicle. A jeep or a five-ton truck would collect them from their homes. The trucks also moved goods and chattels around when officers and their families were posted to another city; a crude removal van.

On the day of the tea party Isabel's nerves made her more and more strung up. She waited to leave, all brushed and made-up, primped and pretty, pacing the floor like a caged leopardess.

She wore the blue suit bought at Barkers; the smartest thing she owned. Underneath was a pretty silk blouse with a floppy bow at the neck and pin-tucks and embroidery down the front; one of the things made from parachute silk by the Italian nuns.

Inspecting herself in the long mirror on the back of the wardrobe door she felt more confident. Pretty classy, she thought. Penny wore one of the gauzy Italian frocks, an ice-cream pink confection with white smocking and a full skirt. One of Grace's hand-knitted cardigans completed the ensemble.

'You look as sweet as a fairy,' Isabel said as Penny twirled the fabric around her sturdy legs. 'Such a pretty girl!'

'Pretty girl, pretty girl,' Penny copied her mother and danced in front of the wardrobe mirror with hem of her skirt held up between her fingers like a tiny soubrette. Her feet, in Clark's sandals and white socks, whirled her across the floor in one of her excited dances.

Downstairs, as ready as they would ever be, they waited for the truck on the edge of the sofa, anxious not become crumpled. Soon they heard the jangle of the bell and went to the door. A smiling Corporal guided them to the kerb. They joined several other wives in the truck, seated on each side on hard wooden benches under the canvas top, after an undignified leap up from the street with a helping hand from the Corporal at Isabel's elbow.

'Steady, ducks.'

He grasped Penny around the waist and handed her to her mother. She was wriggling like a tadpole.

'You're tiggling me!' she giggled.

The Corporal grinned and tickled her again and Penny collapsed on to the bench, still laughing.

There were no other children in the truck and Penny sat close to Isabel during the short journey, her thumb in her mouth until Isabel gently pulled it out. The women appraised each other covertly, only exchanging a few remarks about the weather and the common grumble about the quality of the rations. They were probably also apprehensive about the coming ordeal, Isabel thought. The warm afternoon drugged her senses and Isabel was glad to be the last to be collected and sitting near the canvas opening at the back where a cool breeze stirred the stuffy air.

They arrived at the Colonel's house, which stood in a wide avenue of healthy trees in another part of the Grunewald, back from the road with a drive and a substantial front garden full of mature shrubs. The elegant mansion was even bigger than Bill and Isabel's and seemed to have sustained less damage. The beautiful windows were intact, or had been repaired, and Isabel could see no evidence of artillery fire in the stucco. The Russians hadn't wrought their destruction on this place – a Soviet General had probably lived here for a while until forced out when the boundaries of the zones were settled and he found himself billeted in the British Zone.

A stern-faced maid in a pristine uniform greeted them and led the group of women in to the drawing room. The floral chintzes and cretonnes that furnished the spacious room made it appear as if it had been transported in one piece from the Home Counties apart from the occasional item of heavy Bavarian furniture and the ubiquitous German feature of a massive tiled stove in one corner towering almost to the ceiling. Isabel noticed that these tiles were decorated in a pretty pattern of blue flowers painted on a white background, in the Dutch Delft style, unlike the one in their flat whose tiles were a sombre and menacing dark brown. No heat came from it today as there was no need for a fire on this warm September afternoon. Vases of flowers arranged in the formal English country house style sent fragrance into the air.

Isabel felt the same fear that she had felt on being summoned to the headmistress's office. A hollow feeling at the pit of her stomach told her that she had done something wrong, even though she knew that she hadn't.

Their hostess sailed towards the latest arrivals. A large woman with a firmly permanently-waved head of brown hair and a hard face, she bore down on them with hidden menace. Well-corseted, an imposing battle cruiser, her silk dress swished around her nylon-sheathed legs expensively. A hand outstretched to no-one in particular pointed in the direction of the group of new arrivals.

'Welcome,' she boomed in Kensington tones, 'How nice to see you all.' The warmth of her smile evaded her eyes. When Mrs Stewart-Jones came to briefly shake her hand Isabel flinched involuntarily and her smile wavered. She felt herself being appraised; the shrewd fierce eyes swept up and down, evidently taking in every detail. Impossible to gauge the verdict of this scrutiny.

'Mrs Barton? You're our newest recruit. Let me introduce you to the other ladies.'

Her hostess turned abruptly and Isabel realised she was expected to follow in her wake. Limp hands were thrust out towards her for shaking and she was bombarded with so many names that she was aware that she could not remember one of them. They seemed amiable enough, but no more interested in her than she was in them. But she smiled brightly and murmured greetings to them all. She was glad to sit down at last and accept the delicate Crown Derby cup and saucer handed to her by a maid. At least it's proper tea, she thought, not that awful perfumed stuff or the phoney tea the Germans have to drink.

Penny had been whisked away as soon as they arrived.

'She'll be fine upstairs with the others.' Mrs Stewart-Jones predicted with a dismissive wave of her hand, 'Gerde's in the nursery with them. I'm sure they'll manage to amuse themselves.'

Isabel hoped Penny would be all right as her timidity sometimes overwhelmed her and she was not used to the company of crowds of boisterous children. The teacher at the army school had noticed this when she started at the kindergarten last week and was doing her best to help Penny overcome her shyness. At least she hadn't cried and clung to Isabel's hand, as she had feared she would. But just now she had climbed the Colonel's stairs with the air of someone on their way to the scaffold.

The introductions over, Isabel felt free to look around and take in her surroundings. She noticed with horror that everyone else wore a silk dress in a summery print, or even a proper full length tea-gown in the case of some of the older ladies; some looking a little like Queen Mary at her most imperious. Isabel peered at her suit, which a short while ago had seemed incredibly stylish and now appeared totally inappropriate. She tried to sink lower into the armchair; perhaps she could become invisible. She felt hot colour rise in her cheeks.

'It's amazing, isn't it?'

The voice came from somewhere above Isabel's head.

'I'm sorry?' whispered Isabel, looking up to where the voice came from.

'Amazing – you could be right there, in England, in Weybridge or somewhere in Wiltshire.' The voice pronounced the last word with a long 'i'.

An American, thought Isabel. The voice sounded nearer now as the owner bent down closer to Isabel. She saw a pencil-thin, incredibly chic girl dressed entirely in black, outlined by the light from the window. As she came nearer Isabel saw how very young and pretty she was and the brilliant smile on her face. Those amazingly white teeth again.

'Hi! I'm Zelda. Zelda Hoffstetter. Yes, I know, don't groan. My parents had a thing about F. Scott Fitzgerald.'

Zelda perched on a footstool near Isabel's chair. With a deft hand she stroked back a single stray hair on her otherwise impeccably coiffed head.

'Isabel Barton, isn't it? I thought you might be here – in the Dragon's Lair. I've heard a lot about you.'

'You haven't!' Isabel said, horrified. 'What have you heard?'

'Oh, nothing bad. Don't look so alarmed. Just what a good-looking couple you are an' all. Chuck admires your husband a lot.'

'I'm sorry, Bill hasn't mentioned…'

'That's OK. I know - you hardly ever see him. They're very busy.' Zelda waved a slim hand towards the room. 'Have you met the rest of the *hausfraus*?'

Isabel giggled, 'Yes, most of them. But I can't remember any of their names.'

'Dreadful, aren't they? But don't worry; in no time at all you'll be all too familiar with them. This is it, honey, your social life for the duration. Don't forget the wives take on the rank of their husbands so remember to keep in your place and you'll be all right. I think you British are even worse than us Yanks in that respect – hierarchy and all.'

Isabel surveyed the room full of superior-looking women, of different ages but all so snooty that they made Isabel feel hopelessly *declassée*. She was glad that Bill had been promoted to

Major. At least she wouldn't be too far down the pecking order. Oh dear, she thought with an audible sigh.

'I'll look after you, honey. I'm so glad I've met you at last. We'll have some fun.' Zelda perched on the edge of a chair nearby.

Isabel couldn't fail to warm to her new American acquaintance. She seemed charming and God knows, she could do with a friend. She smiled back brightly.

'I'm dressed all wrong. But I didn't have anything suitable. This is the only thing I've got that's even remotely smart.' Isabel indicated the blue suit.

'It's a great costume, but there seems to be a uniform for these get-togethers. Silk tea dresses, cocktail frocks, evening gowns; everything suitable for the occasion. And so it goes on. Ridiculous when there are such shortages.'

'I haven't got anything like that!' Isabel felt panicky.

'Look, I've got a wonderful dressmaker. She can copy anything. We'll get her to make you some things.'

'I'm sorry,' Isabel said, embarrassed. 'I couldn't possibly afford that.'

'Oh God, I know! You British are so badly paid.' Zelda, whose diamonds at ear lobe and finger indicated considerable affluence, spoke completely without guile or the British embarrassment at the mention of money. 'You don't need cash. You can get anything in Berlin for food or ciggies. Or soap, they're desperate for soap.'

'Oh yes, I know,' Isabel said, thinking of John. 'But we've only got our ration and…'

'Really, it won't be much. I'll talk to her and we'll see what we can do.'

Isabel chatted to Zelda and did her duty in stilted conversation with other guests before the Colonel's wife made it clear that the afternoon was at an end, clapping her hands like a schoolmistress to get their attention.

Her, 'It was delightful to see you, ladies. Thank you so much for coming,' obviously served as their dismissal.

She hustled her guests out of the house towards their waiting transport. Penny came down the broad stairs smoothing down the pretty frock with worried hands, a frown between her brows.

'There was a boy there, Mummy. He was rough. I didn't like him.'

'Oh, you're so cute!' said Zelda, stroking Penny's silky hair gently. 'Rough boys. Gee, we don't like them, do we? You come and visit me; I don't have any rough boys.'

Isabel arranged to call on Zelda as soon as she could; already looking forward to it. Perhaps she'd found a friend at last.

'I don't bring my kids to these things,' Zelda said. 'The maid looks after them, she's a treasure. I've got twins, boys, but only 18 months old, so not rough yet!' She patted Penny's head. 'See you soon, baby. You too, Isabel Barton!' And then she was gone in a rush of displaced air, in the back of an American Army jeep with a uniformed driver. She smiled broadly and waved over her shoulder as they drove away down the centre of the street.

Chapter Eleven

Berlin, Autumn 1946

A heavy burden of loneliness weighed on Isabel. The long hours alone in the flat were submerged in aching boredom, with a valve radio that worked only intermittently and was dependent on the vagaries of the electricity supply and a very old gramophone with a horn, which had to be wound up by hand. Anyway, the selection of records was pathetic; some classical and some German folk songs, many of them scratched, causing the needle to catch at regular intervals. She had read everything she could lay her hands on, from a tattered copy of Jane Eyre to a very racy novel by someone she'd never heard of. An airmail copy of the Daily Telegraph appeared every now and then, bringing news of home. This was soon read from cover to cover.

On some empty afternoons the silence became so oppressive that she wanted to scream. She tried to read, curled up on the old velvet sofa, but the sound of the ticking grandfather clock in the hall disturbed her concentration. She watched the slender beam of light penetrating from the garden and wished she should get out, anywhere, away from here.

She wrote long letters home, but there was little news to tell and she didn't want to worry her family with her loneliness and boredom. She certainly couldn't divulge that her relationship with Bill was not all it should be; that he didn't seem to want to talk to her most of the time. They weren't pleased with her being here anyway and would try to get her to go home if they thought she was unhappy. So she tried to sound cheerful; to emphasise the droll and interesting. She described her meeting with Zelda and the tea-party with the Colonel's wife, hoping it would amuse them.

'What a dragon!' she wrote 'Even worse than our headmistress at school – you remember, the Battleaxe.'

Finally she had found a companion to spend some of those long hours with. Whenever they had time to spare, Zelda and Isabel met. On sunny days, with Penny at school, they walked in the park near Isabel's house. Here the trees had survived the war almost intact, though now some were being felled for firewood. Even in the centre of Berlin most of those trees damaged conflict had struggled into life in the spring. Now the foliage had turned to burnished gold and red as autumn approached. The leaves began to fall in a glory of russet rain and formed a carpet that whispered as they walked. Someone was always trying to make a bonfire and scented fumes filled the chilling air. The long solitary hours were mitigated by Zelda's visits and Isabel relished her cheerful companionship.

Bill had some idea of how she felt and, probably with the best of intentions, he made a suggestion for her amusement.

'You should try to make friends with Emma Masters,' he said. 'She'll be good company for you.'

Isabel quailed at the thought of Dennis's home-counties wife, all twin-sets and pearls, teamed with good-quality tweeds. Her interests seemed to consist solely of sporting pursuits, golf, riding and tennis. Isabel could sense the woman's disapproval; the questions in her eyes, the imperceptible tilt of her nose accompanied by a barely audible sniff. What a snob, was Isabel's first thought and later encounters had not led her to feel any differently.

Emma was a younger, taller version of Bill's formidable mother, with a congenital conviction that her class was the only one worth belonging to and that there was only one way of conducting your life according to rigid and arbitrary rules of behaviour. But Isabel was less daunted by these attitudes now she lived with Bill, who had no interest in or understanding of such distinctions. Her confidence seemed to have grown now. Even the terrifying colonel's wife, Mrs Stewart-Jones, no longer had the power to make her quake in her shoes. She was just a woman like any other trying to make the most of life in a ruined foreign land.

'Shall I ask Dennis and Emma to eat with us?' Isabel asked Bill, regretting the words before they had left her mouth.

'That's a good idea,' he replied. 'A dinner party. Yes, lay that on, darling. Better give me a bit of notice to make sure I'm here.'

'You'd better be,' she warned, 'I couldn't possibly cope with them on my own.'

He kissed her on the cheek as he left. 'Don't worry, darling, I'll be there.'

What had she done? Isabel did not care for the couple upstairs and now she had suggested inviting them to dinner; what had she been thinking? What on earth could they eat? She supposed they should have at least three courses, would that be enough? But there was no chance of a fish course; they were too far from the sea. The nearest thing they saw to a fish nowadays was a tin of sardines and the occasional delicacy that could possibly be a kipper.

Irma suggested a first course of soup; ingredients could always be found for soup.

'I could make *Wiener Schnitzel*, if you can get some veal,' she said. 'And I've got an idea for dessert.'

John managed the veal, from one of his mysterious contacts and the menu was set. Thank goodness for Irma, thought Isabel, what a treasure she is.

The evening began smoothly. Once the table was properly laid, in the way Isabel was sure Emma would expect, and Penny was in bed, Isabel was more relaxed.

Emma and Dennis came down and chatted with rare good humour. Emma was hopelessly overdressed, Isabel thought, in a red silk cocktail dress and, apparently, all the jewellery she possessed. But she smiled.

'How kind of you to ask us, Isabel.' she cooed, with barely a trace of condescension.

They each consumed a strong gin and tonic before dinner.

'This rubbish gin can only be tasted in large helpings,' Bill claimed. 'No point in drinking it if it tastes of nothing.'

By the time Irma announced dinner they were becoming quite jolly and Isabel's nervousness evaporated.

Bill had managed to buy a good bottle of red wine from a French acquaintance. The French zone was awash with everything necessary to make the French occupiers feel at home and anything they didn't import they purloined from the Germans; getting their own back on their erstwhile occupiers.

Irma served a tureen of steaming onion soup with generous sprinklings of croutons. Irma's delectably tender *Wiener Schnitzels* followed, fried in what Isabel feared was most of their butter ration. Mashed potatoes and cabbage (of course), laced with caraway seeds in the German fashion, accompanied the meat.

'This is delicious, Isabel,' said Emma. 'Your maid's a very good cook.'

'I know. She's marvellous, isn't she?'

Finally Irma brought in the dessert. Four goblet glasses filled with a concoction of artificial cream whipped with tiny rubies of wild strawberries.

'Oh my goodness, this is wonderful! Where did you find the strawberries?'

'Somebody brought them in from the country. They grow wild in the woods in autumn. Only ten cigarettes,' said Isabel.

Everyone laughed, all accustomed to this bizarre currency.

'But the cream, it's just like the real thing.'

'Irma has a magic machine that whips up egg yolks and milk and by some amazing alchemy, this is the result.'

'It's incredible!'

They enjoyed the food, Isabel thought with satisfaction, but conversation had become stilted. Isabel found she had so little in common with Emma. She didn't want to keep talking about Penny to a woman with no children. Emma was at least 15 years older than her; what could they possibly talk about?

'Do you like Berlin?' asked Isabel in desperation.

'Not terribly,' said Emma. 'Apart from anything else, there's nothing to do.'

'Have you met any of the other wives?'

'A few. I didn't like them much.'

I'm sure of that, thought Isabel.

'Some of the Americans are nice,' said Isabel, thinking of Zelda.

Emma recoiled. 'Americans? I can't bear them; such brash vulgar people.'

Isabel couldn't reply to that, so she fell silent. Perhaps the men were talking about something interesting, or was it just the usual stuff?

Indeed, the men talked shop, discussing the hopelessness of processing everyone who passed through their centre.

'We'll never be able to root out all the Nazis,' said Bill.

'They can't do much harm now,' said Dennis.

'But they should be punished, surely?' said Emma. 'They did such terrible things.'

'The War Crimes Trials at Nuremberg will see to that. I think that in the end only the ringleaders will be tried. Some of them will be executed, but we can't hang thousands of people.'

'I don't see why not,' said Emma. 'They were evil.'

'It's all a matter of degree,' said Bill. 'They were often forced to join the party to survive.'

Emma shook her head. She'd like to string up everyone who doesn't come from the South of England, thought Isabel. Later, over coffee, Emma dropped her bombshell.

'Actually,' she said, 'I'm thinking of going back to England.'

Shocked, Dennis turned towards her. 'What? You've only just got here.'

'I know. Nonetheless, I intend to go.'

'It's the first I've heard of it,' Dennis said.

'I've only just decided. You don't need me here. I'll go and look after Mother.'

Dennis didn't protest about this sudden decision. Isabel thought she detected a furtive look of relief. I wonder what he's up to, she thought. He doesn't really want her here and she knows it. Why? He doesn't look like the type to have an affair. Isabel couldn't see him taking up with one of the needy German *fräuleins* desperate for a meal-ticket. It must be something else. What a strange, secretive bloke he was.

'We'll talk about this later.' Dennis said, standing abruptly. 'I think we should be going now. Thank you for your hospitality.

We enjoyed it.' The words were stilted and unconvincing. Isabel almost felt sorry for him.

The dinner broke up with the couple climbing to their flat; Emma ahead of Dennis, in complete silence. Isabel was certain the silence would be broken by angry words once their stout bedroom door closed.

One day soon after the dinner party, Zelda arrived with a length of pretty flower-sprigged silk, tiny blossoms in bright colours on a white background; the epitome of spring. Isabel let the fabric flow through her hands like a rippling stream.

'Oh, Zelda, it's beautiful! I love it.' Isabel held it up against her body. How she needed something gorgeous to wear!

'I bought far too much. Anyway, it's too cutesy for me! I prefer to wear plain colours; usually black. It'll be wonderful on you, with you English rose look.'

'But I'm as dark-haired as you,' Isabel protested.

'Never mind that,' Zelda ordered at her most domineering. 'You have it. Do.'

'OK. I give in. How can I resist? What do I owe you?' Isabel laughed.

'Don't be silly. It's a gift. I insist.'

The two spent a happy, productive afternoon, scanning magazines from the NAAFI, for a suitable style to copy. A not too out-of-date Vogue was full of photographs of the latest Paris fashions. It seemed that this year longer skirts were de rigueur. The dressmaker Zelda recommended was a marvel and could mimic a dress from a photograph or drawing for a tin of cocoa or a couple of bars of soap.

Later they went for a walk until the time that Penny came home from school. She was beginning to settle in, to Isabel's relief. The little girl now waited with eagerly for the school truck to arrive in the morning, chattering of friends she had made and things she had learned. She seemed to adore her teacher, Miss Graves.

The autumn air already carried the chill edge of winter. Isabel worried about her wardrobe, lacking in anything much suitable for really cold weather. Grace had knitted her a warm jumper and some amazingly thick socks, but she'd need a good coat. The one she'd had in London was threadbare and shabby and certainly not warm enough for the freezing conditions predicted in Berlin.

'I was here last winter,' Zelda said, 'and although it was supposed to be dreadful it wasn't too bad. But winter's coming again soon and everyone says it's going to be real bad. We'll need to be prepared.'

Bill confirmed Zelda's words.

'You'll have to get Penny and you warm clothes as well as that fancy party stuff, you know.' He scanned her new finery critically where it was spread out on the bed. Isabel was at a loss to know where he thought she was going to get more clothes, warm or otherwise. There were no more clothing ration coupons and certainly no money for them.

One day he came home with a fur coat bundled in his arms. He helped her into it; holding the weight in his hands. Its thick bulk dwarfed Isabel's slight frame and the weight when Bill released it made her shoulders buckle. The fur was dense and dark brown; the hem almost touched the floor. Isabel felt stifled by the garment as if a great woolly body were holding her in its arms. It was certainly warm and no cold wind was going to penetrate the thick folds.

'It's beaver,' Bill said, 'one of the warmest furs around. It's a bit long, but you'll be glad of it later. It'll keep your ankles warm.'

'Where on earth did you get it?' Isabel staggered around the room, trying to become accustomed to the weight.

'One of my "clients" gave it to me. He didn't want it any more. It belonged to his wife, but she died at the end of the War. Now it's too heavy for him to carry around and he can't bear to wear it. Maybe he thought it would be easier to get his *Persilschein*, but he would have got one anyway.' Bill seemed embarrassed by this revelation, as if he had done something wrong in accepting the coat.

'Well, thank you, darling, and if it gets really cold we can all live in it!' She teased as she struggled to twirl. She finally removed it and hung it in the wardrobe, where it threatened to bend the pole.

The same week Bill came home with a less welcome gift. He placed it in her hand.

'This is for you.'

The thing lay in her palm. Isabel looked at it with horror. She thrust it back at him.

'No! I don't want it.'

'You have to, darling. It's for your protection. You heard about Mrs Henderson, stabbed in the chest and no-one there to help her as she bled to death. People out there are bitter – the Germans, the DPs too – they resent us. Remember, we're an occupying army. Living conditions are very difficult. There were five murders every day this summer. Yes, I know they've been spread in all the zones, but it's dangerous out there. You must keep it. All the wives are getting them. I can't be here all the time. Stash it under your pillow or something.' He pushed it back into her reluctant hand and it lay there, mute, cold and menacing.

It was nothing like any gun she had seen before. A mile away from the familiar weapons used by cowboys in the movies - Colt 45s weren't they? They had round chambers, which held the bullets. They killed people. That was the extent of Isabel's knowledge of guns.

But this gun was different. It was tiny and compact and barely filled the palm of her hand - a flat, square-edged piece of molten grey steel, lethal and uncompromising.

'It's a Mauser automatic,' Bill told her. 'This is the safety catch here...' he showed Isabel how to put it off and on, '...and these are the bullets.' He handed her a box no more than two inches square with German gothic script on the sides. It held twenty tiny slugs tightly packed together, each in its own little compartment with no space between them, like the cells in a honeycomb, each bullet capable of killing someone if you were close enough and lucky enough to get a shot at them before they hurt you.

'I'm not going to load it,' Isabel assured him, her voice filled with repugnance.

'You must. There's no point in having a gun that's not loaded, Isabel. It could save your life. We'll go into the country one weekend and practice shooting.'

'I couldn't shoot anyone.'

'Look, keep it close. Then if anyone in an ugly mood turns up when I'm not here at least you've got some protection. I worry about you, darling. It will keep you safe.'

How was that going to happen? She silently turned the gun over in her hand and shuddered. It didn't make her feel safe; it made her feel more frightened and vulnerable.

'I thought the war was over. I didn't think I might have to kill someone.'

Bill's voice became steely. 'There are thousands of starving and angry people roaming the streets. They have nothing. No homes, no food, no jobs and no rights and very little hope. Most of them are totally desperate and dangerous. Think of how I'd feel if anything happened to you. Think of Penny.'

That concluded the argument. Of course, if it was for Penny…

Dutifully she put it under her pillow. At first she felt as if she could discern its malign presence through the pillows. The square hardness, she was certain, would forge a mark on her cheek. Once, when she felt for her handkerchief, her fingers brushed it and she recoiled in shock.

Isabel vowed that she'd never use the thing. But she kept it under the pillow to keep Bill quiet. One day she'd get rid of it somehow; throw it into the river or something. She would certainly never take it out of the flat for any other reason.

Chapter Twelve

Berlin, 1946 – Dennis

Dennis scratched his chin for the thousandth time. God, this beard is driving me mad, he thought. He'd grown it in a spirit of rebellion and self-importance, hoping it would look distinguished, like the neat beards of George Vth and the late Tsar, but it had turned out to be a spindly, haphazard affair, grey in places and ginger in others; not at all what he had in mind. Rules prohibited army personnel from growing beards, but he, as a civilian, could do as he pleased. No stupid strictures could be imposed on him. He'd been conscripted post-war; a civilian sent here to Berlin when the War had been over for more than a year. He was too old for the fighting War, much to his relief, but then they'd come and buggered it up.

Dennis's thinning ginger hair flopped over his eyes. Another rebellion, he didn't have to conform to regulation military hair length either. The ginger, he preferred to call it auburn, was fading to a mottled greyish brown, like an old fox. He remembered the torment he had endured from bullies in his childhood.

'Garn' Ginger, Ginger!' they'd taunted as he made his way home from the grammar school. 'Gingers Nuts!'

He would never forget his cringing humiliation at their hands. But he had ridden above it all; good School Certificates, university and on to be a respected accountant working in Cheltenham for nearly 20 years and about to be made partner. Then this had happened. What a bloody cock-up! Just when things were going well he'd been ordered by the War Office to come to Germany to help with administration in the denazification programme.

Because one of his Higher certificates had been German; he wasn't even fluent in the language. It seemed the useless Army couldn't manage on their own. Anyway, after five years abroad most of them itched to go home. So now they were short-staffed and found help from wherever they could.

The massive deluge of people and paperwork threatened to submerge the Allied Control Council; a bureaucratic nightmare. Amazingly, in 1945 they had found the records of every party member, kept meticulously by the Nazis, waiting to be pulped in a paper mill near Munich. The Army people were incapable of sorting it out, more suited to running around with guns and killing people, Dennis supposed. They'd not been trained in proper business method.

So here he was, nearly 50, with a boss almost 20 years younger. This stuck-up public schoolboy upstart, Major Bill Barton, telling him what to do in his 'oh so polite' plummy voice. But fair do's, the man was an incredibly good interrogator, with plenty of practice during the War. He could teach the police back home a thing or two about extracting information and without the use of thumbscrews. He managed to get to the nub of a person's background in no time. Not that there was much time, what with the numbers that they had to process. The rapid turnaround made his head swim. But Barton knew how to sort out the wheat from the chaff.

Dennis's deep resentment had etched lines of discontent on his already striated features. Always lugubrious and humourless, his present circumstances had rendered him positively morose. I don't see why I should make an effort to be pleasant to people; not to the Army and certainly not to the Germans. I didn't ask to be here.

What am I going to do now? He thought. His wonderful job back in England had been kyboshed, that's for sure. A couple of years in Germany and he could be certain that the offer of a partnership would have vanished. They'd probably give it to that stupid pipsqueak Andrews.

However, after a few weeks at the Berlin job, a way out had presented itself. Well, if not exactly a way out yet, at least a sop; something to ease the awfulness of the situation. Observation had taught Dennis something interesting and he had an inkling of what he could do to save himself. He realised that here in Berlin there pertained the perfect way of making a lot of money to fund his future life in England.

Emma, when he told her about it shortly after her arrival, had disapproved.

'People like us don't get involved in that sort of thing,' she'd said with a sniff, in that infuriating snobby way she had of making her opinions known.

Dennis knew that anything to do with the Black Market was anathema to most people who had struggled in England during the War. It was seen as unfair; somehow not playing the game; not British.

Sod that, thought Dennis. An opportunity this good wasn't going to come again. Berlin was awash with suffering people that he could help out by relieving them of their valuables in exchange for as little as possible. A kilo of sugar here, a pound of butter there and then he could either sell on the goods for US dollars or barter them again for yet more valuable items. Watches. He had a drawer full of watches, the Russians were mad for them and would pay ridiculous prices, even for a tacky Mickey Mouse watch purloined from an American corpse, for a first edition or a work of art. Russian soldiers had no interest in art and culture.

Sometimes he managed to sell half bottles of what might have been Scotch whisky for ridiculous sums. He preferred to be paid in jewellery; more portable and easily stashed away. The dollars the Russians gave him were suspect. They printed their own with US Treasury printing plates implausibly supplied by the Yanks in a spirit of co-operation. They worked when used to buy painkillers from the shifty night clerk in the US Army's pharmacy, to be exchanged for more valuables down the line. So backwards and forwards it went and in the process it was making Dennis rich.

In whatever spare time he had away from the 'office', Dennis haunted the open-air markets at the ruined *Reichstag* or the *Tiergarten*, exchanging as little as he could for jewellery, rugs, furs, *objets d'art* and paintings. He was becoming quite an expert; able to value anything at a glance, with the help of an antiques directory he'd had sent over from London and knowledge gained from observation of his parents' possessions. The sellers were often pathetically ignorant of or oblivious to the worth of their chattels, survival and food having taken precedence over temporarily worthless artefacts.

The 'clients' who came through Dennis's office, whose paperwork he processed daily, also proved a rich source of bounty. The other day someone sold him the deeds to a plot of land in central Berlin (there had probably been a building on it at one time, now bombed out), in the right zone thank God, for a *Persilschein*. Who the hell cared what the man had done in the War? He couldn't do much damage now, Nazi or not. Dennis had found that people would do anything for a clean bill of health, a rubber stamp and a ration card.

He had to be careful that Bill Barton didn't notice that he had let slip through the occasional person that Bill had suspicions of. But so many were processed day by day that it was quite simple to lose some that had suitable payment for their freedom.

A few weeks ago he'd had a stroke of luck. A German civilian came in, probably more to get out of the cold and get a free Red Cross cup of tea than anything. He didn't seem interested in a *Persilschein* or the possibility of a job. A filthy, ragged specimen with the stench of poverty and a graveyard cough, his name was Fritz Keller and only asking for help in getting the ration card he was entitled to as a released work-camp inmate. He had been interned for years because of his communist leanings. He supplied all the right paperwork as proof. His shifty eyes and demeanour gave him away as someone out for the main chance.

'Perhaps you can help me, Herr Keller,' said Dennis.

Keller brightened, somehow guessing immediately what was required of him.

'Is there anything I can get for you, sir?' he asked hopefully. 'Furniture, art ... women? Almost anything can be bought at a price. For medicines, cigarettes, coffee, tinned food, soap.'

'I think it's possible that we could do business, Mr Keller. I'm looking for items of value, for the usual currency. Let me know what you can get and we'll negotiate.'

Since that meeting Fritz Keller had put him in touch with the right people to buy what he needed. He proved particularly helpful over the property deals, knowing just who to approach to seal the legal details in the most discreet way possible. The last deal had cost him an Army vehicle 'lost' from the REME motor repair shop in a hazardous night-time raid. There had also been Fritz's commission of course; several cartons of cigarettes. But it had been worth it.

Sometimes it gave Dennis great pleasure to refuse a *Persilschein.* There had been a bastard the other day that had kicked up the hell of a stink; shouting all sorts of accusations about bribery and corruption. He had been a postman and had obviously been denouncing Jews to the Gestapo when he found them taking refuge in their neighbours' houses. He had nothing worth trading, so Dennis had gleefully sent him to the cells from where he would eventually be taken to a camp, one of those used earlier to house Jews en-route to extermination, and later to trial for his sins. Served the Nazi bastard right. It made Dennis feel quite virtuous.

He wasn't sorry that Emma had decided to leave, even after such a brief stay. Well, it had never been a joyful marriage. Miserable cow, he thought, always moaning, never satisfied. It's true there isn't much to do here, but she could have started a bridge club, if that's what she wanted. She couldn't be bothered and mooched about the flat all day, complaining of boredom. She couldn't even make friends with Bill Barton's pretty wife, who seemed amiable enough.

'Such a common girl,' Emma had said, sticking her sharp nose into the air. 'I wouldn't mix with her in Cheltenham; I don't see why I should here.'

He couldn't see it himself; Isabel Barton spoke and behaved perfectly properly.

'It's subtle,' said Emma. 'I know the signs. She's far too friendly with that maid of hers. She doesn't know how to treat servants. They need to be kept in their place. Anyway, she told me that her father works on the railways,' Emma said this with the tones and expression of someone who had just had something smelling obnoxious thrust under her nose.

'Isabel probably feels sympathy towards the maid. She comes from London, you know, saw a lot of bombing and horror, similar to what they've suffered here. We didn't get much of that in Cheltenham, did we, dear?' Most of their suffering had been in the form of inconvenience, rationing and shortages.

'As for that man, John Marriott,' Emma continued as if he hadn't spoken, 'swanning around like the Playboy of the Western World. What on earth's he doing all the time? He spends half his days gallivanting with Isabel Barton, as far as I can tell. Shouldn't he be making himself useful?'

Dennis decided not to reply to this. He had a fair idea of what Marriott was doing and it didn't require sitting in an office all day. His fun and games with Mrs Barton probably acted as excellent cover. He knew he'd have to watch out for Marriott. He was well aware that if the man discovered Dennis's black market activities he would be arrested, prosecuted and sent home pronto, in disgrace. They were supposed to be getting the German economy back on its feet, not undermining it with illicit trading and removing everything of value from the country.

Dennis had to take more care now. There had been developments making it impossible to use hard currency in payment for goods. American soldiers, doing very much what Dennis did, buying and selling on the black market, had been sending home to their families more dollars than they legitimately earned, swamping the US with currency printed by the Russians willy-nilly without reference to the US Treasury department. This practice would be the ruin of the American economy if it continued unabated. Hence the new currency restrictions, much to the Russians' disgust. Soldiers could now only use Occupation Currency, Baffs. But they still had their cigarettes and rations to trade if they wished to.

None of this affected Dennis. He had his own little business nicely sewn up and so long as John Marriott and Bill Barton kept their spiky, espionage-trained noses out of it, and with Fritz Keller's help, he expected to return to England a very rich man.

Chapter Thirteen

Berlin, October 1946

The foyer of the Hotel Moser buzzed with activity. In spite of threadbare patches in the carpet and the dust on the swagged curtains, the old hotel had managed to maintain an air of grandeur and dignity. Fake Fragonard murals still adorned the walls between the pillars even though the swinging maidens had faded curls and their garlands of flowers and sweeping skirts were washed-out pastels. The hallway remained in remarkable condition considering that this had been the watering hole for Nazi officers and later for the conquering Russians. But, as it had been used exclusively for the entertainment of the officers and had even served as a brothel in earlier times, it had escaped much of the vandalism seen in other buildings. Now it had been requisitioned as the Officers Mess by the English-speaking Allies and was used as a transit hotel for single officers between postings. Many evenings hosted social functions such as this.

Isabel watched as the elderly German retainers, if not exactly bustling, indeed often hobbling with hunched backs and stiff knees, balanced trays of drinks and canapés with dignity and aplomb as they weaved between the arriving guests.

'Entschuldigen, meine Herren; gnädige Frau,' they murmured as they manoeuvred through the throng.

This was a cocktail party arranged for officers and their families to which similar ranks from other forces were invited amid an atmosphere of camaraderie and *esprit de corps*.

'Daahling,' Zelda always pronounced this word as if

it contained a whole string of a's. She stood behind Isabel, a reassuring hand on her shoulder. 'Don't be nervous, you look *wunderbar*!'

Isabel wore a new cocktail dress, courtesy of Zelda's dressmaker, very *a la mode* with a peplum, a long frill at the waist that hung to hip level and longer at the back and a full skirt almost to her ankles. It was in a brilliant peacock blue taffeta that perfectly suited Isabel's colouring. The dress fitted her figure to perfection and had edged her confidence up a few notches. A chic finger-tip length coat in the same fabric, with a swinging double pleat at the back, completed her outfit, protecting her against the sharpening autumn wind, as the jeep that had brought them here was open to the elements. The coat was borne away by a porter with the delicate chiffon scarves that they had used to protect their newly curled hair. Zelda's maid was a wonderful hairdresser.

They spotted Bill and John in the distance in the domed reception hall. Isabel could also see Dennis and Emma on the other side of the room, keeping to themselves. Isabel waved but they didn't seem to see her. They stood huddled together, ignoring those around them in shyness or disdain, their faces compressed in habitual distaste.

'Bill looks so handsome in his uniform,' Zelda purred. 'Yum, Isabel. If you ever don't want him, can I have him please?'

Isabel was getting used to Zelda's often-outrageous utterances. As she regarded Bill from out here, looking at him almost as a stranger would from another room, she could only agree. He did look marvellous with his perfectly tailored uniform tunic moulded to his torso and the beautifully pressed trousers. Isabel shook her head and tore her gaze away as she felt a wave of desire tinged with sadness sweep through her.

'No, you can't, you brazen hussy,' she answered, tapping Zelda playfully on the hand. 'He's mine. Anyway, here's Chuck.'

Charles Hoffstetter had entered behind them and was removing his cap. His cropped hair was greying and he was several inches shorter than his wife, even more noticeable when Zelda was wearing high heels. His kindly, cheerful face mirrored his nature.

'Darling!' Zelda pecked him on the cheek and straightened his already immaculate tie. At that moment the fifteen-year age difference between them was most apparent. Zelda, wearing a black satin cocktail dress, looked like a bright shining jewel beside her homely husband.

'I love him to bits,' Zelda had confided. 'My family thought I was mad to marry him and then having to come to Europe and all. But I adore him. He's so…so steady.'

And it doesn't hurt that he adores you, thought Isabel, there's nothing like devotion to intensify affection. Now, she watched Chuck flush slightly, but characteristically he didn't shake off Zelda's touch as Bill would have done, but grasped her hand and kissed the fingers. Sadly, Isabel realised that Bill would have commented and seen it as an embarrassing affront in this public place. Isabel sighed. Had it come to this?

Isabel heard a roar. A great bear of a man was storming towards their small group with outspread arms and a determined air. He brought with him the odour of cheap wool and strong spirits.

'Chuck! I vas hoping I vould see you.'

To Chuck's obvious embarrassment the huge man drew him into his arms and hugged him vigorously.

'Introduce me to your wife, you old dog,' the man chortled in his rich accent as he released the American, accompanying his words with a playfully rough nudge.

Chuck suppressed a wince and complied. 'Oleg Kolinsky, Russian Liaison. Oleg, my wife Zelda, and Isabel Barton. You know Bill Barton? Isabel just recently arrived from the UK.'

The Russian's eyes narrowed for a second as he regarded Isabel. He recovered quickly. 'Such luffly ladies, I am charming to meet you. Come, we must get you a drink. This evening is to enjoy ourselves is it not?'

Oleg bent over their hands and kissed them briefly, his thick moustache tickling their skin. His huge hand was clad in thick dark grey hair, reminding Isabel of loose wire wool. The massive shoulders were clothed in shabby khaki much like all the other officers, but cut on a generous scale. A spectacular array of medal ribbons was displayed on his chest. They must have represented a considerable weight when he wore his dress uniform and all the medals in full splendour.

Capturing a hand from each lady and tucking them under his armpits he led them into the reception room.

'Wodka,' he bellowed. 'Wodka. If you have any worth drinking in this God-forsaken dump.' He roared with uninhibited laughter at his wit and Isabel and Zelda took the opportunity to slip from his grasp to greet Bill and John.

'Hello, darling. I don't seem to have seen you for days. Zelda...' Bill kissed them both. 'I'll get you a drink. Gin and tonic? The tonic's not up to much, but at least it covers the taste of the dreadful gin.' An old joke, but they all laughed just the same.

John came up beside Isabel. He lifted her hand and kissed it, a smile lighting his beautiful blue eyes.

'Looking as gorgeous as ever, Mrs B. There's someone I want you to meet. Wait a mo. She's over there, flirting with the French. I'll go and get her.'

Isabel looked across the room to where John had pointed. A lovely titian-haired girl was chatting animatedly to a group of French officers who, judging by their uninhibited laughter, were much taken with her. So this must be Anya, the White Russian girl that John saw so much of. She was certainly very attractive, built with a small compact body that reminded her of the pert little blond Agnes she had worked with in London, but with softer musculature and not an ounce of fat, due no doubt, to the shortages of war.

'What's a White Russian, Bill?' she had asked.

'As opposed to a Red, Soviet Russian, you mean? Well, many Russian families escaped the revolution in 1917 and after the First War, and some of them settled in Germany. They hate communism and Joe Stalin most of all. But there are some Russians with the same hatred of Soviet imperialism who left Russia more recently. They took the opportunity to leave during the War. I think Anya may be one of those.'

Isabel watched John go over and whisper in Anya's ear. Poor girl, she thought, to leave your country and family like that. It must be hard for her, harder than for me, I can always go home again. I don't suppose she can look forward to much future if she goes back to Russia. Isabel thought of the pogroms they had heard rumours of. Russia was proving to be a brutal ally and there was disquiet about their behaviour to their own people and those of other countries that they had overrun and occupied at the end of the war.

John and Anya approached Bill and Isabel. Anya stretched out both hands towards Isabel, a high-wattage smile lighting her face.

'Isabel - I may call you that? I have been so looking forward to meeting you. John has told me so much about you and you are just as beautiful as he said!'

Isabel was struck dumb, not quite knowing how to respond to this effusive outburst, delivered in almost perfect English. Somehow she stumbled through what she hoped was an equally enthusiastic reply.

John rescued her. 'There's dancing in the ballroom. Someone's playing the piano and Bertie Haynes has got out his saxophone. Come on, Anya, let's go and jitterbug. You too, Isabel; get that lazy husband of yours to join in. I know you're a wonderful dancer,' he winked suggestively. 'A star of the London stage, I hear.'

'Ssh, John,' Isabel glanced around. 'I don't want everyone to know. The colonel's wife thinks I'm a tart already.'

'Sorry, old thing, won't mention it again.'

Many couples crowded the ballroom and a thick fog of cigarette smoke hung in the air. The pianist and Bertie Haynes were accomplished musicians and they knew all the old standards and more recent popular tunes. Luckily they seemed to be almost inexhaustible so long as they were plied with plenty of beer. Bill and Isabel's jitterbug turned into a virtual exhibition dance as the people near them stood back to watch. Isabel could see that Bill hated the attention so she pleaded exhaustion and they sat down on the dusty banquettes surrounding the dance floor.

'Whew, I must be getting old.' Bill wiped his brow with his handkerchief.

There was little chance of a rest for Isabel as there were many more men than women in the room and a shortage of partners. One of the French officers borrowed her for an energetic polka and John swept her around the floor in a giddying Viennese waltz. Then Oleg grabbed her in a drunken embrace and spun her around the room in some sort of mad Russian whirlwind, nearly overwhelming her with the scent of body odour and vodka and ploughing through anyone in his way. When she finally tried to extricate herself from his sweaty clasp he didn't want to let her go.

'No! No! My darlink – one more dance with Oleg,' He waved his arms around in a frantic parody, trying to grab her back to his embrace, growling playfully. 'You are so beeootiful.'

The others laughed, highly amused, but Isabel detected an air of menace in his protestations and she moved close to the refuge of Bill's side. She was certain that if all the others had not been there Oleg would have pressed himself upon her even more enthusiastically. She had heard too many stories of the Russian soldiers' epic sexual incontinence not to be wary.

Before long it was time for them all to get ready to go home. The time for curfew neared and the streets became much more dangerous late at night, prowled by destitute scavengers and homeless risking apprehension by the curfew patrols. Even with an Army escort it was not wise to be out.

As they gathered in the hallway to put on their coats Anya came over to say goodnight. 'It was lovely to meet you, Isabel. I hope we can get together soon, coffee perhaps. Maybe I could come to tea at you apartment? We can have fun, no?'
Isabel made suitable noises of acquiescence, a little overwhelmed by the energetic young Russian. As Anya turned away Isabel thought she caught the whisper of a note of calculation in the girl's eyes as if the words she spoke bore little relation to her inner thoughts. Outside, Isabel jumped into the jeep, drawing the new blue coat around her. A shiver passed through her that owed little to the biting wind.

Chapter Fourteen

Anya

Anya shivered under her thin coat as she watched the others leave the hotel. Look at those stuck-up bitches, she thought, living in the lap of luxury with their fancy clothes whilst I have nothing but what I stand up in. There they go in their Ami jeep with a driver to take them wherever they want to go; lording it over the rest of us, the victors patronising the vanquished.

John came up behind her and took her elbow. She switched on a bright smile as she turned towards him.

'Where to now, *schatz*?'

'I'll drop you off, Anya. I'm sorry. I've got an early start tomorrow.'

'Oh, come on. Can't I come up to your place? You'll like it.' She caressed his tie with tender fingers.

'Sorry, babe, another time. Like the Americans say, I'll take a rain-check.'

'I'm not sure what that means.'

'No, darling, neither do I. Later, eh?'

John had parked the khaki Volkswagen round the corner and the little engine soon coughed into life. It rattled like a machine gun, but it got you around, thought Anya.

John dropped Anya off at the corner of her street.

'Good-night, baby,' she purred. 'See you soon.' She turned with a casual wave as he drove away.

She never let him come into her home. She knew he'd be horrified at the way she lived, although it was commonplace in today's Berlin. She lodged in the basement of what had once been the block of flats where she had lived with her parents. Most of the block had been reduced to rubble by Allied bombs and its remnants littered the street. She had to climb over carefully stacked heaps of reclaimed bricks, arranged by the *trümmerfrauen*, and down a flight of steps into the basement that she shared with twenty other tenants. This had held the laundry rooms and maintenance areas for the flats above.

Rough partitions now enclosed makeshift cubicles. Luckily drainage and water had been reconnected, even though all water for drinking still had to be boiled. A communal kitchen had been constructed in a utility room. The rudimentary electrical supply had been rigged up by someone who had been an electrical engineer in another life. Wires festooned along the corridors in a haphazard mess. The unreliable supply caused the basement, with only small windows at the front and rear, to be constantly clothed in gloom.

Anya's room was barely larger than a cell. There was enough space for a single bed and an open cupboard with a curtain across the front that enclosed her surviving possessions, her clothes, her books and the cache of artefacts and household effects that she had managed to salvage after the bombing, wrapped in an old sheet. Some of these had come from Russia when her parents fled the revolution in 1917. She had been an infant when they escaped the Bolsheviks. They had gathered together whatever valuables they could; jewellery, furs and money, though their roubles had proved to be worthless in Germany. Anya's mother had insisted on bringing her precious samovar, an irksome burden on the journey that had followed.

As a respectable lawyer and his wife, loyal to the murdered Tsar, they could see no alternative but to join the tide of refugees leaving the country to find a new life. Tales of vicious purges confirmed their fears. After weeks of arduous travel through Czechoslovakia and Poland they reached their goal, Berlin, the golden capital of Germany. But defeat in the First World War had brought Germany to its knees and life proved more difficult than expected.

Anya's memories were all of Germany; of the modest apartment in which they lived and the local school which she attended. Her father, a well-educated man, could only find work as a clerk for a kindly Jewish businessman who owned a manufacturing company.

Everything changed when Adolf Hitler began his rise to power in the 1930s. His impassioned outpourings roused the population into a fever of nationalism and anti-Semitism. Nazis and Hitler Youth prowled the streets and vandalized Jewish businesses. Eventually they found Papa's boss. They dragged him away and beat him up, smashing the factory and putting everyone out of work – Jews, gentiles, Germans, Russians, Poles and Czechs all became unemployed. This happened to Jewish-owned businesses throughout Germany. Many unemployed fled to foreign lands as soon as they could; to England, America and other European countries willing to take them in. Some found jobs in the re-armament industry, some returned to their native lands, all fearing the rise of Nazism. But Anya's parents chose to stay.

'The Germans have been good to us,' said Papa. 'They took us in when we had nothing. This National Socialism will blow over. This lunacy cannot last. They will soon put paid to that madman.'

'But look what happened in Russia,' said Mama, always the voice of reason. 'You said that Bolshevism would blow over too. But look at them, still going strong twenty years later. And now with Stalin it's even worse.'

'Don't worry so, *drogaya*, we'll be safe here.' He reassured her with gentle caresses.

However, as a precaution they took a German name and Papa managed to get papers in the name of Schreiber. Few people remembered that he was Russian.

'Call yourself Anna, sweetheart,' said Mama. 'It'll be safer. Nazis don't like foreigners.'

But Papa had lost his job and by 1939, when the war began, their carefully smuggled valuables had dwindled, sold in the flea markets, and his part-time work barely paid their rent. Anya was 23 by then and worked in the house of a *Wehrmacht* General as a nursery maid, the best job she could find. She didn't mind being a skivvy as she was fond of the two children and Frau Gallen was not too bad and rarely visited the nursery anyway.

Life during the conflict was unrelentingly hard. Rations were meagre and Papa's job at the Records Office did not bring in enough money, even combined with Anya's wages, to supply everything. Constant bombing by the British put them in danger and on many nights they huddled in the basement where Anya now lived, to sit out the air-raids. But their luck held, their block was not hit until the very end, at a time when the war should have been over if Hitler had only capitulated and admitted defeat instead of insisting that Berlin fight to the death even when defeat seemed inevitable. Many high ranking officers, warned of the approaching Russians bent on vengeance, made their escape while they could.

With the Allies almost at the gates of Berlin, Anya went to work one day to find the General's house abandoned. She stood in amazement in the opulent hall. Clothing, books and papers littered the floor as if a whirlwind had gathered everything up in passing and flung them down again. They had left in a hurry.

Anya, gathering with her anything worth scavenging, went home to her parents and told them what had happened. The larder had supplied a rich haul of tinned food that must have been too heavy for the General to carry in their car. A supply of bed linen and blankets was equally welcome as they had lost many things in the bombing.

'They've probably gone to Switzerland or Austria along with the rest of the Nazi gang. They know the war's over. Rats leaving a sinking ship,' said Papa in disgust.

'At last! I can't believe it's almost over. They say the Russians are coming.'

'That may not be a good thing, mama. The communists hate Russians that have left the Motherland,' said Anya.

'Don't worry, Natalya,' Papa told Mama. 'They will be glad to meet others of their own kind when they get here. We speak Russian and German fluently, Anya also speaks French. I could work as an interpreter.'

But when the Russians arrived their inhuman behaviour gave no room to anyone wishing to work for them. They swarmed through the city wreaking havoc with artillery fire, as if the bombing had not done enough damage. They raped and ransacked as they went, nothing remained safe from the onslaught. They ravaged any females that crossed their path; women young and old, children, even nuns.

Inevitably Anya was found one day on her way back from the ration queues. She heard that dreaded call in the street.

'*Komm, Frau.*' The shout came from a gaggle of drunken Russian soldiers; dirty, stinking and overpowering. They grabbed her hair, ignoring her screams, and dragged her behind a heap of rubble, tearing at her clothing until she was shivering in her slip. Terror paralysed her and all her strength seemed to desert her. Her limbs had turned to frail shivering twigs. It was only with a tremendous effort that she could utter a protest.

'*Nein! Nein*!' she yelped, as loudly as possible.

A passing Russian vehicle slowed and stopped. A tall Russian officer strode over to the group. Even in her fearsome predicament his fair hair, blue eyes and slim build made Anya think of Hitler's ideal man; the epitome of Aryan physique. His Russian, when he spoke, was cultured; an educated man.

'Stop!' he ordered. 'Enough. What are you, a pack of animals?'

The men rearranged their clothing, trying not to look at the cowering Anya gathering her torn frock into her hands and slipping into her shoes.

'Come, young lady,' the officer said in German. 'Put your dress on and come with me.'

Anya needed no further prompting. Still shaking with fear she shrugged into her dress; gathered up her shopping and sped to the officer's side; rescued just in time.

'Be off with you. There's been far too much of this sort of thing.' The officer dismissed the grumbling men. They shuffled off and doubtless found easier prey further on.

'Colonel Igor Pravdin,' the officer said. 'Where may I take you?'

'Thank you, sir, for rescuing me. It was frightening, but I'm fine now. I can find my own way home. I was careless.'

'I must apologise for those men. We are not animals. They must learn to show some self-restraint.'

Anya thought that this seemed an unusual opinion

amongst Russian officers, who generally seemed to have given the victorious troops carte blanche to do whatever they wished.

'I will walk a little way with you.' He offered his arm to help her over the rubble and ordered his driver to follow them. They picked their way through the debris to her turning.

'Thank you, sir. I live down here,' she said in her native tongue.

'You speak Russian?'

Anya realised her mistake, it might not be a good idea to reveal her origins to this man. 'Just a little,' she replied.

'Well, it may be useful to you now we are here. You could find a job with our administration. We need Russian speakers.'

So, Papa had been right about one thing.

'That would be wonderful. I need work to be eligible for more rations for myself and my parents.'

'You live down there?' He peered into the gloomy alley. 'Alone?'

'I live with my mother and father; in the basement of that block. We were bombed out of our apartment.'

'They will look after you. Be careful on the streets.' He turned to leave with a mock salute. 'I will see you again soon, I think.'

Within a week Anya was under Igor's protection. He came back for her, meeting her on the corner of the street. He took her to a bar in Potsdam, little damaged by the conflict. Respectful and considerate, it was a couple of weeks before he took her to bed and a month before he moved her into a room in a mansion near his barracks. A passionate man, he showered Anya with love and made her feel secure for the first time in years.

'I have not been entirely truthful with you, Igor,' she confessed, when it became impossible to keep her secret to herself. 'We are from Russia. My parents fled from the revolution in '17.'

'But I am delighted, darling.' He drew her closer into his arms. 'Now I don't have to speak to you in German. Such an ugly language.'

His billet was in a half-bombed-out hospital. When the Russians arrived the few remaining patients had been emptied out to fend for themselves, many of them dying in the process.

Igor no longer spent much time in this depressing place, preferring the room he had found for Anya. The house was barely touched by the bombing and represented considerable luxury in the deprived city.

In the late summer of 1945 the repatriation began. Joseph Stalin had decreed that all Russian citizens in Germany, released prisoners of war, Cossacks and members of the Vlasov army (both of whom had been loyal to the Tsar and wished to remain in Germany) and White Russians who had fled the revolution, any Russians who had spent time in Germany were to be returned to the Motherland whether they wanted to go or not.

The British, now occupying their own Zone and not understanding the motives of the Russians occupiers, helped them and rounded up all the resident Russians they could find. After all, they reasoned, the Russians are our allies; we must do as they wish.

Propaganda held that all Russian expatriates would be welcomed back to the Motherland. Past sins would be forgiven; past allegiances forgotten.

Papa had been reading the works of Karl Marx, forbidden by the Nazis, but now available to those who wished to read them.

'"From each according to his abilities, to each according to his needs",' he quoted. 'I like the sound of it. It seems to make sense.'

For a man brought low by the excesses of National Socialism and almost starving in the ruins of a defeated nation, the idea of communism suggested a bright future of fairness and order where everyone had a job and plenty of food and accommodation would be provided for all.

'But the Russians are appalling, Papa. Igor is an exception, he's an educated man. Look at them, Papa. Dirty great apes; uncivilised and greedy.'

'Those are just the common soldiers, my darling. No more than peasants. Most Russians are like Igor. Back in Russia I am sure society is much more civilised. I think we should return. I miss my country; it has been a very long time.'

'I won't go,' said Anya. 'I don't trust them.'

'You are an adult now, Anya. You must make up your own mind. But it will be hard for your mother and me to leave you here where things are so difficult.'

Igor advised her not to go. 'In fact, if you intend to stay, I suggest that you pretend to be French. You mustn't be part of this repatriation.'

Anya took his advice and changed her name again and Igor obtained papers for her in the name of Anne Ducros, a refugee from Alsace.

Anya would never forget the day her parents left for Russia. They tramped into the Russian Zone with eager expectation, carrying what possessions they could; the precious samovar strapped to Papa's bent back. They were herded onto trains, in much the same way that the Nazis had herded Jews on their way to the camps. But first they separated the young from the old; the soldiers from the civilians; the men from the women.

'*Niet! Niet!*' shrieked mama as Papa was torn from her side. 'He comes with me.'

'*Niet, babouschka*. He goes with the old men.' A uniformed soldier wrenched them apart. Papa fell heavily to the ground and the samovar, cherished for so many years, smashed on the cobbles. Mama wailed in fear and grief.

Anya watched in horror from the parapet of a bridge over the Havel as the swarm of terrified people was prodded onto the transport. The moustachioed Cossacks marched to their doom, stoic and dignified, the last of their protests silenced.

Eventually the segregated carriages shunted away. Later Anya heard that many of the passengers, the old, the soldiers and anyone else deemed to have been disloyal to Mother Russia, were summarily executed barely a few kilometres into Russian territory and their bodies flung into open graves. Others were sent to the gulags in Siberia.

Anya never heard from her parents again and could only assume that they too had met this dreadful fate. Her grief prostrated her for weeks. Dear, deluded Papa, his poor judgement had finally proved fatal.

Shortly after the repatriation debacle Igor received news of his posting to Czechoslovakia. Anya cried with sorrow at his loss and fear for her future.

'I will always be grateful to you, Igor. You saved my life and helped me through a terrible time.'

'Anya, you have helped me also. You have made my stay in this city bearable.'

As he wiped away her tears he spoke of love and gratitude; of redemption and hope and then he was obliged to leave.

She had to leave Igor's comfortable room and return to live in her parents' old home in the basement, turning her back on comfort. Igor gave her what money and food he could and left Berlin for the East, bequeathing her a lasting picture of a dashing blond officer fondly waving his last farewell. She knew she was unlikely to see him again.

She took to loitering in the British Army's NAAFI with other girls. They were frequently offered cups of tea and biscuits by the lonely men in need of a few moments companionship. The relaxing of the fraternisation rules had made this kind of social interaction commonplace. Some girls took it further and went off with men for the night and even, if they were lucky, a longer term arrangement of co-habitation. Anya avoided this commitment until she met John.

She liked him immediately. He didn't take himself too seriously and had an ironic sense of humour, a commodity rarely found in this sad city. It didn't hurt that he was very good-looking too.

'I wouldn't hang around here, dear,' he said. 'You never know what you might find.'

'I'm always prepared to be surprised.'

'Surprised is one thing, darling. A nice girl like you should be careful.'

'You're teasing me. I can look after myself.'

Their relationship quickly blossomed. Anya enjoyed spending time with John and he was a wonderful lover. He made the intolerable drudgery of living in Berlin bearable. He sometimes said, 'I love you, Anya,' in the heat of the moment, but she didn't believe him. Love didn't come into it, expediency, comfort and intimacy were a pretty good substitute and she was satisfied with that for now. She didn't expect it to last. Relationships such as theirs rarely had a future and recently she had become well aware that his heart was elsewhere. She had seen the fond way he looked at Isabel Barton. He was not in the least obvious, but she knew the signs, the attentive tenderness and the hidden smiles. John was smitten. She wondered where that was going and for now she took from him what she could, companionship and sex would have to do.

There was another reason to cultivate John's company, painless though that was. Before he left, Igor had introduced her to a friend of his, a high-ranking Russian intelligence officer, known to her as Pyotr. Igor had confessed Anya's Russian origins and the officer seemed delighted to meet her.

'You'll be living in the British Zone,' Pyotr said. 'That's where your parents' apartment is, just beyond the Brandenburg Gate.'

Anya confirmed this. They had already been informed of the boundaries of the new zones. The population had begun to resettle and everyone was moving into their preferred zone. Many Germans were fleeing from the East, and Russian oppression, struggling to find somewhere to live in the British or American areas.

'We think you can help us,' the officer continued. 'We need information. Anything you can find out about the British and Americans, however trivial it may seem. We're prepared to pay for it. I would like you to get close to the British officers; find out what you can about their plans; their aspirations. Of course, if you disagree, you realise we can always have you repatriated – to Russia.' This lightly-veiled threat was accompanied by a sly smile.

Anya shuddered. She agreed willingly, she didn't have much choice. It meant extra rations and occasionally, very welcome cash. In return she only had to come up with an interesting titbit of information, sometimes true, sometimes not, but she was careful that her lies could not be checked out and that her truths could do no harm to her friends.

Chapter Fifteen

Hartz Mountains, October 1946

A few weeks after the party at the Moser Bill managed to get a few days leave. Isabel anticipated the break with delight; how wonderful to be away from the depressing sights and smells of Berlin. The dreadfulness of it all had begun to weigh heavily on her spirits.

She leaned idly against the window frame of their room, surveying the spectacular view. She couldn't make up her mind if she liked this scenery or not. Before her lay a panorama of pine trees spread like a thick undulating carpet almost as far as she could see, covering a series of hills growing gradually to mountains in the distance. The dense darkness of the forest was veiled in a sinister pall, reminding Isabel of frightening stories told to her in childhood where children had disappeared into forests, never to be seen again. So these were the Hartz Mountains she had been told about; in the depths of the British zone, a couple of hundred miles from Berlin.

When they arrived Isabel found the hotel styled like many houses familiar from parts of England where Tudor and Elizabethan buildings still existed. But its massive timber-framed walls seemed taller, with many more black beams, turrets and gables than on those she knew. The white painted plaster between the beams gleamed in the sunlight. The place had a distinctly Germanic stamp; not least because of the gothic script in which the hotel's name, 'Hotel Schauser', was inscribed on a heavy wooden board across the front.

The hotel perched high on a hill overlooking and surrounded by the dense pine forests. Their room on the third floor was high enough above the treetops for Isabel to see into the morning sunshine tremulously shimmering over the forest. In the distance she could see the glitter of the river Hartz and a lake about a couple of miles away with fairytale cottages on its banks. But downstairs in the baronial lounges and dining room of the hotel, dark-panelled and chill, the forest close outside cast a gloom over everything; oppressive as the inside of a tomb.

They had decided to take their break with Penny in the Officers' Holiday Hotel. A train brought them from Berlin, but it had been a very different experience from that on the train from the Hook of Holland; still remembered with a shudder. Bill, relaxed for a change, entertained Penny with games whilst Isabel dozed between taking in glimpses of the devastatingly beautiful green and undulating countryside, apparently unmarred by signs of warfare. They travelled round hills and through valleys embellished with tiny jewel-like villages nestling in the folds of the foothills, their houses appearing as doll's houses in the distance and the churches as picturesque as a painting.

'Look, Bill, can you see that waterfall; down the side of the mountain. That's incredible!' The cascade drew a white ribbon down the cliff face. From here its movement was imperceptible, but Isabel could imagine the sight and sound of the crash and spray as the water reached the rocks below.

'Is that white stuff on the mountains snow, Daddy?' Penny asked.

'Yes, there's snow right at the top. In the winter snow covers everything, right down to the valleys.'

Thank goodness, Isabel thought, they're beginning to like each other. Bill had been so rarely at home lately that she had begun to despair of them ever becoming friends. Surely every little girl should feel at ease with her father? At least he was making an effort today. She settled down and dozed, shutting out their prattle.

When they arrived, a hotel car picked them up at the station. Herr Schauser welcomed them warmly when they reached the hotel. For him a guest was a guest and he gave the same welcome to the conquering army's officers as he would have given to any customer before the war. His hotel may have been temporarily taken over for the British officers' use but he knew he would have it back into his ownership eventually, when the occupation finally ended. He liked the English. Before the war many of his best customers had been British hikers exploring the mountain trails. Besides, they tipped well, but not as well as the Americans occasionally using the hotel.

'Major and Mrs Barton. *Willkommen*. Come in and get warm. The weather's getting quite chilly now, isn't it? Give me your coats. I'll get one of the girls to show you to your room. Stefan will take up your bags. Can I offer you a little *schnapps* before you go up? *Nein*? Perhaps you would like to take the little one to her room first. Don't worry about leaving her – Hilde will look in on her to make sure she is sleeping.' He gabbled on at great speed without giving them a chance to reply, whirling around taking hats, coats and luggage.

They decided on a visit to their rooms first and after settling Penny in for the night, they ventured down to the drawing room. There, great logs blazed in the hearth obliterating the chill of the room. The promised *schnapps* awaited them on a silver tray. It seemed they were the only guests for the time being, as it was midweek. Resting officers would normally descend at the weekends.

'Cheers, Mrs B,' toasted Bill.

'Cheers, darling,' Isabel took a sip of the clear liquid. 'Oh, my goodness! That's strong.' She blinked back tears. 'I'm not sure I can drink this.'

'It's an acquired taste. It'll grow on you,' laughed Bill.

'I feel really funny at the back of my neck.'

Herr Schauser came in. 'Your dinner is ready. As you're the only guests this evening I am serving you in the breakfast room; it's more intimate.' He beamed at them encouragingly and ushered them through.

The generous dinner was much given to dumplings and potatoes served with a little pork. There was still very little meat, even in the country markets. The *apfel strudel* however, light as air, proved that there was no shortage of butter in this corner of the countryside.

Finally, having finished a bottle of hock and a brandy, they staggered up to bed and, after a brief glance at the slumbering Penny; they collapsed onto the feathery depths of the Teutonic four-poster, its thick drapery shielding them from errant draughts.

They undressed quickly and slipped between the cool sheets. Bill drew her into his arms and made love to her tenderly and urgently, more relaxed and attentive than he had been since Isabel's arrival in Germany. She responded with joy, returning his caresses with gentle fondness and later, with mounting passion. Maybe at last they had turned a corner and could be happy together again. How wonderful that Bill didn't have to rush off to work. They had three days together. For the first time in months they lay in each other's arms, comfortably trusting, able to laugh and murmur softly until tiredness overcame them and they drifted off to sleep.

After breakfast the next morning Isabel and Penny discovered an old dolls' house in one of the sitting rooms. It was modelled in the same black and white timber framed style as the hotel. Everything was there in the tiniest detail, beautifully reproduced. Penny marvelled at it, entranced by the tiny furnishings.

'Look at the china, Mummy! It looks real,' she enthused.

Delicately hand-painted in blue on fine white porcelain, it resembled the Willow Pattern set that old Mrs Barton had in her Kensington eyrie. Penny turned it over in her hands. 'I love it, Mummy, can I have a dolls' house at home?'

'Maybe, one day, when we have a house back in England. I don't think we could get one here. We may be moving a lot and couldn't carry a dolls' house all over Germany, could we?' Isabel knew a posting was inevitable and they would have to uproot and go to another town.

Penny's face fell. Crestfallen, she longingly caressed the dolls' house furnishings.

Isabel tried to distract her. 'Isn't the kitchen lovely? Look, little copper saucepans.' She loved it all too, fascinated by the skill required to make such detailed miniatures. 'Look at the knives and forks. They're so tiny.'

Penny coveted the tiny furnishings and, when her mother wasn't looking, she slipped a tiny teapot into her pocket, thinking –

my dolly will like that. She didn't feel any guilt at this action as she always shared toys with her cousins at home; she was encouraged to do so.

Isabel and Penny passed the morning by the fire, playing with the dolls' house and waiting for Bill to return from a mysterious errand.

'Where're you off to, Bill?' Isabel asked at breakfast. 'I hope you're not working – you promised this would be a holiday.'

'It's all right, darling,' Bill grinned. 'You'll like it, honestly.' His smile faded slightly. 'Well, I hope so.'

Two hours passed and Isabel had begun to pace, her patience draining away. Lunchtime, and she was starving after the huge meal last night. Although she'd thought at the time that she'd never be able to eat again; the mountain air had given her an enormous appetite.

'Daddy's late. Where on earth is he?' She looked at the pretty little watch he had brought her from Switzerland. She joined Penny by the fire and, perched on a long embroidered footstool they read stories together, or rather Penny stumbled through the words, but Isabel wasn't concentrating.

Finally Bill strode in, brushing pine needles from his shoulders, bringing the scent of the forest with him.

'There you are. Where've you been?' Isabel sprang up.

'I've got a surprise for you. I had to go quite a way to get it. Schauser lent me the car.'

'Can't it wait till after lunch? We're starving.'

'Come on. It won't take a minute. It's outside.'

Isabel and Penny followed him to the covered porch where there stood a large cardboard box with an open top.

'What is it?' asked Penny moving forward. 'Is it for me?'

'For both of you - all of us,' said Bill.

They peered into the box.

'A puppy!' cried Penny.

'A puppy?' Isabel raised a sceptical eyebrow at Bill. 'Do we want a puppy?'

'You'll love him,' Bill assured her, slipping a hopeful arm around her shoulders.

The puppy opened a sleepy eye and stood up, wagging

his tail. The rough blanket he had been sleeping on had tangled around his ankles so they could not see his feet. About 18 inches high, he had fluffy, curly black and tan fur and sturdy straight legs and a short, upright tail that never seemed to stop moving.

'Cost me two cans of cocoa. He's a pedigree. His parents were police guard dogs,'

'What make is he?' Isabel asked, regarding the dog dubiously.

'He's an Airedale – a terrier. They're very bright.'

'But they grow to be huge. I bet he's got enormous feet.'

'Not that huge. Besides, he'll make a great guard dog.'

'I'm not sure I want a guard dog, any dog. They're a lot of work, you know,' Isabel said doubtfully. 'I'll bet he's not housetrained.'

'Probably not,' said Bill. 'But he'll soon learn.'

'What's his name?' asked Penny kneeling beside the box and stroking the puppy's head whilst he licked her hand enthusiastically.

'Cyd von Falkenstein,' replied Bill. 'I thought we could call him Prince.'

'Prince! Prince!' Penny helped the puppy out of the box. 'Come, follow me.'

'So Prince it is then,' said Isabel, sensing a *fait accompli.* 'What on earth are we going to feed him on?'

'Some of that awful meat you're always complaining about, I expect. And I'm sure there are dog biscuits at the NAAFI.'

The child and dog raced into the hallway and skidded around the polished floor, the puppy wriggling in paroxysms of joy at this enchanting game. He lollopped about, letting out small sharp yaps of delight.

'Put him back in the box, Penny. It's lunchtime. We'll take him for a walk later.'

Bill was looking at Isabel questioningly. 'Well?'

'Oh, all right, you win. He is rather sweet and he'll make a great companion for Penny.' Isabel glanced back at the puppy; now in the box again. He looked at her with a question in his clever brown eyes. He angled his head to one side, his ears pricked up intelligently, one a little higher than the other. He seemed to be asking a question. Isabel smiled at him. 'All right, I give in. Hello, Prince. Welcome to the family.'

Prince sank down into the box with a sigh and went to sleep. A long, close friendship had begun.

Chapter Sixteen

Berlin, November 1946

'No! Not now, I haven't got time for this.'

Isabel opened the back door onto the frost-spangled garden to thrust the reluctant puppy outside. He gazed up at her with abject apology written in his eyes and his tail between his legs.

'No. Don't look at me like that. You're a bad dog!' She slammed the door firmly behind him and returned to the hall just as Irma was showing Zelda in. The American handed her coat to the maid and whirled forward with her usual energy.

'Darling, I've had a wonderful idea!' She stopped dead just before stepping in the little accident Prince had deposited in the middle of the gleaming parquet; the subject of his dispute with Isabel.

'Let me get this cleaned up, Zelda. I won't be a minute.'

'You should get the maid to do it. I'll wait in the drawing room.' Zelda stepped fastidiously around the mess, put her hat and gloves on the hall table and strode into the lounge.

When she had finished cleaning up Isabel joined her friend; dropping into one of the sagging armchairs with a sigh.

'OK, so what's your wonderful idea?'

Zelda got straight to the point.

'Dancing lessons, ballet! What do you think? You've certainly got the space for it,' Zelda said, waving vaguely at the salon's undoubtedly ample proportions, 'and I know you're qualified. Loads of the mothers would love their little darlings to have ballet lessons. And think, you could actually charge them money for it!' She paused for breath and regarded Isabel hopefully.

Isabel considered for a moment, and then smiled and answered Zelda solemnly. 'You know, I think you may be on to something. I'd have to put up a barre and it would have to be warm enough. Maybe the hall would be better – where the stove is.' She stood up and walked over to regard the hall with speculative eyes.

'Perfect. You like the idea. I've already mentioned it to one or two people and they loved the idea. There's so little to keep children occupied.'

'Oh, Zelda, you could have at least waited until you'd asked me.'

'I know, darling, but strike while the iron is hot and all that. Besides I knew that if I already had pupils lined up, you'd be more likely to take them on.' Zelda made a vain attempt to look contrite.

Doubts beset Isabel. There were several reasons why this might not work. She would have to ask Bill, and Dennis might not like an unruly troupe of small girls gallivanting around in the shared hallway. There would be music. Little girls could be very over-excitable. Would she be able to control them? She hadn't done much teaching before, only a term, to the Elementary School kids when Penny was a baby. It was fun, but it ended when the school was bombed, on a weekend fortunately, so no one was hurt.

'I'd have to teach in the afternoons just after school. Maybe the school truck could drop them off and then the mothers could come and get them later.' Isabel worked out details in her head. 'Do you think they'd be too tired then? And what about music? The gramophone's hopeless and the records are nearly all scratched.'

'We'll get a piano in. I'm sure we could get someone to play'

'What about you, would you like to play? Didn't you learn the piano when you were a kid?' Isabel asked, sure that Zelda would have no trouble with this; she seemed to have every other accomplishment.

'Darling, they tried real hard, but I've got a tin ear.

I preferred to be outside riding horses. And of course Pa encouraged me; he wanted a boy. I should have been born in the Wild West!'

Isabel was only slightly disappointed, suspecting that Zelda might not be sufficiently reliable. 'I understand. I'll just have to find a pianist. But then I'll have to pay them.'

'You'd include that in the fees – people won't expect it to be cheap. A few dollars a session I would think.'

'Do you suppose ten bob a time would be too much? Otherwise it's hardly worthwhile. No, it would be too expensive for most families.'

'Don't be so negative,' said Zelda 'You know it's a great idea.'

'But I'll have to ask Bill. He can be a bit of a stick-in-the-mud, you know.'

'Yes, but you know you can charm him round.'

They worked on the plan while they drank tea and ate some of Irma's delectable seed cake. As it proved, Bill had little objection to the plan.

'We'd better see if Dennis minds, but I can't see why. He's out most of the time and now Emma's going home to Cheltenham, you won't disturb her. A few little girls running around can't do much harm and it'll be good for you to have something useful to do. Keep you out of mischief.'

Isabel thought this was a bit patronising, but said nothing, at least he had agreed. He was right anyway; she longed for a useful occupation. Bill even said he would find a piano for her.

'I'm sure there will be someone with one to sell. A few cigarettes and cocoa will see to it. That's if all the pianos in Berlin haven't been bombed to bits. Then I'll ask my people if they know anyone who can play.'

A ten-ton truck delivered a good quality upright piano within a few days and four hefty Privates heaved it into position in the hall close to the stove and positioned it according to Isabel's instructions.

'Oh, that's wonderful,' she thanked the soldiers. 'Can I get you anything before you go?'

They shuffled their boots, embarrassed, and mumbled gratitude as they accepted a mug of Irma's luscious cocoa.

'It's getting right parky out there, Mrs Barton,' one of them said. 'We have to scrape ice off the vehicles in the morning already.'

'Yes, we're in for a hard winter, I'm told.'

After their departure Isabel sat down and tried to play the piano, running inept fingers up and down the keys. Her sister Grace had learned to play properly - Isabel's skill was limited to little more than Chopsticks and a clumsy rendition of 'Little Brown Jug', that Glenn Miller standard.

When Penny was delivered home from school they sat together and Isabel taught her what little she knew. They strummed for a while, laughing at the discordant sounds.

'No, Mummy, it doesn't go like that.'

'You show me then.'

'I don't know how. How do you make a tune out of just these notes?'

In the bowels of the piano they discovered some sheet music, curling at the edges, the squiggles dense on the pages. The pieces looked far too difficult for Isabel. Anyway, she couldn't read music.

Irma joined in with singing any recognisable songs they managed to produce. 'I have never learned how to play piano. My cousin Willi played, he was quite good,' she added sadly. Willi had died in the siege of Stalingrad, aged nineteen.

'Do you know anyone who can play, Irma? Well enough for my dance lessons?'

'I will ask, Mrs Barton, *Mutti* may know someone.' Irma's mother still lived in squalid seclusion in those rooms remaining of her bombed block of flats. The front of the building had been ripped away, but the rooms at the back were still deemed to be habitable. Most of Irma's wages went to help her survive. Irma was surpassingly grateful for having somewhere warm to stay. It was safe in the Barton's apartment, after the perilous streets of Berlin, awash with marauding Russian soldiers, before the British came. Irma's food was included so she was spared the freezing, starving fate of many people she knew.

In the end Bill found their pianist.

'She was a Nazi Party member,' said Bill and Isabel flinched 'No, it's all right. They forced teachers to join and any one in an official capacity had to sign up to keep their job. I don't think she's a proper Nazi. You'll like her. She's had a hard time, lost her husband and son, this will help her immensely.'

'Does she speak English?'

'Very well. I told you, she used to be a teacher and she didn't just teach music. Shall I send her along?'

'Yes, of course I'll meet her. We'll have to get along; it takes a lot of patience. She may get bored with having to stop and start all the time.'

'I'm sure she'll put up with a bit of boredom for money and any other things you can send her way.'

Frau Hilfe was a surprise. Her rounded frame and blooming complexion, even after years of starvation rations, caused her to look more like a farmer's wife. She appeared stouter because she seemed to be wearing all the clothes she possessed at once, layer after layer on top of one another. Her deferential and wary manner was normal. Not all of the conquering occupiers were kind to the defeated Germans, seeing their role as one of vengeful masters. But she could not suppress her naturally cheerful nature and Isabel was glad she was not as depressed and helpless as many German women.

'Just for two hours a week?' she asked in her excellent English.

'Yes, certainly at first,' replied Isabel 'I don't know how the classes will go yet. I may do more later. Is that not enough for you?'

'It will be fine. Something is better than nothing, Frau Barton. I shall be happy to be able to play again,' she glanced at the piano, longing in her eyes. 'May I try the instrument?'

'Of course. But I don't think it's in tune.'

Frau Hilfe sat and opened the lid. She ran her hands up and down the keys and played a few scales. It sounded amazing to Isabel, like a virtuoso performance.

'It's not too bad, but you should get it tuned, ja. May I arrange it? I know a man who would be happy to do it, maybe for a little cocoa, or tea?'

'Certainly, please ask him to come round.' Isabel was concerned that cocoa or tea might seem insufficient for this important job, but Irma reassured her; the value of these commodities was greater than money in these times.

The piano tuner, a stooped old man, greeted Isabel tentatively. His gaze passed over her shoulder. Shrapnel had almost blinded him in the latter days of the war, Isabel discovered. Before the war he played piano in a symphony orchestra of international renown. His coat looked as if it had been fashioned from a thick blanket and his feet poked through the toes of his demolished shoes. Frau Hilfe led him to the piano. Firstly he ran his hands over the instrument.

'Ah, a good sound case,' he pronounced and probed the insides, 'and an iron frame, *das ist gut*.'

Isabel watched as he minutely adjusted the strings and hammers, playing the notes randomly; tapping his tuning fork on the tiles of the stove and matching the plangent notes. He cured the few sticking keys and when he had finished, he played some majestic chords.

'Splendid, *meine Frau*, you have a fine instrument here!'

'Thank you so much. As long as Frau Hilfe can play for the children, it'll be wonderful.' She felt a wave of compassion for the man. How was he going to survive with only this skill to offer?

'Good luck with your ballet lessons. I hope the children enjoy themselves. We need some joy in these sad times.'

Isabel watched as Frau Hilfe guided him away, carrying his precious payment of Twinings tea clasped to his chest as if it contained the riches of the Orient.

With Zelda's energetic networking, word quickly got around that Isabel was to give ballet lessons to any little girls that were interested. Isabel had more enquiries than expected. One mother telephoned; a worried note in her voice.

'Is it just for girls, Mrs Barton? I have a boy, Andrew, he's just six and he'd love to learn to dance. Could he come?'

'Of course. I'd love to have a boy. I just thought that only girls would want to.'

'Oh no. He's always liked the idea since we took him to see the Nutcracker Suite in London. I think he sees himself as a dashing prince.'

'Well, do bring him. Classes start next Wednesday, after school – as near to four as you can make it. We're going to arrange for the school truck to drop them when we're more organised.'

Isabel explained to the mothers about clothes.

'Normally the children would wear a ballet tunic, but if you haven't got the clothes coupons or can't get anyone to make one for you, vest and pants will do fine. If you can't get any soft ballet shoes they can dance in socks, but they may be slippery on the wooden floor. And there may be splinters, but I'll try to get rid of them all first.'

The dressmaker made Penny a ballet tunic from a pink silk slip. It looked so sweet on her, sleeveless and with a small slit at each side nearly up to the waist, just covering her bottom. Penny already had the pair of soft ballet pumps they had brought from England.

On the day of the first class six little girls and Andrew turned up; with Penny that made eight. One of the mothers had misinterpreted the idea of a ballet tunic and sent her child along in a full-blown ballet tutu, a froth of stiffened white tulle – completely over the top for a beginner, but she did look pretty in it, like a blond fairy.

'We don't want to get it spoilt, Mary. We're going to be rolling around on the floor and getting messy. Better leave it at home next week. I'll speak to Mummy about it.' Isabel smiled at Mary's troubled little face. 'It'll be all right, really.'

Frau Hilfe sat ramrod-straight at the piano, waiting to begin. I'll have to tell her to relax a bit, thought Isabel.

Isabel explained the first principles of ballet to the children. She taught them how to point their toes and turn out their feet and legs; she showed them the five positions of the feet and arms.

'You won't remember everything at once. Don't worry, there's lots of time. We'll go over it again. Now, Mrs Hilfe will play us a little tune and I want you all to dance around the room. Do anything you like. Just listen to the music and let it take you anywhere you feel you want to go. Try not to bump into each other.'

Frau Hilfe struck up a lively light polka and the children skipped around the hall in an undisciplined flurry. They still managed to bump into each other even in that huge space. Their swirling arms beat the air like birds learning to fly.

'Remember to point your toes and try not to be quite as heavy on your feet – light as a feather. See if you can land without making a sound.' Isabel had to raise her voice above the sound of the children's giggles and squeals.

Bill came in early from work before the class had ended.

'Goodness!' he exclaimed. 'A herd of fairy elephants!'

Frau Hilfe stood to attention beside the piano. 'Good afternoon, Major Barton.'

'*Guten Tag*, Frau Hilfe,' acknowledged Bill. 'At ease, please.'

'OK. It's time to stop now, children.' Isabel brought the class to order. 'Give me a little curtsey before you go. Andrew, you bow. That's lovely. Now go and get your shoes and coats. If you sit down quietly your mothers will be here soon to take you home.'

The dancing classes proved very popular and after a couple of weeks Isabel had two extra pupils. She was amazed at how quickly they learned and how in no time a spirit of competition sprang up amongst them. Isabel lavished her praise and the encouragement she gave made them blaze with pride at their successes.

'Andrew loves it,' said his mother 'and he doesn't get teased by the other boys as I feared. I think they envy him when they're playing football out in the cold.'

Isabel planned a concert for the parents around Christmas, if she could get the children to remember a few simple dances. Then she would invite all the parents and their friends.

'How I love playing for the children,' Frau Hilfe told Isabel. 'Chopin. I've always loved Chopin. The little ones look so adorable; so concentrated as they work.'

Isabel persuaded Frau Hilfe to relax and now she was playing for them with a lyrical fluency that would inspire anyone to dance beautifully.

Bill was enthusiastic about the classes at first. But after a few weeks he said that he felt they were taking up too much of Isabel's time.

'But it's only two afternoons a week, Bill. And it's bringing in a little extra money,' said Isabel.

'What are you doing with the money? I would have thought we had enough to get by. There's not much to spend it on around here.'

'I'm saving a bit and I needed to get some new clothes. I'm expected to look smart at the Colonel's wife's coffee klatches, you know.' Inside, indignation began to simmer. 'The things I brought from England were hardly suitable. It's all horribly competitive. You want me to look right, don't you?' She regretted this question as soon as she asked it. It sounded like pathetic wheedling.

Bill ignored her. 'I blame Zelda for this. She's a bad influence. You didn't think about clothes all the time when we were in England.'

'No, I thought about food and where the next meal was coming from and whether we might be killed in the next air raid. It's different now; I'm trying to be a good Army wife.'

'Hmm,' Bill grunted. 'Are you saying I didn't give you enough to live on back then?'

'Oh, Bill. It wasn't your fault. The War was on, you couldn't be thinking about us. There just wasn't much food and we were forced to scrimp and save and make do. It wasn't just a matter of cash. I can't blame you for that. Penny had never eaten ice cream until we bought her some that day last year. Don't you remember? We all laughed because she complained it was too cold.'

'Yes, I remember,' Bill seemed slightly mollified. 'I suppose everyone was in the same boat.'

'Of course, I was luckier than some; at least I had Mum and Grace and Doris. We helped each other out.'

'But you didn't have to work then and now you do.'

'I don't think of it as work. I'm not doing it because I have to, but because I want to. I love teaching the children. It's very satisfying. It's reminding me of how much I loved dancing myself; how much I miss it.'

'Do you? Would you really like to be back in that tacky theatre, dancing your feet off every night for a bunch of ogling men?'

Isabel could see Bill was working himself up into a fury.

'Oh, I don't mean the music hall, though that could be fun, but the ballet, that was lovely. I know I wasn't good enough to pursue it as a career.'

'All the same, I'm glad you don't have to earn your living that way now. My mother thought …'

Oh no, thought Isabel, I have a good idea what his mother thought. Mrs Barton had considered her a thoroughly common piece and referred to her as 'that Cockney gal', which Isabel found particularly irksome as she had spent a lot on elocution lessons.

'I really don't want to know what your mother thought, Bill. I know she doesn't like me. As Penny is her only grandchild I suppose she will have to put up with me.'

'Yes, I suppose she will.' Bill frowned. He hated the disputes between Isabel and his mother. 'I wish you'd make more of an effort with her. You could write to her occasionally and tell her how you're getting on.'

Isabel sighed, 'I'm sure she couldn't possibly be interested.'

Isabel remembered visiting her mother-in-law and how she had dreaded it and how the reality had more than lived up to the expectation. Mrs Barton could barely bring herself to be civil to her. Like many wealthy widows of her generation the senior Mrs Barton had gone to live in a hotel in South Kensington. Living on private incomes they constructed the illusion of stately home living on a reduced budget that could no longer stretch to servants or large establishments of their own.

'I think you neglect her,' said Bill.

'She's your mother, not mine. I went to see her while you were away. She was horrible to me. Kept telling me I'm bringing Penny up all wrong and she had no manners. Poor Penny is terrified of her; you know how shy she can be. It made her clumsy and she forgot to say the right things. Your mother picked her up on everything.'

'She thinks you're vain and spoilt. And you know, sometimes I think so too.'

Isabel was aghast, struck dumb with impotent rage. This was so unjust.

Abruptly Bill turned to leave, 'I've got to go back to work; there's a rumpus on. I may be late.' He strode across the hallway to the front door, pulling on his greatcoat and cap. He slammed the door behind him, causing the hardboard panel protecting them from the elements to rattle. Isabel remained, silent and furious, by the stove. She found that she was holding her breath and as she let it out she was shaking.

Isabel went to check on Penny, already asleep. Isabel hoped she had not heard the arguing. She kissed the child gently on the cheek. 'Bloody Bartons,' she whispered.
She knew that tomorrow he would apologise and say, in soft, loving tones, 'I do love you, you know'.

But could she believe him? He was a sentimental man with a soft inner core that she had recognised before she married him. Since they were together again she had sensed a distance between them. He never followed up his loving words with a tender touch or a secret glance to show her that she was still the most important person in his world and he was still on her side, always. She sometimes felt that if things did not change her soul would dry up and blow away, like a piece of fragile paper.

She returned to the hall and wound up the old gramophone. Tchaikovsky - that would be lovely. She carefully wiped a record and put it on the turntable. She stuffed some old socks into the body of the machine so that it wouldn't be too loud and wake Penny. She rested the needle on the record and immediately the plaintive notes echoed. Isabel shook off her shoes and stepped out of her dress. In her petticoat and stockinged feet she began to dance. She lifted her arms and pirouetted across the floor. *Fouettées, arabesques, pas des chats.* She twirled and skimmed like a wisp of thistledown. She whirled across the floor as if possessed. As time passed and the music ended, her anger drained away and, exhausted, she staggered to her bed.

Chapter Seventeen

Berlin, Autumn 1946

John pulled the coat closer around his neck. God, it's bloody freezing. A malign wind blew between the mass of bricks and rubble. Eddies of grit and brick dust skittered around his feet. It was trying to snow. Icy darts burned John's cheeks in spite of the woollen neck of the old submarine jumper, a souvenir from another life, pulled up as high as possible. He hoped no one would notice that the coat was military issue. He had ground down the plastic buttons to blur the badges; taken off the shoulder flashes. Surely enough greatcoats had been stolen in the last months for this one to be inconspicuous. They had to be the greatest antidote to a penetrating wind.

John stopped to get his bearings. Every street and alley looked the same. This was not an area where the army had organised a clean-up operation; it would be years before progress was made. Fritz's home was a shack constructed amongst the rubble of a bombed-out building. Straight on from the old red *Katze* sign, Fritz had assured him, you can't miss it. I hope he was right. It'll be difficult to explain what I'm doing here after curfew. Peering ahead through the misty gloom, John glimpsed a tiny chink of light. He hurried towards it, swearing as he knocked his anklebone against the sharp edge of a brick.

'Bugger!'

He limped towards the sliver of light. The path ahead was suddenly and brilliantly illuminated as a makeshift door - a wobbling sheet of old board - was pushed aside from the entrance to a ramshackle shelter.

'Not so much bleeding noise. Do you vant to vake the whole neighbourhood?'

The man standing outlined in the light resembled a scarecrow. His hair was matted and his face gaunt, the cheekbones stood out in sharp relief under the lined yellow skin. In the hovel behind him the makeshift walls were plastered with any rotten junk that could be found to fill the cracks against the searching wind. The floor was carpeted with newspapers and what appeared to be books, their backs broken and squashed against the raw ground in a parody of tiling. An old primus stove, emitting the chemical odour of burning paraffin, stood in the centre, caked with grease and supporting an ancient tin kettle. A rough bed, covered with layers of filthy tumbled bedding, filled the remaining space.

Fritz dragged John into the reeking den, looking for the curfew patrol as he pushed him through the door. The light, which had seemed blinding from outside, inexplicably dimmed to a flicker from the oil lamp within with the door closed.

'Brass monkeys weather, eh, old boy?'

'Certainly is, Fritz.' John acknowledged. He often chuckled at the way Fritz Keller had adopted English phrases and clichés. This was particularly odd, as Fritz's hatred of the occupying forces seemed to have no bounds. John knew he was only tolerated because he was useful and supplied him with what he wanted. In no way was John ever going to place his trust in Fritz's grasping hands, ever eager to stab him in the back at the first opportunity.

'What have you got for me today?' asked Fritz, licking his unsavoury lips.

John silently withdrew several cartons of cigarettes from the capacious pockets of his coat, like a conjuror at a children's party. Fritz grabbed them greedily.

'No drugs? We need drugs.'

'Hang on. I haven't finished.' John put his hand into his inside pocket and carefully drew out half a dozen fragile glass vials wrapped in an airmail copy of the Daily Telegraph, tissue soft and whisper thin.

'Morphine. Be careful with it, these things break easily.'

'Wonderful. You are a genius, Johno. Erm..., I don't

suppose you managed a syringe did you – and a few needles?' Fritz's eyes gleamed greedily in the pale light.

'Sorry, almost forgot.' With expert legerdemain John delved into his coat again and with a flourish a narrow cardboard box appeared in his hand. 'There are about four needles. Remember to sterilize them between patients if you can – boiling water will do.' John realised this advice was superfluous as Fritz was unlikely to be the end-user of these precious products. The chain of trade within the black market wound a complex and mysterious route.

'Yes. Yes.' Fritz grabbed the treasure and stashed everything in an old biscuit tin with a faded and scratched painting of a puppy on the lid. 'You have no idea how valuable all this is. You are a good friend.' The last words dragged from him with reluctance.

'Not at all, old boy. Now - sorry to remind you - but what about your side of the bargain?' He sat on a narrow canvas camping chair beside the stove.

Fritz fished around and eventually his hand reappeared clasping a bundle of dirty, crumpled dollar bills and thrust them into John's hands. 'No use to me, John. Fair exchange I call it.' Fritz chortled. He bent double with a rasping cough that seemed to contort his whole body.

'That doesn't sound too good, Fritz. Want me to get you something for it?' John said as he pocketed the cash. Hundred dollar bills, and a lot of them too. They were useless to Fritz because of the new prohibition. That was why the black market flourished so vigorously and goods changed hands for valuables and cigarettes rather than for cash; a complete alternative economy based on barter.

'Just stop the winter from coming, can you? That should do the trick.'

'Oh, I nearly forgot. I've got something else for you.' John delved into his clothing again and withdrew a half bottle of Remy Martin. 'I had a nip on the way here; otherwise it's all there. Good stuff too.'

'You're a lifesaver. Come; let's have some now.' Fritz extracted the cork from the brandy bottle and poured some into a glass jar that served as a drinking vessel.

'*Prosit*,' he swigged and shared the jar with John, who sipped the spirit delicately, not wishing to deprive Fritz of more than necessary.

'There's something else I wanted to ask you,' said John.

'That was *glanzend*, splendid!' Fritz smacked his lips noisily. '*Ja*, what was that?'

'You remember, you said you know other people who would be willing to pay well for goods – coffee, fags and so on.'

'You're a greedy little *Britischer*, aren't you?' Fritz regarded him through narrowed eyes.

'OK, if you say so.' John grinned. 'But is there anyone else I should be talking to? We could expand this enterprise, you know. Even get into bigger items, machinery maybe, vehicles, radios. What do you think?' John felt the tension rising. This could finally be the breakthrough he had been waiting for. If Fritz would only lead him to the people further up the chain, to the Slavs, the Russian deserters and the ex-Nazi black-market racketeers. Many of these were resident in the camps run by the British. They lived in relative luxury, with free bed and board. These were the people to whom Fritz sold his acquisitions, for food and life's necessities.

'Next time, John, I will arrange it. Better bring something to impress them though. Something bigger than your 'fags' or a bit of coffee. Something substantial. They don't like meeting strangers, particularly eager beaver *Englischer* strangers.'

John nodded. 'I'll try. I may be able to lay my hands on some valuable stuff. Ssh!' He put a finger to his lips. Outside they heard the clattering of rubble tumbling. Heavy boots struck the frozen ground.

'Just the curfew patrol. They're always around at this time of night.'

John peeped through a chink in the makeshift door. A couple of heavily armed British Army privates were cautiously making their way through the empty street towards a dark alleyway. They must have heard something there; maybe just a rat. Who would be out at this time of night? It was nearly one a.m.; time to go home.

'I must be off. I'll wait a minute for them to clear off. Enjoy the brandy.'

'I'll save a bit. May need it later; medicinal purposes. Thanks for the loot. I'll do what I can about the introductions. Come the same time next week, I may have some news for you.'

The patrol had passed and John sneaked out of the shack into the dim alley. He could still hear the patrol nearby so he set off in the opposite direction, planning to circle back later. God, he thought, tonight I could be shot by an English patrol, and next week I could be meeting a set of vicious robber barons ready to cut my throat as soon as look at me. Peril lurks in both directions. It looks as if I may have got myself into something quite dangerous. As he moved away the sound of Fritz's fruity cough echoed off the devastated walls.

Chapter Eighteen

Isabel walked along the narrow corridor to the kitchen at the back of the house. The dingy servants' quarters always oppressed her. She would have loved to brighten the walls with a coat of whitewash but this like so many other things, was as scarce as whisky these days.

The kitchen walls were tiled from floor to ceiling like an institution; plain off-white tiles, the glaze crazed and pitted, with a narrow line of dark green at shoulder height. The earlier residents had not managed to destroy this room and the kitchen equipment was intact, albeit rather basic. A huge cast iron stove dominated one wall, the mysteries of which only Irma had managed to master. A large square stone sink with vintage taps stood beside it. A square pine table dominated the centre of the room, the surface scrubbed white with elbow grease and time, with four sturdy chairs surrounding it.

This was Irma's domain. Isabel was so grateful to have her help. As well as being an accomplished cook, making impossibly delicious meals from their meagre rations, she adored Penny and was always happy to look after her and she kept the flat spanking clean. Isabel sometimes she felt redundant in the face of Irma's remarkable efficiency.

A small sound drew Isabel's attention.

Tears streamed down Irma's cheeks and dripped into the sink as she tackled some washing. Sobs wracked her slim body. Isabel hurried to her and put an arm round the girl's heaving shoulders.

'Irma, whatever's the matter?'

Irma wiped the back of one soapy hand across her face.

'Oh, Frau Barton. I am so unhappy.'

'Come and sit at the table and tell me about it. Is it your mother?'

Irma dried her hands and wiped her face. She sat on one of the chairs across the table from Isabel.

'No, *Mutti* is fine. She's managing well now I can help her.'

'What is it then?'

'It's my boyfriend…' Tears threatened to start again.

Isabel felt a pang of remorse. She wasn't aware that Irma had a boyfriend. How little she knew about the child. At first their stumbling language difficulties had made communication rudimentary, but they had cobbled together a mixture of English and German and now they understood each other most of the time.

Isabel clasped Irma's small hand across the width of the table.

'What boyfriend? I didn't know …'

'Oh yes, Hank. So *wunderbar*.' A tentative smile shone through her tears.

'Hank? Not German then?'

'No, he's a big, strong American. So handsome! A corporal now.'

Isabel calculated that this relationship must be a recent one because the American forces had been forbidden to speak to a German until recently. Fraternization was frowned on. The British had relaxed the rules last year in the face of constant flouting and they finally realised the futility of enforcement and took a more lenient view. The Americans had more recently changed their policy.

'Where did you meet him?'

'At the PX. I go there with my friends. You can get chewing gum, chocolate and sometimes nylons, if you dance with the soldiers and I love to dance. They have a jukebox.'

'How lovely!' Isabel longed for nylons – John seldom seemed able to get them for her. She didn't like to ask, but hoped Irma had not given up too much of herself in return for these gifts, she was very young, but Isabel supposed she should be realistic.

Irma must have seen the doubtful shadow that crossed her face. 'It's all right, Frau Barton, Hank is a real gentleman.'

'He sounds a paragon, dear. So why the tears?'

'He is going away. "Posted", is that what you say? To Hamburg.'

'Ah, I see. That's a long way.'

'*Ja*, I may never see him again.' Fresh tears started and her shoulders began to heave. Isabel tried to forestall a further outburst. She grasped Irma's hand.

'Don't worry, dear, perhaps I can do something. I hate to see you so sad.'

A watery smile appeared on Irma's lips. 'Do you think you could help?'

'I've really no idea, I could try. I'll ask Chuck – Colonel Hoffstetter. He may be able to pull some strings. I take it your Hank doesn't want to go?'

'Oh no, Frau Barton. He likes it here, in Berlin. He doesn't want to leave me. I would be so very grateful if you could help us.'

Isabel couldn't resist the appeal in the wide blue eyes, the hope written on the girl's sweet face.

'Try not to worry. And cheer up. Even if he has to go you could visit each other. There are trains to Hamburg. If he loves you he will do everything he can to keep in touch. Why don't you get him to come round here one day, so we can meet him?'

'Yes, I will do that, Frau Barton. Soon.'

Isabel became aware of the delicious smell emanating from the stove. 'What are you cooking? It smells wonderful.'

'*Goulasch*. It has to cook for a long time, so I started this morning.'

'I know, the beef they've been giving us lately must have died of old age. Still, I'll look forward to it. I'm sorry, dear; I've got to go. I'm expecting Captain Marriott. I came down to ask you if you could look after Penny after school.'

'Of course, Frau Barton. I will be happy to. I'm going to teach her to knit.'

'That's wonderful! She'll like that. You have the most amazing patience. I must rush now. Bye!'

Isabel made her way back to the hall thinking how she would always be grateful to Irma for a her help and praying the girl wouldn't leave to follow her man to Hamburg. What a nightmare, how on earth would I manage? Wryly she remembered that only a few months ago the idea of having a servant filled her with horror and now she was totally dependent on her maid.

John was uncharacteristically late. He'd managed to get the *Volkswagen* and Anya sat with him in the front seat, wrapped in a bright blue coat with a luxuriant fur collar that almost covered her face. A gift from John, Isabel thought with a twinge of jealousy, lucky girl.

'Chop chop, darling, we're late.' John saw the sardonic look on Isabel's face and grinned. 'OK, it's my fault, sorry, nearly couldn't get the car. Someone else wanted it for a jaunt, but I managed to pull rank.'

Isabel climbed into the back behind John as Anya emerged from her fur.

'So lovely to see you again. Are you well? You look blooming. Such a pretty hat. You didn't get that in Berlin, I'm sure.'

'No, in London before I came over.'

'Ah, the hat,' said John, 'the first thing I saw of Isabel, that hat. Very fetching, I thought.'

'Yes, darling,' purred Anya, 'you do have an eye for the ladies. It's very rare for a man to appreciate clothes as you do.'

Isabel noted Anya's proprietary tone as she spoke and how she idly stroked his arm.

'Leave off, Anya. I'm trying to drive.'

John half turned his head. 'We're going to the lake. There's a new little *Gaststube* that I've heard about. I've got to stop off on the way; a bit of business – shouldn't take a minute.'

The lovely bright autumn day lifted Isabel's spirits. The sun dazzled between the trees and the sky was as clear and blue as summer. Possibly it would be balmy in the sunshine down by the lake. Anya's strange, exotic perfume filled the car with fragrance. Musky and old-fashioned, it reminded Isabel of an Indian shop in the East End she had been into once; a scent that could lull you to sleep.

They drove through the outer suburbs. It looked as if some reconstruction was taking place. Neat stacks of salvaged bricks stood beside the road and women and old men were trying to dig a foundation. Luckily little traffic travelled the street as John took the corners in his usual style, with a screech of tyres. Isabel's nerves were already frayed and her fingers clung to the back of the front seat.

'I've got to pay a quick call on someone before lunch. It's near here somewhere,' said John. 'I've got the address.' He indicated a slip of paper on the dashboard. 'It's just that these streets all look the same now and the street signs are lost on most of them.'

After a few hundred yards the car skidded to a halt and the women lurched back and forth like a pair of limp dolls, protesting at the sudden braking.

'Sorry, ladies. This is it. Won't be long.'

John leapt and crossed the road, disappearing into the remnants of a suburban villa whose roof was torn in ragged shards leaving the attic open to the elements. A tarpaulin arrangement had been slung over it to cover part of the damage, but the recent winds must have dislodged it because it now hung like a limp curtain over the partly boarded-up windows of the second floor.

Anya narrowed her eyes and watched John closely as he vanished into the house.

'I wonder who he's seeing. Did he say?' said Anya.

'Not to me. He often disappears on mysterious errands. Something to do with his work.'

'Hm. Do you think I should go with him?'

'Certainly not. I'm sure he doesn't need his hand held, Anya. He wouldn't want us to interfere.'

'I know, but… he may not be safe.'

'Oh, I think John can look after himself,' said Isabel. 'He's tougher than you think.'

'I know he's tough. I've seen him in action.'

'What do you mean?'

'We were followed by a couple of thugs one evening after we left the Moser. They looked as if they were going to try to rob us. John knocked them out; both of them. There was some interesting fighting, nothing like anything I've seen before. It involved feet and hands whirling around in the most extraordinary way. The robbers didn't stand a chance. It had nothing much to do with - what do you English call it? The

Queensbury Rules. But very soon they were groaning on the pavement and we walked away.'

'Look,' said Isabel. 'Someone's coming out of the house.'

A tall thin man dressed in clothes almost reduced to rags emerged. He scanned the empty street and registered the car the women were waiting in and stared at them with expressionless eyes in a bearded face etched with deep lines. His stony gaze lingered for a few moments and then he coughed into his hand, turned and hurried off.

'Who can that be?' said Isabel. 'He looks quite young, yet he's not in the Forces.'

'Could be Russian,' said Anya, 'and hasn't gone back to the Mother Country; some Russians escaped the repatriation. Or maybe a German civilian or an ex-prisoner of war. The younger men are reappearing, being let out of the camps.'

'But they usually get work. That's what Bill does, clears them for denazification, gives them a *Persilschein*, and they get sent to retraining or the factories.'

Anya stared at the house. 'It looks as if there are several people in there. I wonder what's going on.'

'It's really none of our business, Anya.'

'Yes it is. It's all our business. The future of Europe depends on what happens in Germany. We can't ignore what's going on in Berlin.'

Isabel, surprised at Anya's vehemence over what appeared to be a trivial matter and let the question rest. She didn't want to know what John was doing; it was probably the under-cover work that Bill had mentioned.

'I hope he's not going to be long. I'm starving,' she said.

Another twenty minutes passed before John appeared in the doorway. He was arguing with someone inside. Throwing his hands up in a gesture of mock surrender he backed away from the door, still talking to the person hidden inside. As he turned away the door slammed, sending down a shower of loose mortar onto the path. John brushed the dust from his shoulders as he crossed to the car.

Isabel saw someone else in one of the upper windows, but they were masked by the drooping tarpaulin. For a moment she thought the outline looked familiar, almost like the stooping stance of Dennis Masters, her upstairs neighbour. But it couldn't be, not here, out in the sticks, he would be in town working with Bill.

John's face bore an expression of glum acceptance until he reached the car. His thoughts appeared to be weighing heavily.

'Well, ladies,' he brightened, but Isabel could see it was with considerable effort. 'Sorry to keep you waiting. Let's get on our way.'

John drove silently and unusually sedately during the rest of their journey to the Wannsee. The silence was an unusual departure from his normal chattering self, but Isabel enjoyed the slower journey.

They found the new restaurant. Someone had gone to a great deal of trouble to make the place attractive. The freshly varnished timber beams matched the furniture, although this was in a mixture of styles and sizes. They must have been salvaged from ruined houses. Someone had managed to cobble together cheerful curtains for the windows out of squares of colourful fabric.

John's party sat on the terrace overlooking the lake. Each of them had a beer in a heavy German beer mug, and they enjoyed the view.

'Goodness, the lake seems to go on for miles. Look at all those lovely trees. It must be wonderful in spring,' said Isabel.

A breeze rippled the surface of the water and the sun reflected in darts of brilliance that dazzled and flickered across the lake like a haphazard message in Morse code.

Isabel shivered. 'I can't stay out here for long. There's a bitter edge to this wind.'

'Don't worry, we'll be going in in a minute.'

The restaurant was sparsely occupied. Only an elderly couple sat near the fireplace, stolidly consuming their *bratwurst* and *sauerkraut.* The proprietor directed John to a table near the window overlooking the lake.

'You tell me if you are cold, please,' said their host. 'I put more wood on the fire.'

The inglenook, complete with spit and kettle hook, already contained an impressive blaze with flames threatening the surrounding timbers and heat radiated into the room. Isabel hoped they hadn't cut down one of those magnificent trees to supply it.

'We're fine, thank you,' said John.

Their meal of clear soup, awash with pasta pieces, and then sauerkraut with all the trimmings - several types of sausage and a slice of pork accompanied by mountains of boiled potatoes - lived up to its promise. The scent of caraway seeds wafted up from their plates.

'Goodness, German food. Certainly sticks to your ribs,' said John, wiping his mouth. 'I'm not sure I'll be able to move.'

'Well, you didn't have to eat quite so much of it,' commented Isabel.

At that moment their host appeared beside the table to offer them dessert.

'I couldn't eat another thing,' said Isabel.

The others agreed and they each drank a cup of strong coffee.

'Interesting,' said John. 'I wonder where they got that from.'

'You know it must be black market,' said Isabel. 'We haven't seen real coffee for weeks.'

'Yeah, American, probably. I expect they've sold off the family heirlooms to get the stuff for this place. Good luck, I say.'

'I thought you were trying to stamp out the black market.'

'Yes, I suppose we are. The big boys; criminals, spivs and racketeers who work on a huge scale. They are gangsters and will do anything. They're dangerous, ruining the economy. But at this level… You can't really blame them, can you?'

Isabel pictured Mum's face. She had stood out against black market goods all through the war. 'It's unfair,' she'd said. 'We should all 'ave the same, rich and poor alike. You shouldn't be able to buy luxuries just because you've got the money.'

Isabel and her sisters had kept quiet about their occasional indulgences – a bit of extra butter or sugar bought 'under the counter'; the butcher keeping aside a little extra meat or offal for his favourites. But that wasn't really Black Market – just the butcher looking after them. Spivs ran the real Black Market and they were genuine criminals.

'Listen,' said John. 'We'll never get rid of the black market altogether, but we'll never get the German economy back on track if we can't get it under control.'

Anya's very quiet, thought Isabel. John must have thought the same. 'What do you think, Anya?' he asked.

The Russian girl shrugged. 'I think people will do whatever they have to do to survive. And I mean anything; theft, murder, fraud, kidnap, anything.'

Isabel trembled at the malign intensity in Anya's voice. Her Russian accent was more pronounced and her eyes glared fiercely at the others.

'You British, you don't know what it is to be on the edge of survival. You have had it easy. You're so naive. You want everything your own way. It's been incredibly hard for us.'

Isabel started to protest, but Anya interrupted her.

'Oh, I know it was difficult for you in England. But you were never starving, diseased and homeless as we were. No, for some there is a fine blurred line between legality and crime.'

'OK.' John stood up; apparently ignoring Anya's outburst, but a thoughtful look lingered in his eyes. 'Home, I think.'

He went to pay the bill and thanked the proprietor and congratulated him on his hospitality.

Isabel smiled at Anya sympathetically and they each linked an arm with John's as he led them back to the car.

Chapter Nineteen

Isabel and Zelda returned from the *Kino* chattering in good spirits. Wrapped up against the cold, they walked from the bus stop. They had been to see the newest cinematic sensation, "Brief Encounter".

'Would you do that, Zelda? Give up love for duty?'

'God, I don't know, darling. It's not likely to happen here, is it? There aren't too many interesting candidates for an affair. Anyway, I adore Chuck, I'd never look at another man.'

'Come off it, Zelda! I've seen you flirting. And there are loads of bachelors around, English ones and those lovely French officers. Or people like Dennis whose wives have gone home. I'm sure they wouldn't say no to dalliance if you offered.'

'Dennis? Give me a break, honey; he's like a wet week in Seattle! All that ginger hair and horrible beard. Anyway, it's just flirting; doesn't mean a thing. "Dalliance" isn't quite what we're talking about here though, is it? I thought that was real love in the movie.'

'Yes, I think it was. So sad. I couldn't even flirt; not even with the French. I'd feel so disloyal to Bill.'

'I know, and being British doesn't help. You should loosen up a little; give him a run for his money.'

'He's not around enough to notice. I could be having a hundred affairs for all he'd know. I've hardly seen him this week.'

Zelda nodded. 'Yeah, they're really busy with this Bizonia thing, joining our zone with yours.'

'Bill says it's because we need to show a united front. It doesn't make sense to have two administrations duplicating everything. It looks as if the Russians are up to something.'

'More than likely. Russians! I wouldn't trust them with my auntie's dog.'

Isabel took her key from her bag and opened the door. As they took their coats off and hung them on the stand in the corner they heard raised voices from the lounge.

'It's not much good complaining about it now,' Bill's voice was angry.

'But it's my neck on the block if it goes wrong,' John replied. 'It's no good supplying refrigeration units that don't work or radios with broken valves. It completely undermines my credibility. I'm trying to drag the bosses out of the woodwork, not bring a shit storm down on myself. These aren't nice gentlemanly businessmen I'm dealing with. They'd slit your throat as soon as look at you.'

'It was all your idea in the first place. You have to take some responsibility for your operation. Perhaps you should have thought it through more carefully. It's not our fault if it isn't working out quite as you expected.'

'I'm not some sort of mad maverick. I did run all this past the Colonel, you know, and he approved it. I thought you'd back me up. We're never going to get these bastards out of the shadows without the right bait. You've got to complete your side of the bargain. At the moment I'm out on a limb.'

'I don't see why you can't fob them off. Offer them something else they want.'

'What? Another armoured truck with no brakes. Bloody thanks!

Isabel thought it time to intervene and she stuck her head round the door. Prince rushed over, all wagging exuberance, to greet her. He drew his lips back in imitation of a grin, showing all his teeth in sheer delight; his body shaking with excitement. Isabel patted him.

'What a lovely smile! Down, Prince, good boy. Hello, John. Sorry to disturb you, Bill. Zelda's with me. We've been to the *Kino*.'

Bill composed his angry features and John stepped forward, all charm as usual.

'Darling! How was the film?' He kissed them briefly.

'We loved it. A real weepy. Shall I tell you all about it?'

'Later, darling,' said Bill, belatedly pecking her cheek. 'It's a woman's film isn't it? I don't think we need to hear about it right now. How about a cup of tea?'

'Righto. I won't be long. Come on, Zelda; help me make the men some tea. Irma's out this afternoon.'

'What was all that about?' asked Zelda as they made their way to the kitchen. 'John sounded really upset.'

'I don't know. Nobody tells me anything. Just the usual argument about the black market people. John's always off on little missions, visiting some very unsavoury characters.'

'Chuck says they're a real nasty lot of gangsters.'

'What? Like Al Capone in Chicago?'

'Yes, I suppose, only more desperate and even better armed.'

'Better armed? How's that?' Isabel flinched with fear.

'Great piles of arms and ammunition were left lying around when the war ended. If somebody died in the street, a soldier say, their handguns were snatched up and stowed away. Or a machine gun dropped by a dying man. Quite a valuable commodity I'd think, to trade for food. Guns and grenades traded for coffee and soap. It sounds obscene.'

Isabel remembered something. 'I've been meaning to ask you. Have you been issued with a gun?'

Zelda looked startled. 'No. Have you?'

'Yes. I've got this little Mauser automatic. It's under my pillow. Horrible thing. It scares me.'

'Gee, Bill must know something we don't. Did he say why he gave it to you?'

'Something about all the wives being issued with them. There have been murders. But I think he may be mixed up in something dangerous. I didn't realise; I thought he was just interrogating ex-Nazis and DPs, and finding people jobs and housing; admin and paperwork. But he seems to be mixed up in the same thing as John, from what we just heard.'

'He's an Intelligence officer, honey. What he tells you is just the tip of the iceberg. All those hours away from here; they're not all spent in the interrogation centre. He could be up to anything, you'll never know.'

'I hate that! He's my husband, I should know if he's in danger, or putting us in danger.' Isabel thought for a moment. 'Perhaps John would tell me.'

'Don't bank on it, babe. He seems very open, but John can be as tight-lipped as the rest of them.'

Isabel put a couple of spoons of loose tea into the pot. She poured canned evaporated milk into a jug and diluted it with water. No sugar this week; luckily none of them cared.

'Bill would like me to go back to England. He thinks Emma had the right idea.'

'Oh, Isabel, why?' asked Zelda. 'Anyway, who cares what that awful woman does?'

'He thinks I'm lonely and not occupied enough, even with the dancing classes. Maybe it's the danger too – for Penny and me. There's a lot of typhus and TB, measles, diphtheria. And with the winter coming…'

'Don't go back. I would miss you. Who would I gossip with about the *hausfraus* if you went home?'

'No, I won't go. I wouldn't leave Bill alone. Five years during the War was enough. I want to have a normal family life. Although I don't see him much, I think he'd miss me.' Isabel looked wistful for a moment. 'Besides, I'd have nowhere to live. I'd have to go and live with Mum and Dad. Can you imagine how awful that would be?'

'Yes, I expect it would be grim. And of course Bill would be bereft without you. But if he thinks it's dangerous enough to need a gun he must know something.'

'He says people are getting murdered all the time.' Isabel finished making the tea.

'Yes, some people are desperate. When you have nothing you will do anything to protect your family.'

'Yes, Anya said something like that.'

'She's right. Don't tell John, but I'm not sure I like Anya. She always seems to be watching, judging. I'm sure she remembers everything we say; stores it up for later. An underhand little minx, Chuck says.'

Isabel laughed. 'She probably envies you, Zelda. You're so glamorous and rich and American too. How could she not hanker after your life?'

Zelda gasped. 'Goodness me! Is that how I look to you? I thought I was just like everyone else.'

'Don't be silly, Zelda. You're not exactly another *hausfrau*, are you?'

They had reached the drawing room door with the tea tray. John and Bill's voices were low now and they stopped talking as the women entered.

'Don't stop on my account, gentlemen!' Zelda said breezily. 'We're all in the same Zone now!'

'Come and sit down, Zelda,' John showed her to a seat. 'Tell us about your little film.'

'Try not to be patronising, John. I think you would have enjoyed it, actually. It was an interesting commentary on the human condition.'

'La-di-da,' laughed John.

Isabel listened to their banter with only half her attention and poured the tea. Her forehead puckered with concern as she thought about the danger she and Penny might be in. Had she been blind, not really seeing things as they were? Was she complacent about the poor souls wandering the streets whilst she was secure here in her requisitioned flat? Just four fragile walls between them and the ghastliness of outside. Could someone sneak into the house when Bill was out? Could there be someone concealed in the shadows, when she came home one day? Would she meet with an accident when she was at the NAAFI or the Kino? Fear of the unknown gripped her.

But the danger, when it came, took an entirely different form.

Chapter Twenty

The doorbell of the Grunewald house had miraculously escaped the vandalism of the Russian occupants. They had probably had no use for it or no conception of its proper function. It consisted of a stout and ornate iron lever, which, when pulled firmly, through a complex system of cables and pulleys, sent a sonorous clanging to the end of the long corridor and the kitchen.

As Bill said, 'It could wake the dead.'

This evening Isabel heard its strident chimes soon after she had put her feet up for a quick rest after a strenuous afternoon's teaching and had finally settled Penny in bed. She had been excited over the promise of a visit to Hamelin. Frau Hilfe had vividly recited to the children the legend of the piper who had stolen all the children of the town away with the lure of his pipe.

'Were they never seen again, Mummy?'

'I don't know, darling. I expect a brave soldier rescued them.' Isabel answered, distractedly tucking the covers around the child.

'Like Daddy.'

Isabel chuckled as she bent over to kiss her, 'Yes, just like Daddy. Now go to sleep.'

She left the little girl with her pretty German bedside lamp, carved in intricate fretwork shapes representing the story of Hansel and Gretel, painting moving shadows on the ceiling and walls of the room. Isabel found it rather creepy, but Penny loved it and her imagination fashioned animals and people out of the shadows and made up stories until she fell asleep.

The bell clanged again.

'I'll get it, Irma,' Isabel shouted as she strode across the hall and opened the front door, half expecting to see John or one of their other friends standing there. But the stranger before her was a tall uniformed GI, his head shorn in a crew cut, and an irresolute smile on his open face. His wide footballer's shoulders filled the doorframe. Cold air wafted around him and a cloud of white vapour fogged the air as he spoke.

'Good evening, ma-am. I'm sorry to disturb you,' His eyes were focussed on his feet. 'May I speak to Irma?'

Something familiar about the boy's stance and soft accent resonated with Isabel.

The soldier looked up from his boots and studied her face more closely.

'My!' He said. 'I know you. The lady with the hat and the kid.'

'Goodness,' replied Isabel, holding Prince's collar with her free hand, trying to discourage him from giving the soldier one of his overwhelmingly welcomes. 'You're right. I thought I recognised you. We met at the station at the Hook. You were so kind and I was so rude; I can only excuse myself on the grounds of extreme stress. Come in. We're letting the heat out. Irma!' she called, making shooing motions to get the boy through the door. 'Your young man's come to see you.' She closed the door behind him.

The boy's face lit up as Irma appeared from the kitchen, her face glowing with kitchen warmth and a stronger emotion.

'So this is Hank! An extraordinary coincidence, Irma. This is the soldier who helped Penny and me in Holland. Fancy meeting him here with so many other soldiers around.'

'Not such a coincidence. A lot of our guys have gone home. There aren't that many of us Yanks in Berlin now. You British have a much bigger contingent,' Hank answered.

Isabel was well aware of that; many British soldiers were marooned here, waiting to be demobbed. After five years of war they just wanted to go home. Isabel felt sympathy for them; oh for a normal life again!

'Well, it's nice to meet you again. Go to the kitchen with Irma. I'm sure she'll be able to find a lovely piece of *Kuchen* for you. She's a wonderful cook.'

'Thank you, ma-am. But I'm here to see you as well, Mrs Barton. To thank you. I believe it was you that spoke to Colonel Hoffstetter.'

'Well, I spoke to his wife, actually. What happened?'

'The Colonel's been very good about it. He says I can stay in Berlin. He's making me one of his drivers. It's really great, because now I can see Irma when I'm off duty.' He held out a broad hand and grasped Irma's tiny fist. She seemed very slight by his side but her face shone, incandescent with happiness as she gazed adoringly at her American hero.

'Thank you, Mrs Barton, for what you have done,' Irma murmured.

'I didn't do much, but I'm really glad it's turned out well for you. Run along. Major Barton will be home soon. What are we having?'

'*Goulasch* again.'

'Wonderful. I know it'll be delicious.'

Isabel turned to the lounge and retrieved her shoes whilst the young people hurried off hand in hand to the kitchen. Prince trotted behind them, doubtless hopeful of a scrap or two from a generous stranger. How lucky those two are, Isabel thought, happy and in love. We used to be like that. Window-shopping in Bond Street, close together, hardly noticing the luxurious goods or the hurrying people; wrapped up in each other's company with no thought for the future. No thought of War, of separation, of sadness and death.

Isabel sighed and, picking up her book from the coffee table, tried to read to pass the time until Bill got home. Hopefully he would be early for once and they could have a quiet dinner. He'd been working far too late recently. He took the placing of his people far too personally and it was getting him down. He couldn't solve the problems of Berlin alone, however hard he tried and now she was worried that he might be mixed up in something more dangerous.

Prince came back from the kitchen, turned around on the threadbare rug and sighed deeply as he settled. She found she couldn't concentrate on the book, there was something she needed to talk to Bill about; a discovery she had made.

Yesterday afternoon Isabel had been in the bathroom upstairs, washing her hair. She had just wrapped her wet locks in a towel. She wasn't looking forward to putting it in curlers, it always took so long and made her arms ache. She really needed a perm, but there was no-one to do it, she'd have to manage on her own until she could use the services of Zelda's talented maid.

She swilled the last of the shampoo down the drain with the shower hose. Standing up, she stretched her back. I need more exercise, she thought. I can't go on sitting around all day like an old lady; I need to get out. The ballet lessons helped, but she needed something more demanding.

Isabel left the bathroom and stood on the landing listening to the silence of the house. Irma was visiting her mother, Penny safely at school and of course Bill and Dennis were at work.

Before turning to descend the broad stairs she noticed that one of the doors to Dennis's apartment stood ajar. He usually locked everything up. Isabel had never been into these rooms as Emma hadn't invited her to visit.

Overwhelmed by curiosity and with a guilty glance over her shoulder, she padded across the landing in her stockinged feet and gently pushed the door open wider. She stood on the threshold in awe.

Sunshine spilled through the four tall sash windows along one side, matching the four on the floor below. But, as the room was above the foliage of the garden, light penetrated into the room in splendid radiance, illuminating it like a film set. Every surface was covered with beautiful treasures, antique lamps and *objets d'art* stood on inlaid tables and marble-topped consoles standing on fine Persian rugs.

Isabel gasped in wonder at the Aladdin's cave. My! Dennis has been busy. She fingered a fine Meissen figurine of a ballet dancer, its delicate lace gown fashioned out of porcelain, on a walnut side table. How on earth did he get all of this up here? He must have done it secretly when we were out.

She examined the artefacts more closely – silver items made by skilled craftsmen stood beside beautiful enamelled boxes and jasper vases. Was that jade? Isabel stroked the surface of the smooth, green figure of a Buddha. This must all be worth a fortune – where did he get it all from?

Isabel turned to the wall above the fireplace. A pair of voluptuously graceful Art Nouveau figures of dancing girls flanked a magnificent antique clock whose mechanism must have been in working order as it showed the correct time. Above the clock hung a painting, a summery landscape with a flower-scattered stream, the representation of sunlight on water so realistic. It looked familiar to Isabel – she'd seen it in a book before the war. Painted by one of those Impressionist artists – Monet, wasn't it? Or Manet, one of those. She stared at it in disbelief, it looked like an original, but surely it couldn't be. She moved closer and found she could clearly make out the brushstrokes, the light from the window made them stand out in relief, and in the corner, the signature of the artist.

My God! He's collecting art and antiques. He surely can't be getting all these things honestly, not on his salary, he's a civilian Civil servant; he probably gets paid less than Bill.

Then it struck her. Of course! He must be getting it all as bribes from the ex-Nazis, to get a clean *Persilschein*. That must be it, how else could he afford such luxuries?

A small sound alerted her to the presence of someone downstairs. It couldn't be Dennis so early, but it wouldn't do to be found nosing around in his flat. She tiptoed to the door and cautiously opened it and slid out onto the landing leaving the door as she had found it. I'll have to tell Bill about this later and see what he thinks about it all.

Isabel rubbed her head with the towel as she descended the stairs. The sound had only been Prince waking from his nap. His overlong claws tip-tapped across the floor of the hall. He greeted her with joy.

'Down, boy! I'll dry my hair and we'll go for a walk.'

At that magic word Prince danced around in excited circles, practically begging Isabel to hurry up. There was no time to waste when a walk in the woods was on offer.

'Wait, Prince. I'll get my coat and we'll go. I won't be a moment.' She rubbed most of the moisture out of her hair; she'd have to leave the curlers until she got back. She reminded herself that she must tell Bill about what she had seen in Dennis' apartment as soon as possible. But he came in late that night, in a surly mood and she did not have the opportunity to speak to him. By the morning it had gone out of her mind. She really must tell him about it when he got home tonight.

When Bill arrived he seemed distracted; his mind on something worrying. Isabel was dying to tell him what she had found upstairs, but didn't get the opportunity.

'Hello, darling,' he pecked her somewhere near an ear. 'Can we eat soon? I've got some people coming over later.'

Isabel's heart plummeted. 'Oh, no, Bill. I thought we'd have the evening to ourselves. I have something I want to tell you...' She tried to keep the dismay out of her voice.

'Tell me later. I've got to talk to these people. What's for supper?'

'*Goulasch*. It's ready now.'

'Oh, not again.'

'That's all we can do with the beef. I could swear it gets worse each week; it could be horse for all I know. Anyway, I'm sure Irma's done wonders with it. There were some tinned tomatoes to put in it for a change.'

Showing little interest in domestic details, Bill took glasses and bottles out of the cupboard and placed them on the small tables.

'Well, let's get on with it then. They'll be here soon.'

Isabel left the room and hurried to the kitchen.

'Irma, the Major's home. Can we have our dinner now, please? We've got some people coming for drinks later.'

The maid bustled about, deputising Hank to finish mashing the potatoes. In minutes she served the food in the echoing dining room.

Bill laid his table napkin across his lap and began to eat. 'It's not very warm in here,' he said.

'We can't heat the hall and here. The warmth from the stove comes in when I leave the door open. It's the best we can do.'

'It's going to get worse, you know. There's already a shortage of fuel and we're only at the beginning of December. As soon as there's a heavy fall of snow I don't know what's going to happen.'

'We'll have to huddle round one fire in that case. We could always decamp to the lounge; it'll be like wartime again.'

Isabel tried not to worry; they would be all right. She assumed the Army would not let them freeze. They were still getting a regular coal delivery and there were the logs from the fallen trees in the garden. She wasn't likely to have to go into the woods desperately foraging for fuel like many Germans; or those who were chopping up their few remaining sticks of furniture and even floorboards for warmth.

'Who's coming tonight?'

'John, Dennis and Oleg. Oh, and I think Oleg's bringing one of his chaps. But I don't think he speaks English.'

'Oleg's such a brute.'

'I know, sorry. But I need to talk to him, unofficially. You'll be able to fend him off, won't you?'

'Yes, of course, it's just that he will grope and he's so sweaty. Those roving hands...' she shuddered. 'So none of the girls are coming? Do you want me to disappear?'

'No, darling. There's no need for that. You can stick around and look gorgeous, as always.'

Isabel felt ambivalent about this remark, which was delivered without so much as a glance in her direction. It was a compliment really, but it sounded a bit condescending. Was that all she was good for, looking gorgeous?

'Never mind, I can talk to John.'

'Not all the time, I may need him. He's better with Russians than I am. My Russian's not up to scratch yet.'

'John? I didn't know he spoke Russian.'

'John has many talents of which you're not aware, I'm sure,' Bill said enigmatically.

Isabel remembered the many hints she had heard about John's unusual and covert skills. He appeared to be an altogether fascinating man.

They ate supper rapidly and Irma cleared away. Hank appeared from the kitchen to help Irma remove the dishes. He had removed his uniform blouse and added a small pinafore over his shirt. Tied round his waist, it gave him a comical air; his imposing bulk reduced to the status of a housemaid.

'Who the hell are you?' asked Bill. Isabel stepped in rapidly.

'It's all right, Bill. This is Hank, Irma's friend. I told you about him.'

Hank stood rigidly to attention, a terrified expression on his face and his right hand hovering in the air, unable to decide whether to salute or not. At the same time he pawed fruitlessly at the apron, trying to discard it.

'At ease,' growled Bill, attempting to keep a smirk from his face.

'Sir.' Hank mumbled, muted by embarrassment. The boy scurried back to the kitchen in Irma's wake.

'Why didn't you tell me he was here?' Bill asked as they stepped into the lounge.

'I didn't know I had to,' Isabel snapped. 'He's Irma's friend; nothing to do with you. I didn't know Irma was going to co-opt him as a waiter. I suppose he should have stayed in the kitchen.'

'He's an American soldier. In our house. Irma's boyfriend!' he snorted unpleasantly. 'A few months ago he would have been court-martialled for fraternisation.'

'Yes, I know. But it's all right now. They're our allies, aren't they? At least they're better than the Russians and you invite them round.'

'I'm not sure that I want my meeting with Oleg to get back to the Yanks at this stage.'

'Well, I'm sure Hank will keep well out of the way. You scared the poor boy to death. He's only got eyes for Irma anyway. I think they're in love.'

Ignoring her, his mind already on other matters, Bill arranged glasses on the table in precise lines and found some mixers, soda and tonic water, in the cupboard.

'It's a funny old mixture of booze; we've finished the gin. But it'll have to do. I suppose we could mix tonic with *slivovitz*...'

'It might even make it drinkable,' replied Isabel. 'I wish we had a lemon - that would help. I'll go and get some of Penny's orange juice and put it in a jug. If I dilute it we can put it in the vodka - I'm sure Oleg will bring some - and make Screwdrivers.

Anyway,' she turned towards the door, 'I must go and powder my nose.'

Twenty minutes later the front door bell clanged. Isabel waited at the drawing room door and watched as Irma, in a spotless white apron, went to open the front door. Several men stood on the step. As she welcomed the guests she made one of her little bobs.

'Guten Abend, meine Herren,' she said.

'*Guten Abend*, Irma.' She blushed at John's cheerful greeting and stiffened when she saw the huge hairy Russian behind him. Irma could not abide Russians and would never forget their brutality when they first invaded and the agonising months that followed.

'They shot my dog,' she related to Isabel. 'I know many girls who were raped by Russians. I was lucky; *Mutti* cut off my hair so they thought I was a boy.'

Isabel could well believe that with her slight figure she would have got away with this.

Irma took Oleg's fur-collared coat; her eyes firmly cast down to the floor. The garment's weight caused her to stumble. She was obviously not going to look this horrible bear of a man in the face. The other men passed by her as if she was not there and strode over to the stove.

John, Dennis and another Russian, younger and slighter than Oleg, with a hard, watchful air about him, all stood close to the stove. There were also a couple of other Russians, silent and stern, who stood at a respectful distance from the other officers. Isabel assumed they were underlings; a sort of bodyguard. She regretted being the only woman there, it made her uncomfortable.

Bill had explained that Dennis was at the meeting only to keep numbers up; a show of British strength. He probably wouldn't have much to say, he was only there as a civilian observer. Or a witness, thought Isabel.

'Come into the drawing room, gentlemen,' invited Isabel cheerfully. 'It's all right; we've lit a fire. You can drag yourselves away from the stove.'

'Mrs Barton, my darlink, how I have longed to be seeing you again. Come; show me your so lovely apartment…' Oleg turned away from the drawing room door, pulling her towards the other rooms. His lack of subtlety made Isabel wince.

'This way, Oleg,' John took the Russian firmly by his elbow and steered him into the room. 'What can I get you to drink?'

'Ah, Wodka,' the Russian produced a bottle from his pocket as Bill had predicted. 'It is nearly cold enough, it will do.'

He plonked the bottle on the table and, opening it, Bill poured some of the oily spirit into a glass.

'More, more,' encouraged Oleg. 'No, nothing with it. I like my liquor strong and pure, like my women.' He guffawed obscenely and took the opportunity to slap Isabel's bottom. She grimaced and moved away to talk to their other guests.

John and Dennis discreetly halted their conversation as she approached. Dennis moved away and sat on the sofa as if he didn't want to talk to Isabel.

'How I loathe that man Oleg,' she murmured.

'Yes, I know, darling,' said John. 'But we have to put up with him. He's our best link to the Russians. Luckily he's got a big mouth, so we learn a lot about what they're up to.'

'Why, is something going on?'

'Well, for a start, they're not happy about us joining our two zones together. You know - the Bizonia plan. Taking it as a personal slight. They say it looks as if we don't trust them and we're ganging up against them.' John chuckled ironically. 'But it makes sense for the Yanks and makes administration simpler. After all, we are co-operating with each other already. We can solve the problems of where to put the DPs more easily if we combine facilities. Anyway, the Americans have better chow.'

'Chow?' queried Isabel.

'Yeah, you know - rations. They get steaks and oranges flown over from the States. We might see a share of it ourselves.'

Isabel had found this out for herself only recently when Zelda had brought these delicacies on her visits.

'We've got far too much, darling.' she'd said. 'We're out most of the time anyway, what with Chuck's diplomatic work and all; those amazing meals at the French Chief's house. Don't even think of refusing, honey. The oranges will be so good for you and Penny.'

Bill had certainly not complained when he had a juicy steak for dinner.

People in England seemed to think that the occupiers of Germany were living in luxury. But it was a struggle to produce reasonable meals from their rations even when augmented by food obtained by John on the black market. The French lived well and expected the Germans to supply them with the best produce from the countryside in their zone. They were extremely unforgiving as their country had been brutally occupied for years.

'It will be a good idea to merge the zones,' Isabel agreed vaguely. 'Maybe it'll mean Bill won't have to work so hard.'

'I'm not sure I can promise that, Isabel. There's a mountain of work to do,' said John.

Bill came over to them. 'I think I need you now, John. This Russian chap's getting heated and I don't know what he's on about. Something about reparations.'

'Sorry, Isabel,' John touched her arm as he moved away and she tended the fire. Luckily this chimney drew well and a good blaze was possible. You feel that the fire was doing something against the chill.

Bill drew John into the group near the windows overlooking the garden.

'I'm sorry, Oleg, can you get Pyotr to explain that again? My Russian's not up to it.'

The younger Russian must have understood Bill. He gabbled off a string of words, clearly annoyed.

'He's not happy,' John commented. 'What have you said to upset him?'

'I'm trying to get them to understand that they can't just strip out everything that moves from their zone and send it to Russia. How can we ever get German recovery if the entire infrastructure has gone? Factories have been stripped bare in the East. They have taken out half the pumps from the pumping stations, for God's sake, and either broken them up or sent them God knows where. What's going next? The electricity generators?' Bill frowned and made an Italianate gesture of despair. 'Someone's got to replace it all and you can bet it will fall to us and the Americans. And what about the food supplies they are supposed to be sending for the Germans? We should have grain by now, what's happened to that?'

Oleg, who had been trying to follow Bill, screwed up his forehead, causing his eyebrows to bristle.

'Who care about the infernal Germans' recovery? They brought it on themselves; don't deserve our sympathy. Let them go hungry. They should return to the land; become honest peasants,' he said.

'It makes no sense, Oleg. There will always be chaos if we can't restore the infrastructure of the country. We can't let them all starve or freeze to death; quite apart from all the diseases going round. There's enough crime and suffering as it is; we shouldn't be making it worse. We made that mistake after the first World War.'

Pyotr, snarled something that sounded like a question.

'He wants to know what we're talking about,' said John. 'They don't get it. They just want to punish and inflict as much pain as possible.'

'Like a lot of bullies,' said Bill.

Pyotr turned to Oleg and barked an order. He seemed to have lost his patience.

'I think they're going,' said John.

'Already? We haven't discussed anything yet. Are they giving up?' said Bill.

Oleg looked apologetic, certainly regretful at having to leave half a bottle of vodka virtually untouched. He swigged down the last of the spirit in his glass and turned to Bill.

'We leave now,' he said stiffly. 'I warn you, Major Barton, it does not - how do you say? – "go down well" if you interfere in the businesses of the Soviet Union. Already there are difficulties. We will administer our zone as we see fit, especially when it comes to people of traitorous inclinations.'

Bill shook his head, baffled by these remarks. Were they a threat? Was he referring to the so-called White Russians as traitors? Bill thought that the ones that the Soviets wanted had been deported to Russia. At least the Americans had saved some of the White Russians from death or incarceration in the gulags.

'I'm sorry to see you go so early, Oleg – Pyotr. I'll get your coats.'

Pyotr spoke again, in English, much to John and Bill's surprise.

'Much trouble, Major Barton, for you and so comfortable family,' he waved his hand around the room. 'Do not put nose in Russian business or much trouble for you.'

That definitely sounds like a threat, thought Bill, bristling beneath his diplomatic smile. He gave a brisk bow of dismissal and walked from the room.

The Russians took their greatcoats and returned their absurdly large uniform caps to their heads and, barely acknowledging Isabel, strode to the front door, their boots echoing on the floor. One by one they left the house, leaving an atmosphere heavy with questions and something close to fear.

'*Das vadanya,*' Oleg turned and waved farewell as the door slammed.

Moments later they heard the roar of a car's engine as the Russians sped away.

Bill turned away from the door.

'Well! What was that all about? They've changed their tune, haven't they? What happened to mutual co-operation? I thought they were supposed to be our allies.'

John looked thoughtful. 'I'd keep your eyes peeled for trouble, Bill. Something's got them angry; they mean business.'

'I'm not afraid of a few drunken Russians.'

'That Pyotr isn't a drunk. He's a dangerous bastard; I've come across people like him before. Don't cross him.'

Dennis and John lingered for more drinks. Dennis sat on the sofa in deep thought, the usual depressed scowl on his face. He might be missing his wife, thought Isabel, but he was such a miserable bastard and taciturn at best. She watched him. What was he thinking? He doesn't look so much depressed as angry, as if resentment had creased his features, and he was impotently enduring his fate. Then she remembered his stash of treasures upstairs. He was probably worrying about how to get it out and reap the rewards. She must tell Bill about it soon. But now was not the moment, Bill was obviously going to be up for a while, mulling over the evening's events with John. Perhaps Dennis's cache wasn't important, everyone was stocking up for the future one way or another.

Dennis glanced up and must have seen the expression on her face. His eyes narrowed, but he did not smile or acknowledge her. She thought it was time to make a diplomatic retreat and leave the men to talk.

Chapter Twenty-One

Berlin, December 1946

Eddies of snow were making circular patterns on the pavements; miniature white whirlpools. Chubby flakes drifted down from the heavy grey sky. Prince amused himself by trying to catch them and lick them off the end of his nose. Isabel's hand lay loosely on his collar. She wore the beaver coat over her dancing clothes, grateful for its embracing warmth.

She was on the front steps of the house shepherding her pupils into the waiting truck. The corporal stood by to help them up. The children wearily dragged the cloth bags holding their dancing shoes and their feet, clad in Wellingtons or snow boots, scuffed the new snow. The excitement usually brought on by snow was absent; their exuberance quelled by weariness. Well wrapped-up in coats, hats and scarves, they resembled a troupe of gnomes on their way home from a tough day's work. Hey-ho, hey-ho.

'Come on, sweeties, time to go home. Buck up, Helena, the truck won't wait forever,'

They had had a longer lesson today, concentrating on the steps for a little show for parents and friends at Christmas. With only a few weeks to go there was much work to be done. Some were catching on like little troopers, but others lagged behind, unable to remember the step sequences and stumbling over their own feet; moving without rhythm or grace. They had to repeat everything over and over and Isabel's patience had begun to fray. By the end of the afternoon she had snapped in exasperation. God, she felt tired. She couldn't wait to sit down.

Andrew rushed into the house to collect the shoe-bag he had forgotten.

'Hurry up, Andrew; or the truck will leave without you,' Isabel called back to him.

Penny stood beside Isabel. She had insisted on coming out to watch everyone leave.

'Put on your coat and hat and gloves, or you'll catch your death. It's freezing out here.'

Penny wrapped up cosily and had added a bright blue scarf of her mother's to the ensemble, the fringes trailing in the snow. She waved to her friends. The army driver stamped his feet on the compacted snow on the pavement in an attempt to keep warm and remove excess snow from his boots. Other people who lived in the street were trudging home from work or from shopping, after patiently queuing for food from their ration allowance. It reminded Isabel of the hours of queuing outside Sainsbury's or the butchers during the War; would it never end? Some of them greeted Isabel as they passed.

'*Guten Tag*, Frau Barton,' they called and she waved back.

'Get a move on, Andrew, we're waiting!' Isabel yelled into the apartment, turning her back on Prince and Penny for a moment and peering into the gloomy hallway. Distracted, she let go of the dog's collar and moved slightly into the house.

'Where have you got to? Andrew!'

At that moment another truck rumbled into the street. The ration wagon. The drivers were always in a hurry; they had many homes to get round, depositing a box of rations on each doorstep. They drove fast and pulled up behind the children's vehicle with a squeal of brakes and a slight skid in the snow.

'Give us a hand with the box, mate,' the soldier in the back yelled to his colleague on the pavement. The children's driver took the box from him and put it on the steps.

'Ta, mate!' The man gave a whistle as he retreated into the back of the truck to grab the box for their next stop and the ration wagon started to move away.

Prince chose this moment to cross the road. He may have spotted a cat or someone he knew and he shot across the road at great speed into the path of the oncoming vehicle. The driver did not see him from high above street level.

Isabel, as she turned from the front door pushing the tardy Andrew before her, had the horrible sight of Prince turning over and over in a grotesque somersault under the body of the truck as it accelerated away.

Isabel's hands flew up to her mouth. 'Oh no!' she screamed. 'Prince!'

The dog did not hear her but, as the truck passed over him, the wheels missing by inches, with a great howling cry of pain he galloped off along the road apparently unharmed but frightened out of his wits. He disappeared between two houses on the other side of the street.

'Oh God! Poor Prince. I hope he's all right. He can't have been hurt too badly if he ran off like that.'

She helped Andrew into the truck, turning from the house. She steadied herself against the vehicle's frame as the ground was unexpectedly slippery even though most of the snow was loose. The corporal held her arm for a moment. Her feet began to chill in her thin shoes; the toes numbing with cold. I should be wearing my fur boots, she thought.

'Bye, bye, everyone. I'll see you next week.'

She waved from the kerb and watched as they waved back and the truck disappeared around the corner. Isabel turned towards the front door and climbed the steps. Penny must have gone in. She would be upset to see Prince run over like that. She probably thinks he's been killed.

'Penny,' she called, closing the door behind her. 'It's all right, darling, Prince is fine. He ran off, shocked, I suppose. He wasn't hurt badly. He'll be back later. Don't worry, darling.'

She looked into the drawing room and Penny's bedroom.

'Where are you, Penny? Are you hiding? Prince is fine.' Isabel tried to sound reassuring.

She walked towards the kitchen. Penny would have gone to talk to Irma. She seemed to go to Irma for comfort more often than to her recently. Isabel was wrapped up in her own troubles she admitted. How selfish of her; Penny needed her Mummy.

Irma had washed her hair and was arranging it in a chignon. So much more flattering than the thick plaits wound around her ears. Her best dress lay on the bed; a demure blue with white lace collar and cuffs.

'Irma, have you seen Penny? Poor Prince was nearly run over; I think he's OK. The truck went over him, but he wasn't hit by the wheels. He ran off. Now I can't find Penny. Is she here?'

'No, Frau Barton, I have not seen her since the lesson. I was getting ready to go out. I have a date with Hank tonight; a dance at the Sergeants' Mess.'

'How lovely, it'll be fun for you. But I must find Penny. She will be hiding somewhere. Could you give me a hand finding her, Irma? It won't take long.'

'Of course,' said Irma.

They searched the flat from back to front. Although the rooms were large the furniture was sparse and left few nooks and crannies where a small child could hide. They looked under beds and even searched inside the huge wardrobe in Isabel's room and in the chilly larder. The door to the back garden was locked and the key hidden in the desk, so she couldn't have got out there.

'I can't find her, Frau Barton.'

'No, Irma, I can't either. I don't think she's here!' A horrible thought assailed her and a note of panic entered her voice. 'That means she must be out in the street. She may have run after Prince. I didn't see her. Oh, God…!' She hurried across the empty hall to the patched front door and flung it open.

The snowfall had gathered pace and the sky had darkened in the half hour they had spent searching the flat. The flakes now resembled small lumps of cotton wool flung carelessly from a lady's dressing table. It was hard to see across the street.

'Penneee!' Isabel yelled, her breath fogging the air. The snow deadened all sound and there was no echoing reply. 'Are you there? Don't hide, darling, it's time to come in.'

'Perhaps she went after Prince,' suggested Irma, echoing Isabel's thought.

'I don't think so. He was moving very fast. You can't run, it's very slippery. I would have seen her.' She called out as loudly as she could. 'Penneeee…'

They set off in opposite directions along the road, hugging their coats close around them. Isabel had grabbed the heavy beaver coat and heaved it on to her shoulders. Her fur-lined boots were now on her feet with Grace's thick socks inside.

'Penny, Penny. Where are you? Don't hide, darling, it's too cold. Come inside and we'll have cocoa.'

She reached the corner and squinted up her eyes to stare vainly in each direction through the cloud of snow. Up and down; straining her eyes and ears. But she could see no movement except for the falling flakes and could hear nothing at all. Every sound was muffled by the snowfall; a reminder of the thick fogs in London. Surely Penny would call out, Isabel thought, if she was hurt, or lost. Surely I would be able to feel her presence nearby or hear her smallest cry.

Isabel ran back towards the house, frantic with worry, sometimes stumbling on the slippery paving stones. She had to do something. There must be someone who could help however bad the weather. Irma was approaching from the other direction, beginning to shiver in her thin coat.

'She's not there, Frau Barton. Oh - *die kleine. Wo ist sie?*' She blinked away tears of distress starting in her eyes.

'No, she's not here. I must call someone for help. Penny wouldn't have gone off alone. Someone must have taken her. I ought to call the *Polizei*.'

Irma looked doubtful and followed Isabel inside.

'But she would have cried out if someone took her, wouldn't she, Frau Barton? She would not go quietly with someone she didn't know.'

'I know, but I might not have heard her. Prince was making an awful noise and the two trucks were moving off. You know how much racket they make and the children were shouting goodbye. I didn't hear a thing. Why would she go with anyone; why then?'

Isabel fumbled off her gloves and gripped the telephone receiver with fingers clenched in a frozen spasm. Panic was building. Agitated, she jiggled the cradle up and down for a line. Nothing but a useless buzzing answered her.

'There's no line. Bloody phone, why does it never work when you need it? What if I can't speak to the police? I'll get hold of John; he'll know what to do.'

She thought of how Bill had told her that when they first arrived in Berlin, the only thing that worked was the telephone system. That had obviously gone for a Burton, she thought.

With Bill away at an Intelligence Conference in Hanover Isabel felt anchorless and irrationally angry.

'Bloody Bill. Why is he never here in a crisis? Typical!' She swore under her breath, still jiggling the phone. 'Oh, it's hopeless. It must be the weather.'

She replaced the lifeless receiver and paced up and down the hall.

'Oh, Penny, where are you? What can I do? If I had a car I could go and find someone, but I can't walk anywhere in this.'

Irma stood mute and helpless a few feet away. They jumped convulsively as the door bell jangled. Someone's brought her home, Isabel thought, thank God!

With a wave of relief nearly overwhelming her, Isabel dashed to the door. 'Penny! Darling! She's come back!' She grabbed the handle and swung the door open. A tall male figure stood on the step.

'Oh, Hank, it's you.' Disappointment patent in every muscle, she turned from the door. Silently, tears began to pour down her face. The beaver coat hung from her shoulders, dwarfing her, emphasising her helplessness.

Hank, paralysed by the obvious distress his arrival had caused, stared at her uncomprehendingly. He mutely questioned Irma over Isabel's shoulder.

'Come in, come in. I'm sorry. I'm so glad you're here.' Isabel took his hand and dragged him over the threshold, dashing tears from her cheeks. 'How did you get here?'

'Marty dropped me off in the jeep,' he replied.

'A Jeep? Oh, good! Is he still here?'

'No, he's gone to get Janine. But he's coming back for us. There's a dance…'

'Yes, I know, Irma told me. Never mind that. Penny's disappeared. We can't find her. I can't make the phone work and it's snowing and I don't know what's happened and Prince was run over and I don't know what to do.'

The stream of words pouring from Isabel's mouth ended in such a wail of fear and sorrow that Hank was prompted to put an arm round her shoulders. He steered her into the warm drawing room where she collapsed onto the sofa and began to cry despairingly.

Irma and Hank stood over her like a pair of guardians, perplexed as to how to proceed. What on earth could they do?

Isabel sniffed and wiped her nose on the beaver sleeve.

'Do not worry, Frau Barton, we will find her. Hank will know what to do.' She gazed at him with hopeful adoration.

Hank shook his head, obviously alarmed. 'No,' he muttered. 'I don't. We'll have to think about it.' He paused. 'Well, ma-am, I could go and look around the streets again.' His lack of enthusiasm for this course of action was apparent.

'I know you're trying to be helpful, Hank, but I don't think we can. You can't see a thing now it's dark and what with the snow and everything… Oh, my poor baby!' Isabel disintegrated into tears again. Uncontrollable shaking took over her body and she turned her head from side to side. 'No! No – no,' she cried, the tears running in channels down her cheeks, taking with them trails of mascara.

Hank whispered to Irma, 'Perhaps you should make a cup of tea or something, honey.'

Irma dashed to the kitchen and soon returned with a tray. By the time it was on the table and Irma had poured it into cups, Isabel's tears had slowed.

'Ugh, it's sweet.' She shuddered as she sipped the brew lavishly laced with sugar.

'Sweet tea's good for shock. Drink it up and you'll feel stronger.' Hank assured her.

Isabel's shaking gradually subsided. The strong tea helped her to think straight again.

'We've got to get help. Hank, how long do you think Marty will be?'

'Well, ma-am, he's picking up his girl, and then he's coming back here. About half an hour.'

'That's not too long. He can take us to John's; he'll know what to do.'

'Captain Marriott's not at the conference?'

'No – just Major Barton. It's some kind of high level thing.'

Isabel leant back and tried to relax. Not long now. They had to find Penny. Out there somewhere in this dreadful cold. Maybe all alone. Where on earth could she be?

Chapter Twenty-Two

The apartment block where John lived bore none of the splendour of the Barton's house with its vestiges of Art Nouveau grandeur. These flats had been built more recently, in the 1930s, of strictly utilitarian concrete along the brutal lines of gun emplacements or bunkers, in keeping with the Nazi ethos.

Inside, John had managed to instil some semblance of comfort with things he had picked up around Berlin. The market outside the ruined *Reichstag* proved an excellent place to buy household goods. Every day desperate crowds of Berliners sold their possessions in exchange for food and medicines. John had procured a magnificent pair of red velvet curtains, which, though overlong for these slight windows, gave his living room an air of luxurious comfort.

One day John found a beautiful Art Nouveau table lamp for Isabel, using some of his precious coffee allowance in payment. It was Bill and Isabel's anniversary, their ninth and only the third that they had spent together. John was delighted she appreciated its opulent artistry.

'Oh, it's lovely, John,' she exclaimed, caressing its smooth asymmetric lines and ornate glass shade, intact in a miracle of survival. 'Thank you so much.' She hugged him and gave him a big sloppy kiss.

Isabel. Ah, what a lovely girl. How easily he could fall in love with her; perhaps he was already on the brink. He treasured her dark beauty and grace and her gentle kindness more than he liked to admit even to himself. If it weren't for Bill… but after all, if it weren't for Bill she wouldn't be here in Berlin and he wouldn't be able to admire her, even from a distance.

His mind had wandered. He dragged his attention back to the here and now.

He was lying on his bed, decidedly 'out of uniform', and Anya was performing a slow striptease at his feet. She was down to her creamy silk underwear, bra and panties, a lacy suspender belt and the pair of black silk stockings that he had found for her. She stooped to nonchalantly unhook a suspender.

'Come on, darling,' he growled, holding out his arms to her. 'I can't take much more of this. Get a move on.'

Anya grinned, wagged a finger and produced one of her gurgling giggles.

'Don't be in such a hurry, *liebling*. We've got all night.'

She must have thought better of keeping him waiting any longer, removed the rest of her clothes and in a swift, agile movement she was straddling him and tenderly stroking his chest whilst he drew her body closer to his.

God, he thought, what luck I found Anya. A beautiful girl and great in bed. She might not have Isabel's class, but hell, who needs it when you've got an enthusiastic young body like this on top of you? He pulled her down until she lay flat against his stomach. He buried his nose in the Russian girl's neck and nuzzled her gently.

'Mmm. You smell nice.'

'Chanel, darlink, you got it for me, remember?'

'Mmm,' John mumbled as Anya's practised caresses stirred his senses and he stroked her into purring submission. From then on his brain and body took him into another world and little conscious thought crossed his mind.

Their lovemaking was progressing very satisfactorily when John heard an alien, strident sound that should not have intruded on them. He ignored it, but moments later, he heard it again. Persistent. Urgent. The front door bell.

'Christ!' He sat up abruptly, almost striking Anya with his arm. 'Sorry, darling. There's someone at the door. I'll have to go. It had better be something important.'

'Who can it be at this time of night?' Anya sat up in the bed, drawing the sheet around her breasts.

'It's not that late. Only about nine.' John glanced at his

watch on the side table. 'Yes, 8.45. I'll see who it is. Probably just one of the neighbours wanting to borrow some butter.'

'They'll be lucky. We haven't seen butter for a month.'

John slipped on a pair of trousers and walked to the door in bare feet. Opening it he saw a broad and lanky young American soldier shuffling his boots on the concrete floor of the hallway.

John scrutinised him. 'Who are you and what the hell do you want, Corporal?'

'Mrs Barton…' the American lad managed to articulate. 'Outside. In the jeep. She needs your help.'

John's attitude changed abruptly. 'Isabel? Well, bring her in, man. What's up? Is she hurt? I'll just go and put some more clothes on.'

Leaving the door ajar he retreated to the bedroom.

'Sorry, darling,' he said to Anya. 'Better get dressed. Isabel Barton's here. She's in some kind of trouble. I've got to help her.'

He was getting into a shirt and a khaki sweater. Anya hid a frown of annoyance and slipped off the bed and began to dress with considerably more speed than she had undressed. She tried not to look sulky, but her disappointment prevailed; it was so rarely that they managed to spend time together. She had hoped to stay all night, which meant the possibility of some real talking and exchange of confidences and hopefully some useful information that she could profit out of.

'Poor Isabel! What can have happened?' She managed to produce a voice full of concern.

'We'll find out in a moment. Be a good girl. Go and put some coffee on. There's some of the real stuff in the red tin. I expect she'll need it, it's freezing out there.'

By the time he had dressed and Anya was in the little kitchen, Isabel arrived at the flat with the American and Irma inexplicably hovering behind them. Isabel had been crying copiously. She paused in the doorway, a briefly framed portrait of anguish.

'Come in, Isabel,' he guided her tenderly towards a chair. 'Now, what on earth's the matter? What can I do to help?'

'Oh, John!' Isabel launched herself into his arms and began to sob on his shoulder. As she was usually so reserved, John was amazed by this display of emotion.

'It's Penny; she's missing. We can't find her anywhere. I think she's been kidnapped!' Her voice was muffled by the huge fur coat, but he could just make out what she was saying.

At this moment Anya appeared in the doorway carrying a tray with coffee and cups. She gasped and swayed perilously, choking back words. No! She thought, aghast. They wouldn't have. She must have articulated her thought because the others turned to look at her.

'Coffee, everyone?' she asked as if nothing had happened. She put the tray down on the table and sneaked out of the room into the bedroom, leaving the door ajar so that she could hear everything that was going on.

'Come, Isabel, sit down and tell me about it,' John repeated and settled her in the chair. 'And for goodness sake, take off that bear coat. You'll be cold outside if you don't.'

Isabel did as she was told and let the coat fall in a heap beside her.

'Hello, Irma,' said John, turning to the others. 'Take a seat and introduce me to your friend.'

'This is Hank, my boyfriend,' Irma replied. 'He has a jeep to drive us here. The telephone wasn't working, *Kapitän* Marriott, we didn't know what to do.'

John sensed an onslaught of tears was imminent. 'Pour out the coffee for us, Irma, whilst I talk to Frau Barton.'

He turned to Isabel, collapsed in and dwarfed by the big leather armchair. He noticed how haunted her eyes were; huge in a very white face. He took her hands in his.

'Try not to worry, darling. We'll find her. I'll see if my phone's working and we'll get the MPs round and send them to search. I don't think we should involve the *Polizei* at this stage. Tell me exactly what happened.'

Isabel related all that she knew. She was vague about when exactly she had last seen Penny.

'She was standing beside me on the steps. Then Prince dashed out and was run over, and I was looking at him and the other children and the ration man and I didn't notice – I didn't notice where she went. And when I was paying attention again she wasn't there, she just wasn't there!' Her voice rose into a wail of fear.

'Where was Irma when all this was happening?' John glanced at the girl.

'I was in my room, Herr Marriott. I was getting ready to go out - with Hank.' Irma blushed and the American drew closer to her, a protective barrier at her side.

'There's a dance at the non-Com's Mess, sir. We were going there.'

Isabel looked up at him, stricken, and spoke through a haze of tears. 'Oh, I'm so sorry; you're missing your dance!'

'That's of no mind, ma-am,' said Hank. 'With the little one missing an' all.'

John nodded at the young man approvingly. He could see that his calm, competent manner soothed the women, staving off hysteria.

'That's right, soldier. Now we must do what we can to find her.'

Inwardly John was doubtful. That sweet little girl; out in the cold and dangerous city with who knows whom. He had heard ghastly rumours – he tried to put this thought to the back of his mind, but it forced its way forward. There had been rumours that, because of the lack of fresh meat, people, including children, had been disappearing and cannibalism was practised. Completely barbaric. Surely not; not a child, it was unthinkable.

John strode to the phone and tapped for a line. A few seconds later he gave the thumbs-up sign to his assembled guests; it was working.

'Hello. Yes please. Get me the Military Police... Marriott, Captain Marriott. 21 Messerplatz, second floor. I need an officer here. Pronto. I must stress that it's very urgent. It concerns a missing child. Yes, please. As quickly as you can.'

Once he had exchanged all the relevant details he hung up and sat down next to Isabel.

'They're on their way. They'll know what to do.' He turned to Hank and Irma. 'You two could go off now. I'll look after Mrs Barton and see she gets home. I've got the car. You needn't miss the entire hop.'

'Are you sure, sir? We don't mind staying.'

'To be honest, Hank, there's nothing more you can do here and when the MPs arrive the flat will seem a bit crowded.' He indicated the extent of the already cramped room. 'Go on. Be off with you, and try and have a good time. Thank you for bringing Mrs Barton.'

'Thank you, sir. Marty and Janine will be glad. They've been waiting in the jeep for us.'

'Good God! They'll be freezing by now. Go and rescue them. There's nothing more you can do. There'll be no more news for a while.'

He realised the dire truth of what he was saying. It was pitch black outside and the snow was still falling and likely to do so all night. By morning there'd be inches of the stuff. What on earth could the police do at this time of night? They probably wouldn't set up a search until the morning; he wouldn't tell Isabel that.

'You've done very well so far, Corporal, getting Mrs Barton here. Now go and enjoy yourselves.'

He ushered the young people to the door. Irma left reluctantly, turning back before walking out. 'All will be well, Frau Barton,' she said. 'You must be hopeful.'

These words brought fresh tears to Isabel's eyes. Hopeful, how could she be hopeful; where was her baby?

Chapter Twenty-Three

The Military Police, when they arrived half an hour later, were embodied by a Major and a Sergeant, introducing themselves brusquely – Major Goddard and Sergeant Cox. The Major marched stiffly into the room holding his tall frame to rigid attention. The Sam Browne belt across the chest of his immaculate uniform tunic and the pistol holster at his hip were polished to a wonderful sheen. He represented the picture of discipline and rigid self-control. The Sergeant was similarly burnished and unsmiling, the webbing on his gaiters sparkling white with well-applied Blanco. A white armband had the letters MP written on it in large black letters.

John and Major Goddard faced each other like gladiatorial combatants and saluted. Isabel had the feeling that John wouldn't have bothered with this formality had not the other officer done so first. Sergeant Cox joined in the formal greeting and then stood, apparently on guard, in the centre of the room. Isabel suppressed a surge of impatience. Enough of the military nonsense, she thought, get on with it, my little girl is missing.

'Well, what seems to be the trouble?' the Major asked.

Isabel almost laughed. These were exactly the words that the family doctor used when they went to consult him. She usually felt that he had absolutely no interest in her answer. It seemed strange to hear the words coming out of the mouth of a policeman, as if a spoon of medicine would solve their dilemma.

'Mrs Barton's five year old daughter has disappeared. She may have been kidnapped,' John explained.

Isabel watched a frown cross the major's face. He wouldn't have much to do with children or families and possibly deplored the presence of so many officers' families in Berlin. More for him to worry about, as if all the usual mess wasn't enough. His duties would normally involve chasing up Other Ranks that had gone AWOL, or committed other misdemeanours. He wouldn't like the idea of looking for a child.

'Why did you call us in?' he asked John, studiously ignoring Isabel. 'Wouldn't it have been better to speak to the civilian police, the *Polizei*?'

'There wasn't the opportunity. The phone's are down in Mrs Barton's residence. In any case, I thought that as this is the child of a serving officer and as a gesture of courtesy, it would be more appropriate to call you first.'

'Hmm…' the Major looked doubtful. 'Nonetheless…'

'If I may say so,' John interrupted him, 'I hardly think we should be arguing protocol at this stage. There's a child missing. What are you going to do about it?'

The officer drew himself up and bristled. His mouth tightened into a thin line under his even thinner moustache and he looked as if he might be about to protest. After all, he did outrank this Captain Marriott. But glancing at Isabel huddled miserably in the chair, he evidently thought better of it.

'I might as well find out what's happened. I'll question the mother,' he announced.

John indicated Isabel with his hand. Sarcasm edged his voice. 'Yes, you might as well, now you're here. Go ahead.'

The Major started to shoot off hard, staccato questions in Isabel's direction; bullets from a machine gun. She cowered into the chair as each question bombarded her, blow after blow.

'No - I explained, there was so much going on...' Isabel's voice was rising in distress.

'And where was your husband?' Goddard paused to look at John.

John began to answer. 'Major Barton. He's…'

'Let Mrs Barton answer please,' the Major snapped. John shook his head in annoyance.

'He's at an Intelligence conference in Hanover,' Isabel said. 'He won't be back until next Wednesday. It may be later, it depends how it goes.'

'Have you looked for the child? Perhaps she's hiding somewhere.'

'Of course we've looked for her. We searched for over an hour inside the house and out. We couldn't find her anywhere. Then it got dark and it was snowing hard and freezing, and the phone didn't work and I had to come and get Captain Marriott's help.'

'How did you get here? You live in Grunewald you said.'

'I was driven in an American jeep.'

'American?' The major managed to inject outrage into his voice. 'Why?'

'It's a long story. My maid has an American boyfriend.'

This explanation clearly filled Major Goddard with disgust. 'And you say you also had a German national with you? It must be against regulations, even in the American forces, to drive civilians around in jeeps without prior permission.'

In triplicate, thought John as he stepped forward to halt the interrogation. 'Enough of this, it's getting us nowhere. I think we may be missing the point. Look, Mrs Barton is very distressed and you're not helping. With all due respect, it may be better if I explain it to you. I've heard the whole story. Sit down and I'll go through it. It's really not very complicated.'

Goddard reluctantly unbent sufficiently to perch on the edge of one of the dining chairs. His Sergeant stood at his elbow.

'Perhaps you'd like to take notes, Sergeant,' suggested John. 'Then you'll know where to go and so forth.'

The Sergeant flinched and withdrew a small notebook from his battledress blouse's top pocket.

'Sir,' he said, the first word he had uttered since entering the apartment.

Within ten minutes John had related the story of Penny's disappearance, the Sergeant scribbling down the details of addresses. When John finished the Major rose to his feet.

'That seems clear enough. I'll instigate a search in the morning. I'll inform the *Polizei* and get them in on it. They may be able to spare some men. But I must warn you, with all the snow, there may not be any traces. If we don't find her soon, I don't know what we can do. You may have to prepare for the worst.' A sharp cry came from Isabel. 'Who can we question beyond the drivers of the two trucks? They may have seen something.' His tone implied that he did not hold out much hope of this.

The Major had voiced the fears that John had silently thought. Isabel stared at Goddard in despair.

'There were people in the street. There always are at about five thirty; coming back from the shops. People walk to the park to find firewood. Someone may have been looking out of a window,' she said.

'I suppose we'll have to do a house to house.' The major said grudgingly, implying that this was the last thing he wanted. 'If we have enough men.'

'Oh please! You must do everything you can,' Isabel begged, fighting back renewed tears.

'We will, of course, Mrs Barton. But for now I must go. Try not to worry. I'll be at your address tomorrow morning at nine.'

He turned sharply towards the door and, with his Sergeant in his wake, left the apartment. John slammed the door behind them with undue firmness.

'Well!' Fury blazed in his eyes. 'What an insensitive, stuck-up prig! He'd got a poker up his arse, hadn't he? I'm sorry, Isabel. Obviously he's not prepared to do anything until the morning. I just hope he'll get his finger out then.'

'It's all right, John. I know he can't do anything now. It's cold and wet and horrible, as well as totally black. We'll have to wait until the morning. I'm sure someone must be looking after her,' she added hopefully.

'Would you like to go home now, darling?'

'Yes please, John. I know it's unlikely, but just in case she's come home.'

'OK. Just a minute. I'll get ready and then drive you; the car's outside. I'll stay the night; you'll need me there to deal with Goddard in the morning. And I'll try to get hold of Bill in Hanover. Hopefully the phone will be on again by the morning.'

'Oh, I'd be very grateful, John. I hope it's all right with Anya.'

'Don't worry, love, she won't mind.'

He went to his room to pack a small bag with necessities. Anya was still there. God, he had completely forgotten about her. She was lying, fully clothed again, on the bed with a small magazine, Lilliput, in her hands. She waved it in the air.

'This is quite funny you know, John.' She stretched lazily, like a contented cat.

'Yes, I know. I'm sorry, darling. You quite went out of my head.'

'I know. I thought it best to get out of the way. There was enough drama without me being there.'

'I've got to go. I have to take Isabel home and I'll stay there. I can't leave her on her own. She's very upset.'

Anya leaned across the bed. 'It's fine, *schatzi*. I understand. I don't expect you to stay. But you owe me,' she laughed provocatively.

John bent over the bed to kiss her. 'You, madam, are a bad girl. I'll see you soon. You can stay if you like; I'm sure it's warmer than your place. It's nearly curfew anyway. You shouldn't be walking about in this snow, it's getting deeper. Let's hope it stops by morning.'

'Thank you, darling, I will.' Anya snuggled into the pillows and picked up the magazine. 'Sleep well,' she murmured.

A few moments later the door to the flat slammed and soon after that the rattle of the car sounded as it left for the Grunewald.

Chapter Twenty-Four

Anya

When she heard the door close behind John and Isabel, Anya leapt off the bed. I have to get out of here, she thought, whatever the weather's like. She snatched up some of John's clothes and started to dress again. She removed her frock; the silk underwear was soon concealed by a long shirt and John's old submariner's jumper swamping her tiny figure. Pulling on a pair of trousers cinched tightly around her waist with a leather belt she rolled up the hems to prevent them dragging on the ground.

She pulled her fur boots over a thick pair of socks and tucked the trouser legs into the boots. She topped the outfit with a pea-jacket that was short on John but covered her like an overcoat. Finally she found a pair of gloves and, clumsy though they were on her tiny hands, she knew she'd be grateful for them out in the freezing streets. She topped the lot with a woollen hat that had seen better days. No-one will recognise me in all this, she thought, I look just the same as the other vagrants wandering the streets.

Warmly dressed, she left the apartment, quietly closing the door behind her so that no curious neighbour would look out to see who was leaving at this hour. The demise of the Nazis had not diminished the watchfulness of the German residents.

As she stepped into the street an impish gust of wind blew a blizzard of loose snow up in front of her, obliterating her vision. She bent her head and hurried on. She had to reach her destination before curfew.

Christo, this is going to be awful, she thought.

The cloud of snow alighted on the smooth surface of untrodden whiteness and the perverse wind died down. The snow was falling more heavily now and settling on the thick blanket already spread over the street. The pavements were indistinguishable from the road and all sound was absent. No footprints marked the surface of the snow; pure whiteness radiated as far as Anya could see. The tyre tracks of John's car had already been erased.

I must go and see Pyotr, she thought. He may know something about this kidnap. Perhaps he is behind it. He was certainly angry with the British. But why would he take the kid? What could the Russians gain from it? Was it supposed to be some sort of punishment? Surely that could only cause trouble. It would make the Brits angry; they were very protective of their children and didn't let them out of their sight. Poor kid, she must be scared to death and cold; this weather is a bastard.

Anya felt some sympathy for Isabel's plight. She didn't like children much, but could imagine how painful it must be if your only child was missing. She had an inkling that the Russians might think that they would have a hold over Bill Barton and John if they took the child. Would they ask for a ransom? Demand some sort of reward for her return? Anya knew they weren't happy about something. The Bizonia 'threat', as they saw it, had caused heated discussion, as had the rapid withdrawal of negotiable American dollars.

She stumbled forward, occasionally losing her footing on the slippery surfaces covering submerged bricks and stones that caught her unawares. She managed to stay upright. A nasty fall in these conditions could prove fatal as an injured person unable to move was not likely to be found for hours, or until the morning when it would be too late to save them. She didn't fancy death by hypothermia.

Soon she arrived at the border to the Russian zone. There was still easy freedom of passage between the zones. At this time of night the border was only loosely guarded; few people attempted to cross so near to curfew. She passed close to a small guards' hut with light and heat pouring out over the snow. Anya avoided the area of radiance and slipped past in the dark. The guards are probably asleep by now, drunk on vodka and the heat from their kerosene heater, a dangerous combination.

Although the route through the eastern zone to Pyotr's billet was familiar to her, the camouflaging effect of the snow made landmarks almost invisible. She stumbled on, afraid of getting lost. Eventually she recognised her surroundings, hurried down the street and banged on the door of Pyotr's drab and anonymous house.

Moments later a Russian voice grumbled from within.

'Who's there? Who can it be at this time of night?'

Anya heard the stomping of heavy feet as someone came towards the door and fumbled noisily with something inside.

Anya banged again, frozen now she was standing still.

'Wait a minute, can't you? I'm unlocking it.'

Oleg Kolinsky stood outlined in the doorway.

'Anya! Is that you? It's very late.'

God, she thought, that bastard Kolinsky's here.

'Can I come in, Colonel? I've some interesting information for you.'

'News? At this time of night?'

Another voice called from the kitchen at the rear.

'Who is it, Oleg? Bring them in for God's sake. The cold air's coming in.'

Oleg waved Anya in with one of his great paws. He presented an unappetising picture in his grubby shirt-sleeves. A pair of wide braces held up his trousers and the usual odour of vodka came from his sweaty skin as if his pores were secreting the stuff.

'It's Anya,' he called over his shoulder, 'she's got news.'

Pyotr was slouched in a chair in the filthy kitchen, which looked as if no-one had touched it for months. It smelled revolting; of rotting food and grease. Oily deposits covered every surface and dishes were piled high in and around the stone sink. Housekeeping was obviously not his strong suit.

'Sit down,' Pyotr gestured towards one of the wooden chairs at the table, the surface of which was littered with dirty plates and glasses. Close to hand stood the ubiquitous bottle of vodka still with the bloom of ice on it.

Anya noticed that the bottle was half-empty. If they had consumed that this evening they must be half-drunk by now. But she already knew that Oleg's capacity for alcohol was prodigious and that he could consume enormous amounts without ill effects.

She removed the pea jacket, the hat and gloves and perched on the rickety chair.

'So, what's this news that you have to come here in the middle of the night through the snow? Couldn't it have waited till tomorrow?' Pyotr asked.

'The Barton's daughter has disappeared. It looks as if she was snatched from right under Isabel's nose.'

With a deep bellow of laughter Oleg's face brightened grotesquely. 'Ah! The lovely Mrs Barton.'

'Quiet, Oleg,' snapped Pyotr. 'Listen to what the girl has to say.'

'I was at Captain Marriott's...' Oleg grinned and winked salaciously. Anya ignored him. 'Isabel came round in a dreadful state - driven by an American Corporal, incidentally - she can't find the child anywhere. She's gone; probably kidnapped. Do you know anything about it?'

Pyotr looked at her thoughtfully. 'Why would you think that? We don't kidnap children.' But he didn't deny it.

'I thought ...I thought you might know someone who would,' Anya replied.

'It's more likely to be something to do with the black market people. They're getting pretty fed up with all the investigations going on. It's cramping their style.' Pyotr laughed. 'So many greedy people trying to make themselves rich and John Marriott and Bill Barton trying to stop them. A hopeless task, of course. It's too big and a dangerous game to get mixed up in. They're practically encouraging it, giving those criminals free board and lodging in the DP camps.'

'But you know something about it, don't you?'

'About what?'

'The black market.' Anya shook her head with annoyance. Why did they always prevaricate so?

'Of course. We do what we can to disrupt the economy and make things difficult for our British and American Allies.

The black market is an efficient way of achieving this.'

'But why? I don't understand.'

'Because those bastards, our so-called allies, want to take over and rule Germany. All this talk of getting the economy running again – it's rubbish; they just want the power; to move their capitalist industries in to take over. They want us to fade into the background; slink away home and leave it all to them. After everything we fought for, the men we lost; our country in ruins. But it's not going to happen, we won't allow it. Field Marshall Stalin has given orders for us to prevent it and we shall. Even if it means starving them out of the city.'

'I don't think...' Anya began.

'No-body cares what you think, miss. A tart like you.' Pyotr said.

'I'm not a tart!' Anya retorted, outraged. 'I may be a British officer's girlfriend, but that's to help you too; to get information.'

'And you're well paid for it, don't forget.'

Anya fell silent for a moment, thinking. 'But what about this child? Who do you think may have her?'

'I'd certainly look at the black market people. That chap Fritz Keller may know something; he seems to be involved in everything that's going on. Do you know where to find him?'

'I think so, John showed me once.'

'Chances are he'll be in the know. He's got his dirty fingers in many pies.'

Anya stood up and began to put her outer clothes on. 'I'd better go. It's getting late. The curfew patrols will be out.'

'Stay if you like, *liebling*,' growled Oleg, stroking her . 'We could have a good time.'

'No thank you,' said Anya, shuddering. 'I'll get away now.'

'Have a little vodka to keep out the cold.'

Gratefully, but steeling herself against the unhygienic glass, Anya took a swig. The strong spirit burned her mouth and throat; made her teeth tingle, but she knew it would fortify her against the cold.

'Keep in touch,' Pyotr purred nonchalantly, not moving from his chair. 'Tell us what happens.'

Anya turned and left the kitchen, traversing the corridor alone and opening the front door onto the frozen night. I haven't really found out anything, she thought. I'm sure they know more than they're saying. How was she going to find out what had happened to Penny?

As Anya left Pyotr's lodgings, she faced a new onslaught of snow. It fell in heavy whirling scuds, making the surroundings almost invisible. The cold penetrated every inch of her body. She drew the pea-jacket closer round her and set off again.

I'll see if I can find Fritz Keller, she thought, he may know something. She couldn't see him grabbing the child – Penny, so fastidious and armed with dire warnings from the adults about the danger of strangers, would never have gone off with the smelly, scruffy German. But still, he might have an idea who had taken her; he always seemed to know everything that was going on in the underworld of Berlin.

She struggled through the snow and concealed rubble, trying not to think about how cold she was. Why on earth am I doing this, she thought? The child's no concern of mine. But fellow-feeling with Isabel drove her on. She had no particular love of Mrs Barton. If anything she should be jealous of her, after all, John was devoted to her and Anya was sure he would leave her for Isabel in an instant if he had the chance. But somehow she felt sorry for the woman in spite of this; it must be dreadful to lose a child and have no idea what had happened to her.

Eventually she arrived at Fritz's shack, marooned in a landscape of broken buildings and a sea of rubble. Ragged walls stood around it, their tops randomly crenellated by artillery fire and now topped with a grotesquely pretty fringe of pure white snow. Heat from the shack had melted the snow on its roof and in a ring around it.

Good, thought Anya, he must be there. She crept closer to the hovel, taking care not to trip. As she drew closer she could hear voices inside. Two men. She recognised Fritz' voice with its harsh, throaty sound and occasional hacking cough, but the identity of the other voice eluded her. It sounded familiar, not German even though it spoke in that language; English or American perhaps.

She crouched behind a broken wall and tried to listen. The foreigner seemed excited about something. She couldn't make out the words and crept nearer to hear more clearly.

'...Are you mad?' Fritz's voice; almost a shout and then more muffled as the men moved around the shack. Anya strained her ears to hear more, but at that moment the sound of a vehicle being revved up came from a nearby street. It drowned out all possibility of hearing the men inside.

A few moments later two men came to the door of the hovel, wrapping scarves around their necks and pulling on gloves. Fritz was ahead of the other man and Anya was unable to see him properly. He was taller than Fritz and seemed to have a beard, but that could have been shadows falling on his face or a scarf wrapped around it. He wore one of those Russian *shapka ushankas*, a big, peaked fur hat with ear flaps, an efficient disguise.

She slipped behind the wall to be invisible. Her heart was pounding; they were up to something. She felt she should follow them and as soon as they had walked a few metres away, she slipped out of her hiding place and crept along behind them.

The blur of the falling snow obscured her view, but she could hear the men moving ahead of her and followed at a safe distance, making as little sound as possible. If they looked back she could hide behind a heap of rubble now increased in height by the snow lying on top. So long as she was quiet they wouldn't know she was there.

A meandering walk through the streets brought them to a secluded alley that appeared to be a dead end. Anya waited outside. What were they doing? The answer soon came with the sound of a heavy vehicle starting. The engine caught first time and roared in the narrow alleyway, reverberating off the walls. Anya had to duck down as a battered truck backed out at speed, sending a storm of displaced snow into the air which came down on her, blinding her for a moment. But she was still able to see the direction it took – towards the Grunewald.

Anya shook the snow off John's coat and watched the truck disappear up the street. There's nothing I can do now, she thought. All the walking in the snow had made her incredibly tired. Weariness was making it difficult for her to think straight.

What on earth is going on? Where are those men going? Has it got anything to do with Penny's kidnap?

Anya turned towards John's apartment block a few hundred metres away. She knew it would be warm there, with a furnace in the basement warming the whole block, in the modern way. The thought of her own cold room filled her with dread. She willed her feet to carry her as far as the apartments and climbed the stairs. She retrieved the key from above the door and tumbled into the flat, exhausted. She noticed that John had left his cigarette case on the table. She opened the case and put most of the contents in her bag. John wouldn't mind and they would buy her a good meal tomorrow to make up for the trouble she had gone to tonight.

She undressed and soon fell asleep in John's bed. I'll go and see Isabel in the morning; she may have some news. What on earth were Fritz and that other man doing? Something strange was going on and it wasn't good. That was Anya's last thought before drifting off.

Chapter Twenty-Five

Time moved with leaden steps and it seemed an age before John and Isabel stumbled through the front door of the Grunewald house. The journey back had been nightmarish; the blizzard swirled in a reinforced frenzy. Huge clods of snow circled and danced around the puny *Volkswagen* threatening to engulf it as they battled through the arctic weather. John leant forward over the steering wheel, trying to see through the murk.

'I hope we're going the right way,' he said.

'Don't say that. It would be awful if we got lost. It's curfew soon.'

'I don't suppose the patrols will be able to see us. Don't worry; it's more or less in a straight line.' John peered through the windscreen and squinted at the small portal intermittently cleared by the struggling wiper blades and promptly filled again by more snow.

The headlights cast a feeble beam onto the snow ahead of them. It was warm inside the car as the engine generated enough heat to keep them from freezing. But from time to time icy draughts would strike from nowhere, causing them to shiver.

John tried to suppress his doubts. He was attempting to sound confident but he wasn't entirely sure where they were. Hopefully they were going in the right direction. It would have helped if he had a compass with him. Landmarks he thought he recognised floated in and out of his vision, distinct one minute and obliterated the next, in the manner of a nightmarish dream where the landscape was constantly changing or a kaleidoscope held by a nervous hand. He couldn't see a thing, but the stolid car rattled on as if it knew its own way and soon they were able to distinguish familiar buildings.

'We're nearly there. Look, there's that ruined house at the comer of Kirchen Allee.' Isabel pointed out the looming shape of the bombed property, its ravaged walls outlined against the snow.

'Thank God for that,' breathed John, whose concentration was beginning to falter as tiredness threatened to overwhelm him. He drove the last few hundred yards in a stupor; his eyes heavy and his hands numb with cold.

As they parked in front of Isabel's building John patted the vehicle in an absurd gesture of gratitude. 'Wonderful.' he said. 'Anything else would be frozen by now.'

They hurried up the steps and into the house and, both having the same thought, rushed across the cavernous hall to the *Kachelofen*. The tiles still gave out waves of stored heat and they leant against it, soaking up warmth into their bones. There was no exuberant greeting from Prince. He's not back yet. No sign of Penny either, no discarded hat and coat, no wet boots in puddles of melting snow on the floor. No letters, no messages, nothing.

Irma appeared from the rear of the apartment.

'Oh. You're back already!' exclaimed Isabel. 'I wasn't expecting you yet. How was the dance?'

'I couldn't enjoy it, Frau Barton, we left early. I was too worried about Penny. I asked Hank to drive me home. He was so good, there's so much snow and the jeep was so cold! Is there any news?'

John answered for Isabel, who was suddenly reminded of the hopelessness that threatened to engulf her. 'The police are coming in the morning. They will start a search and question everyone. They'll do what they can.'

'I do hope they will find her soon. I am so unhappy with her not here.' Irma's English foundered and she muttered some words in German. Isabel roused herself sufficiently to speak.

'I'm sorry to bother you so late, but could you make up a bed in the spare room for Captain Marriott? He's staying the night so he can talk to the police in the morning.'

'Of course, Frau Barton, I will do that immediately.'

The girl hurried away, glad to be busy. 'But first, shall I make you some cocoa?' she asked over her shoulder.

'That would be heaven, Irma. We're still freezing inside.' She turned to John, 'Let's go into the drawing room.'

John and Isabel sat in separate chairs near the cold fireplace, staring at the spent coal and wood in the hearth. Isabel curled her feet up into the beaver coat. They contemplated the ashes in silence, neither wanting to express their fears or hopes.

'Prince hasn't come back either.' Isabel finally broke the silence. 'He would be a comfort.'

The dog always seemed to understand her moods. He would be sitting here now with his head on her lap gazing into her face with tragic eyes. Isabel felt tears threatening to fall again. And Bill, she thought, he's not here and I can't even speak to him. Why is he never here when I need him?

An irrational wave of irritation flooded through her. I can't even tell him his daughter's missing; perhaps he wouldn't care. He hadn't taken much interest in them lately. Isabel shook her head and admonished herself inwardly. Of course he'd care. He'd become very attached to Penny in the last few months. He'd be as distraught as she was; maybe he'd have some idea of what to do.

John's thoughts were running along similar lines. As Bill's away I've got to look after Isabel. It's what he would expect and he'd do the same for me in similar circumstances. In any case, John wanted to help in any way he could, he hated to see Isabel so distraught.

John ran through the possibilities in his head. The child was unlikely to have run off on her own. She was a shy little thing; not adventurous and most of her friends had been there, on the truck, so she wasn't running off to see any kid she knew.

Perhaps she'd seen an adult that she liked and gone off with them. But, apart from Zelda and himself, he couldn't think of anyone else Penny was fond of in the adult world. Also, Zelda would have been in touch by now if Penny were with her. She would have spoken to Isabel first; wouldn't have just walked off with the child.

Frau Hilfe perhaps. No - she had left much earlier, after the class ended, hurrying to get home before the snow began to come down heavily; Penny was still here then. She had met Anya of course, but they seemed to view each other with mutual suspicion. Anya didn't like children; never wanted to have any of her own and Penny seemed to sense her antipathy. She kept her distance, disappearing to her room or the kitchen whenever Anya was there.

'Children have such sticky fingers, don't you think?' Anya had complained to Isabel one day when John had brought her to the flat.

'I hadn't noticed,' Isabel had replied, surprised. 'Actually, Penny's quite fussy about her fingers, she hates being grubby.'

John chuckled inwardly as he recollected Penny's tidy habits and the way she brushed her own hair and didn't have to be told to pull her socks up. Quite impressive for a five year old.

His thoughts came back to the present. This must be what Sherlock Holmes would have called a 'two pipe problem'. This thought prompted him to consider a smoke himself. He groped in his pockets for a cigarette but found that they weren't there. Damn, he must have left the case by the bed. Anya would probably smoke them or take them to pay for something; always out for the main chance. Oh well, good luck to her. But he could do with a smoke and there wouldn't be any cigarettes here. Damn!

The only other explanation he could think of for Penny's disappearance, with regret, was abduction. He knew that people did steal children for unspeakable reasons. Someone may have thought that if they kidnapped an English child there would be a ransom forthcoming for her safe return. The ransom was unlikely to be money as cash was pretty useless at present, barter being the currency of the day. But it might be for some other reward. Who knows what reasons the warped mind of someone who would steal a child could conjure up?

Kidnapping for a ransom seemed to John to be the mostly likely scenario. So there would be a ransom demand in due course; they should wait for that. He hoped that Isabel could hold out and not be completely overcome by her fear.

'Cocoa, *Kapitän*?' Irma murmured, interrupting his thoughts, as she placed a steaming mug on the small table beside his chair.

John dragged his thoughts back. 'Bless you, Irma. That's wonderful.'

'Thank you, Irma, how delicious this is,' said Isabel, sipping from her own mug. 'Why don't you go to bed now? There's nothing any of us can do until the morning.'

'I have put hot water bottles in your bed, and in the spare bed, for *Kapitän* Marriott.'

'You're an angel, Irma. Good night.'

Shortly after finishing their drinks in silence, each deep in their own thoughts, John and Isabel got up to go to bed. John followed Isabel into the hallway.

'I hope you'll be warm enough, John.' Isabel said. 'That room's a bit chilly – it's not near the stove.'

'I'll be fine darling. I'm dog tired. You must try to sleep, won't you?'

'I will, but I don't hold out much hope. How I wish Bill was here.'

'I know, darling. I'll see if I can get hold of him tomorrow.'

'I would be grateful. Goodnight for now.' Isabel kissed him gently on the cheek; a warm hand touched his sleeve. 'You've been a great help already. I would have gone completely to pieces without you. You know that, don't you?'

'It's nothing, Isabel.'

She smiled at him sweetly, knowing it wasn't 'nothing' at all. The air was chilly in her room; the benefit of the stove had barely raised the temperature a couple of degrees. She quickly slipped into bed blessing Irma for thinking of the hot water bottle. She pulled the heavy beaver coat over the top of the blankets for extra warmth and the comfort of its weight.

Feeling under her pillow for her handkerchief she encountered the hard outline of the Mauser. She drew her hand away in a spasm of revulsion. Horrible thing!

Sleep was elusive at first as she went over and over in her mind the events of the past day. What could she have done differently? She should have been watching Penny more carefully, But she was such a sensible child; she rarely needed to be told off. I hope Prince is all right too and comes home soon. Penny, I pray you're warm enough, my darling. Mummy is thinking of you.

Eventually she drifted off into a troubled sleep beset by mad dreams of running and searching futilely for some nebulous and unidentifiable object - finding nothing and not able to remember what it was that she had lost. She woke fitfully at dawn with tears coursing down her cheeks, unable to recall what was wrong. Remembering, she lay in quiet despair for hours until it was time to get up and prepare for the police.

Chapter Twenty-Six

Tentative light peeped through the bedroom curtains. Isabel had been sleeping restlessly for about an hour. I can't stay here any longer, she thought. She forced herself out of the warm bed and slipped on her dressing gown and slippers. She picked up her watch, six o'clock; no-one else would be up yet.

Isabel shuffled down the freezing corridor to the kitchen, pulling the gown closer around her, and found she was mistaken; Irma had already made a pot of tea.

'I thought you would wake soon, Frau Barton,' she said. 'Such a terrible night, I hardly slept. I'll go and light the stove.' She picked up the bucket of fuel waiting for this purpose.

'Bless you, Irma. You're a marvel.'

Isabel sat at the table, her hands moulded around her cup, drawing energy from the warmth. She started to think about breakfast. John will want something more substantial than a piece of toast, she thought, it's a pity there's no bacon and eggs. She dug out the box of porridge oats from the larder and started to prepare it.

John was fully dressed and, though tousled and unshaven, he appeared to be remarkably wide awake when he emerged from the spare room and sat at the table. She tried not to notice how gorgeous he looked like this; a strong man but vulnerable, with the ghost of sleep hanging over him.

'I won't ask you if you slept well, Isabel, I'm sure you didn't,' he said, running a hand over his bristly face. 'Can I borrow a razor of Bill's? I forgot to pack one in the rush.'

'Yes, of course. I'm sure there's a spare in the bathroom. First left at the top of the stairs.'

'Yes, I know. It must be very inconvenient for you, having to go up there all the time.'

'We've got used to it.' Isabel replied and was instantly reminded of something.

'Actually John, there's something I'd like to talk to you about. All this terrible business with Penny put it right out of my head. I was up in the bathroom one day, washing my hair. It's about Dennis' place. I'm afraid I was a bit nosy and had a look in his flat as it was unlocked.'

Isabel described all the wonderful things she had seen in Dennis's flat. John listened intently but didn't seem to be surprised.

'I've never seen anything like it outside a museum or one of those country houses you can visit,' she concluded.

John looked at her thoughtfully, interest lighting his eyes. 'Dennis Masters? Well, he is a dark horse. He may be a miserable bastard, but he's obviously getting together an art and antique collection to take home with him. A lucrative little nest egg. I bet he didn't get it all by honest means either.'

'Yes, it's extraordinary.' Isabel set a bowl of hot porridge in front of him with a jug of diluted tinned milk.

'Perhaps we can go and have a look later, when I've spoken to the police about Penny?' said John, spooning the porridge into his mouth.

'Oh, no. I expect Dennis is in there now, this early. He's not at the conference in Hanover with Bill. He'll be going to work later; I think Bill put him in charge whilst he's away.'

'You'd have thought he'd have come and talked to us last night, when he heard us come home. He'd be curious. Surely he must have heard all the hoo-ha.'

'No. Dennis isn't like that. He keeps to himself and hardly ever speaks to us unless he has to.'

'Yes, I always thought he was a bit of a weird one.'

Isabel sat opposite him at the table. 'I'm sure he wouldn't want to get involved with all my wailing and crying. He's not interested in what we do and even more reclusive since Emma went home.'

'Really? Do you think he misses her? They didn't exactly look like a devoted couple.'

'I don't think it's that. I think he hates it here and is just keeping his head down until he can go home.'

'And cash in on his loot,' said John.

'It looks like it,' said Isabel.

They ate their porridge in quiet companionship until Irma erupted into the kitchen.

'Oh, *komm*, Frau Barton. Prince! He was on the doorstep whining to come in. He is home; in the hall now.'

Isabel leapt to her feet. 'Prince! Oh good, he's home. Is he hurt badly?' She didn't wait for an answer, but rushed to the hallway.

The forlorn dog lay on the parquet, panting vigorously. Caked blood coloured the fur on his scalp where a deep graze still seeped, the fur pushed back grotesquely. He held a paw pathetically in the air and gave a gentle whine while at the same time wagging his tail, though with little of his usual enthusiasm.

'Poor Prince! How are you?' Isabel examined him, soothing with gentle hands. 'It doesn't look too bad, but I can see you're feeling very sorry for yourself.'

The dog staggered to his feet, nursing the front paw, and licked Isabel with his rough tongue.

'Come on, boy, let's go to the kitchen and I'll bathe your poor head for you.'

Within a few moments she had diluted some Dettol in a bowl of warm water and was bathing Prince's wound with a piece of cotton wool from the First Aid kit kept in the larder, crooning to the dog as she worked.

'There, there,' she said. 'Look, it's not too bad, just messy. Now give me your paw. Oh dear, you've lost some skin there too, it does look sore. It'll be better soon.' She bathed the foot and wrapped it tightly in a gauze bandage. 'Now, leave that alone, it'll help to keep it clean.' She patted the dog reassuringly and he relaxed with a deep sigh into his box lined with a blanket, in the corner near the oven.

This distraction caused her to forget for a moment, but as she completed her task and petted the dog everything came rushing back to her in a great wave of emotion. Tears sprang to her eyes.

'Oh, God, I was almost forgetting about Penny; I was so happy to see Prince again. We must get on to the police. Is the phone working yet? Those MPs will be round soon. I'm not looking forward to Major Goddard.'

'Don't worry, I won't let him bully you,' said John.

She was throwing away the blood-stained Dettol and cotton wool as she spoke. John came up and put an arm around her.

'Calm down, Isabel,' he said. 'Go and get dressed and I'll get on to the police and try to get hold of Bill in Hanover. He needs to know what's happening.'

Surprised, Isabel looked down. She had forgotten that she wasn't dressed yet. She left the kitchen and climbed the stairs to the bathroom, clinging to the banisters as if her life depended on their support.

She felt much better after a wash and change of clothes. As she prepared to leave her room the sound of the bell reached her. That'll be Goddard and his men, they're early.

Irma was already at the door. The visitor wasn't the MPs but Zelda, bringing with her a whirl of snow and energy.

'Darling! There you are. Oh my poor baby, how can you bear it?'

'You've heard about Penny?' Isabel asked, puzzled, 'so soon.'

'Yes, dear, Hank told me, first thing, when he came to get Chuck. We're both devastated. Chuck says if there's anything he can do, anything...'

Zelda, always immaculate even at this early hour, enveloped Isabel in her mink-clad arms, exuding exotic scents.

'Let's go into the drawing room,' she said, 'sit down and talk about it. What's being done? Have you heard anything yet?' Arm in arm they went and sat by the newly-lit fire. Irma was tidying cups and cushions from last night.

They heard the click as John replaced the receiver and he joined them in the lounge.

'Oh, John, you're here,' said Zelda, raising one questioning eyebrow.

'Yes, I went round to see him last night,' Isabel explained. 'I had to. The phone wasn't working so Hank took me to John's flat in the Jeep. They were supposed to be going to a dance. I explained it all to John and he got the MPs. He kindly brought me home and stayed the night. The MPs will be here again any minute.'

"Morning, Zelda,' said John. 'You'll be glad to hear that your phone's on again, Isabel. I tried to get hold of Bill but he wasn't around so I left a message at HQ Hanover. We'll hear from him later. I also called the *Polizei* and they said Goddard's Sergeant had already been in touch. But they're very busy, something about all the snow, and they can't spare more than a couple of men. We'll have to see who turns up.'

Irma brought them coffee and they drank it whilst Isabel retold the story of Penny's disappearance and answered Zelda's many questions.

'Aw, poor Penny and poor Prince too. What can I do, honey? Is there anything...?'

'Thank you, Zelda, but there's nothing at the moment. We're waiting for Major Goddard and he's going to organise a search and a house-to-house; questioning the neighbours, I think. Maybe we'll find out something. Of course your moral support is always welcome. Stay and hold my hand, do.' Isabel's fugitive smile told Zelda all she needed to know.

'You betcha, honey, I'll be here for as long as you need me.'

The telephone rang, but it was only the *Polizei* to say they were on their way and would be at the house within the hour, snow permitting. There was nothing from Hanover. Isabel felt that Bill was deliberately avoiding the message and didn't want to hear about Penny's disappearance. What would he do? Could he just leave the conference and come to Berlin to help find his daughter? A steely resolve swept over her. No, she thought, I can do this alone, with John, I don't need Bill's help, he can stay at his Intelligence conference for as long as he likes.

The strident bell broke into her thoughts. Since Irma had retreated to the kitchen John went to answer the door. Isabel heard murmured voices from the hall, but stayed on the sofa close to Zelda. John came into the room followed by Major Goddard and two private soldiers with MP armbands and white holsters at their hips carrying side arms. They scanned their surroundings uncomfortably.

'Good morning, Mrs Barton,' said Goddard in his usual gruff tones. 'I hope you slept well.'

'Not really, Major Goddard,' replied Isabel. 'But thank you for your concern.' The man's only trying to be pleasant, she thought, he's just not very good at it.

'I thought we'd have a look around your flat first, get the lie of the land, so to speak.'

'They've already searched the flat from top to bottom,' said John. 'I really don't think there's anything to be gained by doing it again.'

'You never know,' said the Major 'there may be something that you missed.'

'All right,' said John. 'As you wish.'

'What about the apartment upstairs? Have you looked there?'

'No. That's Dennis Masters' apartment. He's on civilian secondment and probably at work by now. The rooms are kept locked.' John glanced at Isabel. 'Most of the time, anyway. Did you check, Isabel, when you were looking for Penny?'

'Yes, Irma and I looked everywhere. Dennis's rooms were locked then. But he will have come back to sleep. He's up there now for all I know. I haven't heard him leave.'

'Right,' said the Major. 'We can leave that for now.' He turned to his men. 'You two, go and search this apartment again. Be thorough, mind; see if anything's been missed.'

'Sir,' said one of the privates and they marched off, their boots striking loudly on the wooden hall floor. I must go and warn Irma, Isabel thought, she'll be terrified when those armed soldiers charge into the kitchen. She rose and started to leave the room.

'Where are you going, Mrs Barton?'

'I've got to warn the maid about the men. She's in the kitchen.'

'All right, but please be quick,' said Goddard. 'We have a lot to do.'

John looked at Isabel quizzically. Her wan smile showed him that she understood his concern.

'It's all right, John. I knew it would be like this.'

I've got to be practical, she thought. Do whatever is necessary. Getting hysterical won't help Penny.

But there was little she could do whilst the MPs searched the house. She could see that the soldiers were trying to be tactful, but of necessity they had to move furniture around. Even the huge wardrobe in her room was shifted so that they could look behind it after riffling through her clothes and moving her shoes about. They crawled under the beds and dragged out the trunks from the storage room, put there after their arrival from England. But, as Isabel already knew, Penny was not to be found.

They returned to the drawing room and shuffled around looking embarrassed, probably dreading to go out into the cold again.

'She's not in the apartment,' announced Major Goddard.

'I know,' said Isabel suppressing a futile sigh.

'We'll start questioning passers-by. I'll get a verbal report from the *Polizei* to see if they've found out anything in their house-to-house. I will keep you informed.' He snapped to attention, saluted and left the room abruptly, the soldiers following. They gathered their outer clothing and left, slamming the door so that the wooden panel masking the gun-fire damage rattled like distant castanets.

'Well! That wasn't very helpful,' said John, without getting up from the armchair by the fire where he was pretending to read an old newspaper. 'I suppose they'll be back later if they find out anything.'

He looked up at Isabel, who seemed to be visibly wilting, distant and not able to concentrate on what was happening.

John stood up and turned to the drinks cupboard. 'I think it's time for a drink, it's nearly lunchtime and it couldn't do any harm. You too, Zelda?'

'Yes, please John, that's a great idea. A G and T please.' Zelda emerged from the sunken springs of the sofa from where she had been silently observing events. 'Then I must go home for a bit, Isabel honey. I've got to supervise the twins' lunch and get them down for their nap. I won't be long.'

John poured the drinks and he and Zelda sipped theirs, but Isabel threw the gin down her throat in one gulp as an alcoholic might and stood with the empty glass outstretched in her hand, ready for another.

'Steady on, old thing. I think one's enough for now.'

Hardly conscious of what she was doing, Isabel stood in the middle of the room like a zombie; glass suspended in the air, pointing in John's direction. He took it from her gently. Zelda came up and gave her a hug.

'I'm off for now, Isabel. I'll brief the maid that I may out of the house for a while and then I'll come back. Try not to worry too much, it won't help.'

They soon heard the sound of the front door closing behind Zelda. Dazed, Isabel shook her head and seemed to register her surroundings again.

'Oh, John! I'm frightened we'll never find my baby, never see her again!'

'Sit down, Isabel. There's nothing we can do now. We'll wait here for the MPs to finish whatever they're doing. Maybe they'll get some clue.'

Obediently Isabel sank on to the sofa and stared at the fire. Her head felt as if it was stuffed with cotton wool, not like a cold, but fuzzy, soulless and accompanied by a complete inability to concentrate. Perhaps it was delayed shock.

John, with no idea what else to say, paced the room aimlessly, hoping the MPs wouldn't be long and that they'd come up with some useful information.

About an hour later the doorbell rang again. There was murmuring from the hall as Irma opened it to the visitor. Shortly after that Major Goddard strode in.

'Well,' he said. 'That's about it for now. We've talked to everyone we can think of. No-one seems to have seen anything. They were all too busy thinking about what to have for supper as far as I can see. No-one saw a child, most of them didn't even notice the children going home from their dancing class. One person saw the ration truck arriving – he complained about it going too fast – and someone else heard the sound of the dog yelping. But no-one saw your daughter, Mrs Barton. Later they all went indoors, out of the snow and tried to keep warm. No-one so much as looked out of a window for the rest of the night. There's really nothing more we can do here. I will report to you immediately if I have more news.'

The Major seemed satisfied that his report had been received and understood. His duty was done. Isabel's blank face reassured him that there would be no more histrionics, at least while he was on the premises. He gathered his things together; gave a stiff salute and marched from the room.

John and Isabel breathed out audibly.

'Well, at least he's gone,' said John. 'Not very helpful, I agree, but he'll keep his ears open, I'm sure.'

'Oh, God, is that it?' Isabel sighed. 'I know we didn't like him much, but he was at least doing something. Now, what are we going to do? We can't just sit here waiting for something to happen.'

'There are one or two things I can do. People I can speak to. And we still haven't heard from Bill.'

'I need him home, John. I can't bear this waiting.'

'I know, darling. I'm sure we'll have news soon.'

But whether he meant news of Bill or of Penny, Isabel wasn't sure and didn't want to ask. A wave of despair washed over her and she turned and left the room. She went into the bedroom and put on the beaver coat. She needed a dry handkerchief and felt under her pillow where she knew there was one. Her hand brushed the gun and, almost without thinking, she withdrew it and put it deep into her coat pocket. She opened the tiny drawer in her bedside table and took out the box of bullets and dropped them into the pocket with the gun. Maybe she'd have a use for it after all. Vindictive fury filled her – whoever had taken her child was going to suffer if she had anything to do with it.

She crossed the hall and opened the door. The MPs were getting into their jeep to leave. A small crowd of curious people had gathered on the pavement. A pity they weren't paying a bit more attention yesterday, she thought acidly. She recognised one or two of them as people she often saw in the street, neighbours, and waved to them.

From the top of the front steps, just where she was standing yesterday when Penny disappeared, she watched the MPs drive away. The gears of their jeep ground alarmingly and they did not bother to turn to wave or acknowledge her presence on the steps, or her hand feebly raised in farewell. She turned into the house and dragged into the drawing room. John was deep in thought in the big armchair, his feet stretched towards the fire.

Suddenly overwhelmed with grief; desperate for comfort, Isabel turned to him and launched herself into his lap, her body trembling and face shrouded in tears. Bemused by this outburst of emotion John gathered her into his arms.

'They're never going to find her,' Isabel wailed. 'She's gone; lost forever.'

John whispered reassurances into her damp ear.

'They will, darling, they will. She can't have just disappeared into thin air. We've got to be patient.' He gently kissed her cheek and stroked her shaking back – the beaver coat threatened to engulf them both.

'Take this thing off, Bella, it's swallowing me whole.'

Isabel shrugged out of the fur and flung it onto the floor. She returned to John's arms, feeling calmer, but still needing the comfort of his closeness.

'Darling Bella,' John murmured into her hair. 'You know I'd do anything for you, don't you?'

Isabel leaned even closer, her eyes never leaving his face. For once she didn't mind being called Bella, which John said as if he knew the name's true meaning – beautiful, my beautiful girl. Her heart fluttered with that familiar sensation, a distant memory from when she had first met Bill and they had been carefree. Her body filled with warmth. For a few moments they clung together. Isabel raised a hand and softly touched John's face.

'You're so kind to me, John. I shouldn't be taking up all of your time. I'm sorry I'm such a wreck.'

John hugged her close to his chest. 'You're entitled to be, darling. It's all been too much for you. This is very delightful,' he squeezed her softly, 'but I'd better get up now, there's things I should be doing.'

Isabel shook her head to bring herself back to reality and slowly rose from the chair.

'Have you got to go in to the city? Work, I suppose.'

'Not exactly. There are people I need to speak to, contacts. Someone may know what's happened to Penny; who may have taken her. I'm going to ask for a few days' leave. Don't worry, Isabel, I'm not going to abandon you.'

Isabel smiled her gratitude. She certainly felt abandoned by Bill, however unreasonable that was; he couldn't help being away at this crucial time. But he should be here, with her, supporting her and helping her through the crisis, searching for Penny.

Once he was standing John gathered her into his arms again and drew her close. After the briefest hesitation he looked into her brimming eyes and kissed her, full on the lips this time, slowly, tenderly, but with an underlying passion that conveyed itself to Isabel in a moment of revelation that stunned her. He released her and, without looking at her again, turned to gather his coat and cap and strode from the room. Soon after that the front door slammed.

Astounded, Isabel fell into the chair. In wonder she traced the imprint of John's kiss with her fingers. The sensation still trembled there and in the quickening of her heart. What did this mean? Was John in love with her? She tried to remember if there had been any earlier signs. He had always been such a good friend; perhaps she hadn't noticed that his feelings towards her were growing warmer. Then there was Anya. She was supposed to be his girlfriend, but perhaps it was just a casual thing, just a matter of proximity and expediency.

Isabel couldn't work out how she felt. She was in such emotional turmoil about Penny's disappearance that she couldn't process this new emotion. How did she feel about John? He was lovely, of course, so generous, kind, funny and strong. But what about Bill, to whom she had given her heart all that time ago, before the War, when life had been easy and they were at peace? He had changed. Of course he had, but that didn't mean she no longer loved him even though it had been nearly impossible to recapture that earlier feeling, that closeness and complete trust and openness they used to share.

Confusion filled her mind. Her head felt as if it enclosed a vacuum; as if all the joy had been sucked from the world. All feeling had gone; replaced by a dull ache. Would she ever feel safe again?

Weariness overcame her and she decided to lie down in her room. She had slept so little last night. Perhaps a nap would help her feel better. Later there might be some news. She picked her coat up from the floor where John had discarded it and carried it to her room. She slumped down on the bed, spreading the coat over her feet, closed her eyes and let tiredness take over her body. In a few moments she was in a heavy stupor of drug-like sleep.

The susurration of whispering outside the bedroom door woke Isabel. She forced her body from the bed and shook her head to clear away the cobwebs threatening to smother her.

She opened the door. Irma and Zelda stood in the hall hissing at each other in heated dispute.

'She needs rest, Frau Hoffstetter. She slept very little last night; we shouldn't wake her.'

'But she should know about this, Irma. It may be important.'

'What is it, Irma?' asked Isabel from the doorway.

'Oh, you're awake, honey.' Zelda turned towards her. 'We've found something in the hall.'

'What is it?' Isabel came forward.

Irma handed her a sealed envelope. 'We found this on the floor. I don't know how long it's been there. It was tucked under the blue rug.'

Isabel took the typed envelope that Irma was holding. Was this about Penny? A bubble of excitement rose within her. 'There have been so many people coming and going this morning – it could have been left at any time. Do you think the postman brought it?' she asked.

Their post from home was normally collected from the NAAFI by whoever was there, but a civilian postman delivered local mail sometimes. Hope surged through her.

'It seems unlikely that he'd come today, with the snow. Anyway, someone would have seen him,' said Zelda.

'I know, but it got here somehow.'

'Aren't you going to open it?'

Isabel turned the letter over in her hands, shaking nervously. 'Do you think I ought to wait for John? He'll know what to do. I don't want to destroy evidence.'

'Slitting open an envelope's not going to do much damage.'

Zelda and Irma leaned forward in anticipation.

'For goodness sake, Isabel, open the thing. It may be news of Penny,' said Zelda.

Isabel ran a fingernail along the flap of the envelope and tore it open. Carefully she withdrew the piece of paper within. It was a sheet of ordinary foolscap with a typed message. She read it rapidly but couldn't take in the sense of it. The only information that stood out was that Penny was safe. Relief swept over her in a rush that made her feel faint. She walked into the drawing room, Irma and Zelda following close behind her, and sat down heavily on the sofa.

'What does it say?' Zelda asked, impatience nearly getting the better of her. 'Is it a ransom note?'

'I suppose it is, in a way. You read it.' Isabel thrust the letter into Zelda's hand.

'Mrs Barton,' Zelda read. 'Your daughter is safe and well and will be returned to you if you fulfil certain conditions. She is being held in a safe place in the Hartz Mountains. For her return we require the following goods to be supplied to us within three days, at a rendezvous to be arranged later... There's a great long list of things they want, Isabel, I don't know what half of them are, drugs and spare parts it looks to me. They obviously expect Bill or John to get them.'

'Why the Hartz Mountains, for God's sake. It's miles away.'

'I know, Isabel, but perhaps they want to get you away from Berlin for some reason. Anyway, they couldn't very well keep Penny near here, could they? You would have found her in no time.'

'We're going to have to speak to John, to see if he can get all this stuff - this ransom. He knows how to get anything, I'm sure he'll be able to.'

'I suppose so,' Zelda sounded more doubtful. 'This is very valuable stuff, you know. They'll have to clear it with the powers that be. We have to hope they can arrange it in three days, it isn't long.'

Isabel looked at Zelda, aghast. 'What will they do if we can't get this ransom for them? They wouldn't kill her, would they? Not a little girl!'

'You can never know what these gangsters might do. We must hope they wouldn't go that far,' said Zelda, trying to sound reassuring.

'Unless they're Russians,' murmured Irma, who had been listening in horror. 'They would kill a child.' Then she pressed her hands to her lips as if ashamed that the words had escaped them.

'Oh, Irma, don't say that! Where's John? He should be back soon; we've got to tell him.'

The three women waited in the drawing room for what seemed hours and speculated on the origins of the ransom note.

'Why didn't we notice it earlier? When Prince came back? It must have been on the floor then. I suppose someone must have kicked it under the rug in the excitement,' Isabel said.

'There were so many people coming and going. Major Goddard and his men - and the *Polizie* came into the hall for a bit too. They must all have trampled on it.'

'But it wasn't wet, Zelda. It would have been if someone had trodden on it. The pavements are thick with snow. Look, there are no footmarks. It's quite clean and dry.'

'Someone must have put it through the letterbox later then.'

'We haven't got a letterbox. It was sealed over when they put on the panel to cover the bullet holes.'

'That can only mean someone in the house left it and pushed it under the carpet.' Zelda said. 'But who else was in the house yesterday?'

Isabel's head lifted, a spasm of revelation crossing her face. 'My God, Zelda! There's only one person that could be – Dennis!'

Chapter Twenty Seven

'You're not serious!' exclaimed Zelda. 'That Dennis couldn't do anything so – so courageous.'

'Courageous! To kidnap my Penny? That's not courageous; it's evil,' retorted Isabel.

The women were in the drawing room, Zelda pacing the floor as she talked and Isabel stoking the fire.

'You know what I mean, honey. He hasn't got the guts of an ant. Always looming around looking down his nose. Forgive me, baby, but he's so English.'

'We're not all like that, you know; all stuck up and reserved.'

'Sorry. I don't mean to insult you, Isabel. I know you're not like that, but you must admit, some of you are.'

'It's all right. I can't believe he'd take Penny either. And why? What would make him do such a thing?' said Isabel. 'He always seems angry, but I didn't realise he might take it out on us.'

'Perhaps he's finally gone crazy. Let's face it, a lot of people round here are close to the edge.'

'He is a strange man, I think,' said Irma, who was sitting in one of the chairs. 'I have seen him coming into the house in a very secret way.'

'Yes,' said Isabel. 'He has got a secret. His flat is full of valuable things.'

'What sort of things?' asked Zelda as she finally sat down.

'Oh, you know; antiques he's bought on the black market. Porcelain, silver and so on and some really good paintings.' Isabel picked up the ransom letter and waved it in the air. 'He'd be quite capable of writing something like this. He's obviously a greedy so and so and would see this as a chance to get even more out of us.'

'Can we go and see?' asked Zelda.

'His flat's locked. Anyway, that's what I told the MPs. I'm not sure that anyone actually looked this morning. Did anyone go up there, Irma?'

'No. It was locked yesterday afternoon so I thought it still was. I do not know if he came home last night.'

Zelda jumped to her feet. 'Let's go and take a look.'

The women climbed the stairs with Irma following nervously behind.

'Gee, he's got a whole bunch of rooms up here,' said Zelda.

'Yes, there are eight bedrooms and two bathrooms. One of those is ours. One of the smaller bedrooms was made into a kitchen and the biggest one is the sitting room. He doesn't use all the rooms, obviously. This is it.'

Isabel turned the door knob on the sitting room door and to her surprise it yielded,. She opened the door and stepped into the room.

'Oh, my goodness! It's empty.'

Apart from the original few bits of furniture and some discarded boxes and packaging materials, the room was bare. Not a trace of Dennis' treasure remained. Isabel gazed around the room, astonished.

'Well I never! He's got rid of it all.'

The three stood, staring, in the centre of the bare room which, like most of the rooms in the house, bore traces of the Russians' occupation with damage to the plaster and the woodwork. Their breath steamed in the cold air.

Isabel pulled an armchair away from the cold electric fire and went to sit in it. As she did so she noticed something on the floor.

'God! This is mine!' She lifted a bright blue scarf from the floor. 'Penny was wearing it. This proves it – Dennis had her here! He must have brought her upstairs and kept her here. How did he keep her quiet? Why didn't she call out to us when we were looking for her? She must have heard. How did he sneak her out without us knowing?'

Zelda took the scarf from her. 'Yes, this is yours. I've seen you wearing it. He must have brought her up here yesterday afternoon and snuck her out later when you were out of the house. When Irma and Hank took you round to John's place. Crafty devil!'

Isabel stood rock-still, in shock, clutching the blue scarf to her chest. Penny had been here all the time! Zelda guided her to the door.

'Come on, honey. We'll go downstairs.'

The three returned to the drawing room and warmed themselves by the fire. Bafflement – that was their most obvious emotion.

'I still don't understand why he did it. How did he think he'd get away with it?' asked Zelda. 'He must have known we'd find out pretty soon.'

'He probably still thinks he has got away with it. After all, he may not know about the scarf and the letter didn't really give anything away,' Isabel replied. 'Still, he must be stupid not to realise that we'd work it out.'

'Herr Masters is a very bad man,' said Irma. 'I think he has no conscience and he does not care what happens to him. He thinks we cannot catch him.'

'You may be right, Irma. But now we've got to find him and make sure he gets arrested. And Penny of course; we've got to find Penny. I hope John gets back soon; he doesn't know about the ransom letter. And Bill; we still haven't heard from him. I don't even know if he's had the message that John sent; I haven't heard a word.'

'I'll go and make more coffee,' said Irma, 'Would you like something to eat, Frau Barton?'

'Thank you, Irma. Could you make some sandwiches please? Captain Marriott shouldn't be long and he's bound to be hungry.'

Irma left for the kitchen. Isabel curled into her chair, suddenly remembering John's kiss and feeling a powerful longing for his strong arms around her again. She shook her head and tried to suppress the sensation and concentrate on what had to be done now. She and Zelda sat and contemplated their options for a while.

'We've got to get to the Hartz as soon as possible. We

can stay at the Hotel Schauser. You will come with me won't you, Zelda? To hold my hand.'

'Of course. I've told the maid I may not be home for a day or two. She can manage the twins and Chuck will be around.'

'I'm not sure how we'll get there. John's *Volkswagen*, I suppose.'

'I've got a better idea. I'll ask Chuck if we can borrow the Mercedes and Hank. He'll get us there in no time. How far is it?'

'About 250 kilometres,' said Isabel.

'Three hours or so. That's not bad. If we set out before dark we should be there by bedtime.'

'That's if John gets back soon. I'm not going without him. Anyway, he's got to get this ransom together first. That's not going to be easy and we haven't even told him what the demands are yet. We may not be able to go till the morning.'

'It looks as if we've got no option but to wait. Never mind, honey, here's Irma with the coffee.'

'I can't bear this waiting, Zelda - sitting around doing nothing when Penny is in danger. Even if she's safe she must be frightened. What on earth must she think is happening to her?'

'I know he hasn't got any children of his own, but I don't suppose Dennis will be mean to her.'

'Don't be daft! He could kill her. He must be desperate to kidnap her in the first place. Killing her isn't going to worry him.'

'It's no good working yourself up imagining things. He doesn't know we're on to him. He thinks he's way ahead of us and that we don't know anything. Calm down, try not to upset yourself.' Zelda soothed Isabel with soft strokes.

They ate and drank in languid silence. The stillness of the room became oppressive. Pale sunshine stole in from the garden. The snow had stopped falling for now and the afternoon had brightened. They could hear a snow plough outside, piling the snow into walls at the sides and making the street passable. Residents were out on the pavements shovelling the snow away; the scraping sounds of their spades on stone invaded the women's thoughts.

'It won't take so long for John to get here now they're clearing the roads. Especially the way he drives. But it'll still be bad out in the country,' said Isabel.

They jumped as the telephone rang. Irma was the first to spring up and run to the hall to answer it. Isabel stood in the doorway listening. Is it Bill? She thought. Let it be Bill.
Irma held the receiver out to her.

'It's Captain Marriott,' she said.

Thank goodness; John was her saviour, even if Bill couldn't be bothered. She rushed over and snatched the receiver from the maid's outstretched hand.

'Oh John, I thought it might be Bill. We still haven't heard from him.'

The line crackled and John's voice sounded strangely alien.

'No, I know. I've left another message. I've arranged a few days' leave, Isabel. I'll be back soon. I thought I'd better let you know in case you were worried...' John paused.

Isabel interrupted him, 'Something's happened; something important. We know where Penny is. She's safe for now.'

Isabel explained about the ransom letter and discovering that it must have been Dennis who took Penny. She read the note aloud, detailing the ransom demands. She had to repeat some information several times as the line buzzed and crackled, making it difficult for John to hear her.

'Do you understand, John? We've got to take this ransom to the Hartz. Can you get all that stuff – the drugs and everything? God knows what we'll do if you can't.'

'Don't worry, darling, I'll do everything I can. I'm sure I can persuade them to let me have it, to save Penny. They'll see how urgent it is. It'll take me a couple of hours, but I'll be back as soon as I can.'

'Oh bless you, John. I don't know what I'd do without you.'

'I'll see you later.' John hung up without further comment.

She replaced the receiver and returned to the drawing room. The tension in the room was palpable; thick as a heavy blanket. Irma had started to chew her fingernails and Zelda twirled loose tendrils of hair in her fingers. Isabel felt that she couldn't stand this for much longer. If they didn't do something soon, she would scream.

Another visitor broke the afternoon stillness. Isabel went

to open the door as Irma had gone to the kitchen, aware that they would need a meal that evening and she might have several extra mouths to feed. Anya, wrapped up in what looked like some of John's clothes, stood on the doorstep.

'I came to see if there was any news about Penny,' she said. 'Have you heard anything?'

'How kind of you to come,' said Isabel. 'Come in – you must be frozen, did you walk?'

'Yes, but it wasn't too bad. I had John's jacket and the roads are being cleared and at least you can see where you're going. I meant to come earlier but I overslept and then I tried to find John. I thought he might be at the Moser, but he wasn't.'

'He's been at HQ, arranging some leave and ... other things. He's coming back here later.' said Isabel.

Anya unwound a scarf from her neck and took off the pea-jacket and left it in the hall. She stepped into the drawing room and greeted Zelda.

'So,' she said, 'is there any news?'

'Goodness, yes. We found a ransom note and worked out that it must have been Dennis who took Penny,' said Zelda with poorly suppressed excitement.

'Dennis Masters?' Anya looked surprised. 'Why would he do that? I thought...'

'What did you think, Anya?' asked Zelda.

'Oh, it's nothing. I thought it might have something to do with John's dissatisfied black market contacts or even the Russians trying to get their own back for something. They don't seem happy at the moment.'

'And you should know,' murmured Zelda.

'What do you mean?'

'Oh, we all know how close you are to the Russians, Anya. The juicy little tit-bits you give them when you can.' Spite edged Zelda's voice.

Anya had the grace to blush a little. 'Yes, well, you've got to what you can.'

'It's all right,' said Isabel, 'we don't blame you. I know life is hard. God knows, it's been hard for us all, but you've had it much worse.'

Zelda shrugged. 'That doesn't excuse spying and betrayal of your friends,' she said.

'It's not that bad. I'm careful not to tell them anything that could hurt you. They only seem interested in how you supply the city. How you get enough food for your forces and keep going. In any case, I don't know anything important to tell them.'

'You'd be surprised. Even the smallest detail could be useful. Like who's coming and going from Berlin and when.'

'Leave off, Zelda. There's not much we can do about the Russians. We all know they're not our friends now. They're going to make things very difficult for us soon, Bill says, and his people are keeping a close eye on them. There's no point in having a go at Anya. She may be Russian originally, but she's on our side now.' Isabel poured fresh coffee and handed a cup to Anya.

'Thank you, Isabel.' Anya took the cup and it was obvious that her gratitude was for the drink and also for the kind words.

'Anyway, our concern now is not about Anya, but about what's happened to Penny. We've got to work out how to get her back safely and quickly.'

The women sipped their coffee, contemplating this conundrum.

Darkness fell early and the atmosphere in the silent house pressed down on the women waiting by the fire. Each was deep in her own thoughts. Isabel's fear had dissipated a little now that she knew Penny was safe. She no longer tasted that seamless terror now that she knew approximately where Penny was and that the person that held her would do her no harm until he had what he wanted. All that was needed was to go and get her from wherever she was being held.

I wish John would hurry up, she thought. How long can it take to get a few drugs?

Irma had kept the fire banked up and the room, except for the farthest corners, felt cosy. The beaver coat was spread over Isabel's knees and she hadn't taken off her fur boots all day. Zelda dozed in the corner of the sofa, her mink wrapped around her. Isabel smiled. Her friend seemed to manage to keep her hair and makeup immaculate even when in a relaxed stupor. Anya was deep in thought in the other armchair.

The sound of the front doorbell made them jump; woken from various degrees of sleep into wakefulness. Irma went to answer it and John strode into the room, shaking a few snowflakes from his head, a triumphant grin on his lips. Isabel jumped up and ran towards him.

'You'll be proud of me, darling, I've managed to arrange everything.' He greeted the other women, managing to look only slightly surprised at Anya's presence.

'Hello, darling, I wasn't expecting to see you.'

'Anya's giving me moral support,' said Isabel. 'What's your news? Have you heard from Bill? Did you get the ransom stuff? Were they all right about it?'

'Hold on. Let me get a word in.' John sat down. 'Well. My news is good, as far as it goes. I've got the drugs – I'll tell you about that in a moment. I haven't spoken to Bill in person but to a liaison officer who will pass on the message about the Hartz and the urgency of getting there as soon as possible. I expect Bill will go directly from Hanover.'

'So I won't see him till we get there,' said Isabel. 'I'd hoped to talk to him sooner.'

'Yes, well, I'm sure he'll do whatever he can. At least he'll know what's happened by now.'

'Why doesn't he ring?'

'I expect he's on the road and can't. Don't worry, Isabel, we'll hear from him soon.'

'Did you get everything Dennis asked for?'

'Yes and no. I've put together some packages that look as if we've got everything. It's cunningly packed. Boxes of morphine and penicillin and the other things arranged on the top of the cartons and then the same sort of boxes underneath, but there's nothing actually in them. It's all in the car.'

'But won't he guess? Won't it be lighter than he'd expect?'

'Ah, no. That's where the cunning bit comes in. The chap in the pharmacy had loads of empty boxes and we weighted them with aspirins and other pills and bits and pieces, and then sealed them again as if they came straight from the drug companies. You wouldn't know, really. Dennis is hardly likely to open every box. Anyway, I hope to get Penny away long before that, so there's no need to worry.'

Isabel frowned. 'He's a clever bastard. He might guess we'd try to trick him.'

'I really wouldn't concern yourself, Bella, we'll sort him out; get Penny back and probably still get the drugs back intact. I hope so anyway, I made some rather rash promises along the way,' John grinned.

Zelda's voice cut in. 'This is all great, guys, but when can we get going? Shouldn't we be leaving for the mountains by now? It's getting dark.'

'Too dark to leave tonight. In this thick snow it could be lethal.' John replied. 'We'd do better to leave early tomorrow morning. I know it's hard, Isabel, but there isn't so much urgency now. Dennis isn't expecting his ransom for a day or two. He'll keep Penny safe till then. Don't forget, he's not aware that we know he's responsible. I'm sure if he did he'd be panicking by now. I hope the VW will be able to manage the journey. I've got her full of petrol, but the snow's going to be thick in the country and going will be tough.'

'Oh, I haven't told you,' said Isabel. 'Zelda's asked Chuck and he's letting us borrow the Merc and Hank is going to drive. Zelda, you'd better ring and tell them that we shan't need him till the morning. About 7.30? It should be beginning to get light by then.'

'OK, honey. I'll do that now. I'll ask the maid to pack me a small bag and Hank can bring it. I'll stay here tonight, if that's all right with you.'

'Of course, if you don't mind sleeping in Penny's bed. I'll lend you anything you need.'

Zelda left the room and was soon delivering her instructions on the phone. It sounded as if Chuck was being very accommodating. Anya got to her feet, stretching her arms, cat-like, and pulling on John's coat.

'I think I should be going. There's nothing I can do here. I hope all goes well, Isabel. Do not be afraid; John will look after you.' She glanced at John under her lashes and smiled a small sad smile. 'Goodbye, *schatz*. Look after Isabel.' A silent message passed between them and John nodded in understanding and held her in his arms for a moment.

'Goobye, darling. Use the flat if you want to; it's warmer there.'

Anya turned and left. Isabel thought she detected a tear on her cheek, there seemed to be finality in their parting, as if Anya knew that this was the end. She followed the Russian girl to the front door and hugged her warmly.

'Thank you for your support, it's greatly appreciated. I'll be in touch.' She watched as Anya disappeared into the cold darkness leaving behind a faint waft of that exotic scent.

Irma produced a warming meal, pork stew with dumplings and boiled potatoes, redolent with caraway and herbs, which they ate together in the kitchen. Prince gazed at them longingly, hoping for titbits, but they were all so ravenous that he was lucky to get a little leftover gravy on his dog biscuits.

'You're looking a lot better, boy,' said Isabel, stroking his head, where the scab was already shrinking. The dog wagged his tail.

Soon after they'd eaten they went to their rooms with hot water bottles to warm the sheets.

'We'd better go to bed early,' said John. 'We've got to be up at dawn and there's a long journey ahead. It might be a good idea if Irma makes a flask of coffee and some sandwiches for us, what do you think?'

'That's a good idea. Do you mind, Irma?'

'Of course I will do that, Frau Barton. I will have it ready for when you leave. Also I will pack some things for Penny; she won't have any clean clothes.'

'How clever of you to think of that,' said Isabel.

'Goodnight for now,' they chorused and left the warm kitchen for their chilly bedrooms.

Isabel fell into bed with relief. She was not expecting to sleep, having napped earlier in the day, her mind still full of worry. But she found that her body was more relaxed and before long she had drifted into a deep slumber, obliterating the chasing, darting thoughts of what tomorrow might bring. The fear she had felt had been quashed, but at the back of her mind she wondered, just how crazy was Dennis Masters and how far would he go to get what he wanted?

Chapter Twenty-Eight

Creeping dread was overtaking Dennis; fear consuming all rational thought. His limbs ached with cold and discomfort; his head throbbed. What had he done?

What had seemed so simple yesterday, he realised, was a stupid and dangerous enterprise. What would they do to him if he got found out? He couldn't bear it if they sent him to prison. What on earth would he say to Emma? He almost wailed in fear and desolation. He had burned his boats and if it all went wrong he would have lost everything.

With Bill Barton away at the Intelligence conference in Hanover Dennis thought he'd take a few unauthorised days off. How boring these snivelling Germans were, with their endless excuses about why they had to join the Nazi party and how deeply they regretted it and how they had never done anything wrong. Dennis was completely fed up with the whole lot of them, so he decided to spend a few days at home while he had the chance. He'd arranged for the other staff to concentrate on paperwork and had stopped all appointments, so there were no 'clients' to see. The staff would all be glad of the break. If Barton asked why he'd done it he'd say that he wasn't feeling well. There was a lot of flu about as well as the more serious ailments.

His solitary life without Emma around to nag him about his many shortcomings had become relaxed. He could lounge about in the apartment at ease, admiring his growing collection of art, enjoying the craftsmanship and beauty of everything he had acquired. Some of it had been looted from empty houses when the city was first overrun and sold on for more valuable goods, like drugs and coffee. Some had been in the homes of people now desperate for food; easy pickings for a person in possession of a generous cigarette ration and, of course, the power to deliver a *persilschein* to the less than innocent. Best of all, Dennis could sit and calculate the value of everything; working out how he could live the rest of his life in luxury on the proceeds of his spoils.

He stretched his boots out towards the electric fire, all three bars blazing. Well, he didn't have to pay for the electricity, the Army saw to that. He couldn't be bothered to have an open fire up here. It meant lugging the fuel up from the store outside the Barton's kitchen. He didn't qualify for the services of a maid, so he didn't have someone to order about and fetch and carry for him. Mind you, it might have been pleasant to have a girl at his beck and call, especially one as pretty as Irma. He sipped at a cup of tea.

The tinkle of the piano in the hall reached his ears. Those kids are having a ballet lesson, he thought. He quite enjoyed seeing Isabel Barton, all grace and beauty, with her hair twisted into one of those buns at the back of her head that all ballet dancers seemed to have, instructing the children. He watched quietly from the top of the stairs, keeping in the shadows. The music was pleasant; lyrical and familiar, something his mother would have played on summer afternoons in Cheltenham.

Dennis pondered his dilemma. He had managed to smuggle his illicit treasures into the flat in the evenings and afternoons when the Bartons were not at home and Irma was working in the kitchen. Now he had to work out how to get it all away and into the arrangements he had made for shipping it back to England, where he could sell it all for a healthy profit. In England the rich and the collectors would be scouring the dealers looking for antiques now the war was over, hoping to replace those things they'd lost in the bombing.

How was he to get it out without anyone seeing? Bill would be back from the conference on Wednesday so this would be an opportunity, in his absence. But Isabel and the kid were here most of the time, how could he get them away from here? With all this snow they were unlikely to go out without good reason.

He rose and softly opened the door to his sitting room. He stood at the top of the stairs and watched the children dance.

They looked quite sweet, he thought, whirling around like little undisciplined dervishes. Penny Barton followed the movements of the others devotedly, her forehead creased in concentration; such a serious little girl. Isabel clapped her hands; the music stopped and she got them all to curtsey and bow and the children rushed in all directions to change and get ready for the truck that would take them home.

Dennis watched as dumpy Frau Hilfe packed up her music, gathering several coats around her and pulling on a stout pair of boots. He noticed when the door was opened that snow was falling and the air issuing through the front door was freezing; the cold reached him at the top of the stairs.

The truck arrived and he could see it at the kerb whilst the corporal helped the children in. They chattered and giggled; a happy crowd of kids. Isabel waited on the doorstep, her hand loosely holding the dog's collar. Penny, wrapped up warmly, stood beside her.

A little later Dennis heard the sound of the ration truck speeding down the street. The dog vanished from Isabel's side and there was a great deal of noise and screaming and Penny, looking terrified, turned and ran into the house, emitting distressed cries.

'Prince! Oh, Prince!' she cried.

Dennis had a flash of inspiration. An opportunity like this might not occur again. It was risky, but worth a try.

'Penny!' he called softly from the stairs. 'What is it, sweetie? What's happened?' He tried to inject avuncular sympathy into his voice.

'It's Prince,' the child sobbed. 'I think he's been run over by the truck.'

'Come up here, Penny. It's nice and warm. I'll look after you.'

'But Mummy ...'

'Mummy's busy at the moment, come up and I'll give you something nice to drink.'

Penny climbed the stairs and stood shaking, still in her outdoor clothes, in front of Dennis's electric fire. He made a drink of grenadine, the sweet syrup that he had bought in the French zone. He diluted it with warm water and covertly put in the contents of a couple of the sleeping capsules that Emma had left behind. He hoped they wouldn't be too strong for the child, but he took a chance; he couldn't miss this marvellous opportunity.

'Here you are, Penny, you'll like this. It'll make you feel better.'

'Thank you, Uncle Dennis,' she said politely, sipping the drink. 'It's very sweet, but I like it.'

She settled in the armchair and Dennis was surprised at how quickly her eyelids drooped and she drifted into a deep sleep. She should sleep for hours now, he thought, while I think what to do next.

From downstairs he could hear the sounds of Isabel and Irma searching the house and Isabel's wails of fear and loss. He couldn't help smiling. Little did they know that the child was upstairs here. He'd have to be very quiet for a while; they wouldn't know he was here, probably thought he was at work.

He tucked a woollen rug around the child and settled in the other chair to wait, after locking the door to the room. Just in time, he realised, as one of the women came up and rattled the handle. He stayed as silent as he could. Go away, he breathed, nothing in here.

He heard the doorbell ring and a lot of talking, some of it hysterical, before he heard the front door slam and the sound of a jeep driving away taking Isabel with it. Dennis, in the meantime, had formulated a plan of sorts. He would have to get that villain, Fritz Keller to help, but he had to get the child away from here, somewhere safe, where the Bartons couldn't find her until he was ready. This might be the opportunity not only to remove his stash from the house, but also to get some even more valuable items out of them in ransom.

He'd have to leave the child alone for a time while he went to fetch Fritz and fill him in with what had happened. Penny seemed to be sleeping soundly, but he didn't want to take any chances, so he slipped another sleeping pill into her mouth and watched as her reflexes took it down her throat. That should keep you out for a bit, princess, he thought, locking the door to his room.

As he left the house he checked that there was no-one who knew him in the street. He would have to walk to Fritz's hovel. It would take him about half-an hour in this snow. Bugger, it was cold. Dennis shivered even though he had put on fur lined boots and a *shapka urshanka*, with flaps over his ears, as well as his overcoat over several thick sweaters. He set off with plodding gait into the frozen whiteness. Luckily the wind was not strong and he could see where he was going.

By the time he arrived at Fritz's filthy dwelling he was cold to the bone and, having greeted the German, he accepted a swig of brandy and stood beside the rank paraffin stove with outstretched hands, shivering from cold and agitation.

'What's happened?' asked Fritz. 'You're very excited about something.'

'I've got the Bartons' kid.' He rubbed his hands together to get some feeling back.

'What!'

'Yes. I snatched her practically off the doorstep, right from under Isabel's nose.' He sounded smug.

'*Mein Gott*! Are you mad? What did you do that for?'

'Think about it, Fritz. I've got to get the Bartons out of the way to clear the flat and we could get a ransom as well. Yes, you and me! They'll do anything to get the child back. How do you like the sound of a juicy ransom? Enough to set you up and get you out of this squalor.' He waved his hand at the insanitary shack.

Fritz' eyes lit up. 'That would be bloody good,' he said. 'What do you need me to do?'

'I want you to take care of things this end. When everyone's out of the house, I'll let you know and I want you to start moving all my stuff out and into that building that I own, off the *Ku'damm*. Later we can get it into the truck and off to the UK. It's all arranged, I've got official papers for it, Bill Barton signed them himself; he had no idea what they were for. There just hasn't been such a good opportunity to move it before.'

'And why should I do this for you, Herr Dennis?'

'Don't worry, Fritz. You'll be well paid. We're going to get a ransom out of the Bartons. We'll get some of those drugs you're always going on about. Like gold dust aren't they?'

'*Ja wohl*.' Fritz thought for a moment. 'I like the sound of this; it may work. Perhaps it would be best if I come back with you and we can get started.'

'Yes, that's a much better idea; to do it all now. We'll have to be quiet in the flat when Isabel gets back. She's gone off somewhere, looking for the kid, I suppose. But she'll be back later.'

'We'd better get a move on and move your stuff before she arrives.'

'I'm not sure how long she's going to be. We can do it now, whilst she's out, and hope there's time. Can you drive the truck?'

'*Natürlich*. We go and get it now and then I can take everything to your storage before curfew.' Fritz was prepared for going outside and he extinguished the paraffin stove.

The two left the shack and walked to where Dennis kept his stolen five-ton truck. All signs of Army involvement in the vehicle had been obliterated. It looked like any other tired, knocked-about truck in Berlin. But in spite of the cold the engine roared into life immediately; well-maintained by REME in its previous life. The tank was full of purloined fuel, enough for the night's work.

The truck, unimpaired by the snow as it was well above the surface of the road, made good progress back to the Grunewald house.

'Park round the corner,' said Dennis. 'I don't want it right outside the house until we load up. Someone may see it and ask questions later.'

The pair entered the house quietly. It was empty except for the sleeping child upstairs in front of the electric fire. She stirred in her sleep as Dennis checked on her. Fritz stared at her doubtfully, obviously thinking that this could all be a very bad idea.

'Have you drugged her? You may have poisoned her, you crazy man,' he said.

'Don't worry, Fritz, she's all right,' Dennis said. 'Let's start getting things packed up.'

The two men started to wrap the smaller artefacts in old newspapers. Dennis tore up sheets and wrapped them around the paintings. In crates that he had collected earlier they packed the smaller items. Clocks, statuettes ornaments, lamps and vases were wrapped and carefully arranged in layers. One by one they stacked the boxes on the landing and then carried them down to the hall.

Dennis listened nervously for sounds of anyone returning, getting increasingly jumpy as each moment passed.

'We'll have to be quick now,' he said. 'Bring the truck round and we'll get it all in there.'

Opening the front door they found that it was now quite dark and snow was falling heavily. There was no-one in the freezing street. Fritz brought the truck to the front door and they filled it with the crates of packed treasure. Delicate pieces of antique furniture, swathed in blankets and sheets, were the last to be placed inside.

'That's everything. Time to go, Fritz,' said Dennis. 'You know where to take it, don't you?'

'*Ja.* I will see you tomorrow; where we agreed. You had better be there. I will find you if you're not, you know.'

'Don't worry. I'll be there.'

Fritz jumped into the driver's cab and drove away. Just as he rounded the corner an American jeep coming the other way passed him. Irma and her friends were coming home. Dennis saw them, turned and hurried into the house. He climbed the stairs rapidly and had only just reached the sanctuary of his room when the front door opened.

How bare his room looked with everything gone. Just the bare necessities remained; all luxury had been peeled away. He felt bereft, all his wonderful things, so carefully collected over the last months, gone. He knew that he would soon be reunited with them, but meanwhile he had things to do and plan. Somehow he had to get the child out of the house without anyone seeing him. Irma was home, but where was Isabel?

Dennis stared into the glowing bars of the electric fire, gnawing at his fingernails. He tugged at his thin beard and glanced at Penny, sleeping peacefully in the other armchair. She looked like a slumbering cherub, but her cheeks seemed rather red.

Dennis stood and examined Penny more closely. She was very hot. He had not taken off the overcoat and hat or the mufflers she was wearing when he brought her into the flat. Gently, trying not to wake her, he pulled off the gloves. They were connected by a cord of ribbon through the arms of the coat. He pulled away the two scarves; a small child's scarf and a much longer, bright blue one. He slipped the coat from her shoulders and arranged it around her. He did not move the child off the coat as he knew that if she woke she might make enough noise to alert Irma. There, she would be cooler in a minute. Perhaps he should turn off the fire too. No, not a good idea, it was so cold outside that the temperature in the room would drop rapidly without it.

He slumped into his chair again and tried to get his thoughts in order. Everything had happened so fast that he hadn't formulated a proper plan. At least Fritz was taking care of the loot. He hoped he could trust the slimy rat. But he didn't think Fritz would let him down with the knowledge that there was more bounty to come. He was a greedy little sod.

He had to get the child out of the flat or he would be found out. There were bound to be police around soon, either the *Polizei* or the Military Police. That meant carrying her, sleeping, out into the snow and taking her somewhere safer.

Perhaps he should take her to Fritz's hovel until the morning and then – well he'd have to take her to the country, away from the city. His cottage in the Hartz Mountains would be perfect. Hidden away, down by the lake near the woods, no-one would find him there; no-one knew he owned it. But he'd have to tell them something, give them some instructions, or they wouldn't know where to take the ransom and collect the child. He didn't want them to know that he was responsible for snatching Penny if he could possibly help it. How could he arrange that?

Dennis sank deeper into thought until the heat from the fire lulled him into a stupor. He woke with a start, afraid that hours had passed, but his watch told him that he had only napped for a few minutes. He had to do something, now, before Isabel came back. More than likely she'd have that spook John Marriott with her, pushing his nose into everything.

First he'd have to write a letter of some sort to tell them what to do. He started to scribble a draft on a piece of rough paper. No, he couldn't write it by hand, they'd be bound to recognise his handwriting, so he dragged out his old Olivetti portable and began to compose a ransom note. His typing was pretty accurate after years in an office where the typists went home on the dot of 5.30.

Would there be time for them to get to the Hartz by tomorrow? No, he wouldn't be there himself by then probably, the weather being as it was. The day after, then, sometime in the afternoon. Maybe he'd not say definitely, just say something vague about a rendezvous being arranged within three days. They'd have to come to a meeting in the forest, not too near the cottage; someone local might know he used it. There was that place where two streams met on their way towards the lake; that would do, but he needn't tell them that till later or they might set up an ambush. His head was spinning with confusion.

He wrote a list of the drugs and other things he required as ransom. Fritz' instructions had been comprehensive. He doubled the quantities he had first thought of; might as well be hung for a sheep as for a lamb.

He tapped away at the typewriter, his confidence growing. Yes, this should work. They needn't know it was him and if they did guess, he would blame Fritz and say that he had rescued Penny from the old villain. Everyone knew Fritz was a crook and a leading light with the black market gangs. A lot of ruthless thugs, they would think nothing of kidnapping a child, he thought.

Dennis pulled the typed letter from the machine and found an envelope for it . He typed Isabel's name and address on the front so that they'd think the postman had delivered it, inserted the letter and sealed it, well satisfied with his plan so far.

He stood up and stretched. Now what? Time to get the kid out of the building. He leaned over the chair and dressed Penny in her warm clothes again and turned off the fire. She stirred slightly, so he fed her another of the sleeping pills and put the rest in his coat pocket for later. He went into the bedroom and took the old service revolver that he had acquired from the bedside table. A rucksack was filled with the few items of food he had left from his rations and a flask of strong coffee. A couple of bars of Cadburys Dairy Milk chocolate completed his hoard. He hoped the coffee would keep warm; he would need it to help keep him awake.

Returning to the sitting room, he wrapped Penny in the rug again and prepared to leave. First he had to check that there was no-one downstairs. He went to the landing and peered over the banisters. No sign of Irma; she must be in her room. He stole down the stairs and placed the ransom note on the floor, under one corner of the blue rug. They would think it had been delivered earlier in the day. He supposed someone would find it quite quickly.

He climbed the stairs again and picked up the sleeping child. Even swaddled in the blanket she was not heavy. He lifted her onto his shoulder and left the room. He had to be quick; he couldn't be seen or everything would be over. Holding his breath he crept down the stairs, opened the front door, praying the panels wouldn't rattle, and stepped out into the snow. He didn't breathe until he reached the corner, not able to relax until he knew he was out of sight of the house. Then he hurried towards Fritz's cabin for the second time that evening, the weight of the child on his shoulder increasing with every step.

But Dennis had been careless. Upstairs in his sitting room the bright blue scarf lay on the floor beside the armchair.

Chapter Twenty-Nine

Fritz drove the truck with Dennis's collected treasure away into the white streets. He knew the location of the building in which he was supposed to stow Dennis's loot, but he wasn't going there. With a tank full of fuel he thought he'd take the opportunity to visit some friends who might be interested in these new developments.

Extraordinary, he thought. What was that idiot thinking, kidnapping a child? Did he seriously think he could get away with it? I'm pretty greedy myself, he acknowledged, but nothing like that, the man is *verückt.* He'd be lucky if he hadn't killed the child, overdosing her with sleeping pills. She looked all right at the moment, but if he carried on giving them to her it must have a bad effect. Still, it was none of his business; let the mad Englishman do as he liked.

Fritz negotiated the snow-covered streets out to the suburbs close to the Wannsee. He parked outside the house with the damaged roof. At last someone had been up and rearranged the tarpaulin so that the snow had not filled the loft. It seemed that the occupants were either out or gone to bed because it took some time before someone opened the door; finally he was inside.

The burly Serbian, Lujic, who ran one of the biggest black market rings in Berlin, roared with laughter when he heard of Dennis's antics.

'These British,' he said. 'So high and mighty, but so venal too. Well, this is very interesting. You say you have this truck full of valuables outside?'

'Yes,' said Fritz. 'All packed up and ready to be shipped to England.'

'We'll see about that,' said the Serbian. 'Where did you say he is taking this child?'

'To the Hartz. He's got a summer cottage there.'

The Serbian's eyes narrowed. 'So that's where this drug ransom is going to be delivered?'

'That's what he told me. He didn't want to stay in Berlin. Frightened of British Intelligence, I think.'

'Yes, he's probably right to be. Is that man John Marriott involved in this?'

'He is a friend of the parents, I believe.'

'Good, good. I have a few scores to settle with the clever Captain Marriott. Too much interference. He pretends to be my friend, but I know he just wants to sabotage my business. I can't allow that. Come, Fritz Keller, we have work to do.'

The Serbian called some of his men from upstairs and reluctantly at first, as they were groggy with sleep, they unloaded the cache. Fritz stood by nervously as they man-handled the more delicate antiques into the house.

'He has done very well,' said the Serbian, examining some of the finer pieces. 'I can find a good home for these. We have a trip to Switzerland scheduled for next week. These can go in that consignment. You've done well, Fritz. Don't worry; you'll get your share of the proceeds.'

Fritz's back stooped with weariness. He had been involved in the packing and transporting of these goods twice today and had had enough. He sat on the front step of the house sucking on a cigarette until the unloading was complete. The Serbian sat beside him.

'What should I do now?' Fritz asked, fighting back one of his rasping coughs.

'Just carry out the rest of the plan as agreed with Mr Masters. He thinks you've put the goods in his storage, does he not?'

'Yes,' said Fritz.

'So, you go back to your lodging with the truck, pick him up, with this child he's taken and drive to the Hartz as agreed. We will follow later. Don't worry, Fritz, we will get the ransom for ourselves. No stupid civilian idiot can stop us and if we have any more interference from the British military, we know how to deal with them.' He slapped Fritz on the back. 'Off with you. I'll see you soon, my friend.' His loud insincere laugh guffawed from his deep chest. 'Good luck.'

Within minutes Fritz had climbed back into the empty truck and was on his way back to his hovel.

Dennis peered out anxiously into the darkness. Behind him Penny slept soundly on Fritz's unsavoury bed. Her thumb had found its way into her mouth and she looked like one of those Botticelli cherubs, round-cheeked and content.

Dennis heard boots approaching. He pulled the cardboard door inwards so less light fell onto the snow reflecting out like a beacon on the whiteness.

'Fritz, is that you?' he whispered as loudly as he dared.

'Of course, *dummkopf*,' said Fritz from the darkness. 'Who else were you expecting? Close the door. Do you want the curfew patrol to come round? That would spoil your little plan, if they saw the kid. Get inside for God's sake.'

He stumbled in, pushing Dennis aside.

'Great! Now where are we going to sleep? If I don't get some rest soon I'm not going to be fit to drive to the Hartz tomorrow.' He sat on the edge of the cot and pushed Penny over. She stirred in her sleep.

'For God's sake don't wake her up,' said Dennis. 'There'll be hell to pay if she starts making a fuss. Kids can make an unbelievable amount of noise when they want to.' He soothed the child whilst moving her to the side nearest the wall.

'There's room for you to sleep there now, just try not to kick her in the night or she'll wake up.'

'And you, Herr Dennis? Where will you sleep?'

'I'll sleep on the floor or here in the chair. I'd better keep watch. Don't worry about me.'

'Fair enough, old boy.' Fritz turned his back to Dennis and curled up on the bed, pulling a blanket around his shoulders. 'Good night.' It soon became clear that he was asleep. For Dennis this relief came less easily.

The next morning they started on an uneventful journey to the Hartz Mountains. Dennis had drugged Penny again and she slept. I can't keep doing this, he thought. I'll have to let her wake up soon; at least she'll be pretty groggy for a while. I'll have to tell her some story about where we're going and why. He searched his brain for an inventive reason, probably involving cats and dogs or fairies or some such thing to convince her. He knew so little about children; perhaps she would be overcome with fright and become hysterical.

When they arrived at Bad Hartzburg Dennis took over the driving for the last few kilometres. Snow had been falling gently but steadily for the past hour.

'I don't want to drive up to the cottage,' he said. 'The tyre tracks will give us away. We'll get as close as we can, to the edge of the forest, and I'll carry the child from there. The snow will soon cover my footprints. You can park the truck in the village. Try not to look too obvious, and join me later on foot.'

Fritz was fine with this and, having been told the directions to Dennis's cottage he left him on the edge of the forest and watched as he disappeared into the trees with Penny's tiny form draped over his shoulder. *Verückter Englander,* he thought as he climbed back into the truck; he really seemed to think this would work.

Dennis couldn't see where he was going through the forest as the gloom cast by the covered trees made his route obscure. He staggered on, avoiding exposed roots and thick undergrowth, his burden heavier on his shoulder with every step. Eventually he could see the glimmer of the lake in the distance; his destination was near. Penny began to stir, but he didn't want to give her another sleeping pill and hoped he would reach his sanctuary before she was fully awake. Somehow he'd have to think of a plausible story to keep her calm.

His arms became cramped and he stopped for a moment and, laying the child on the cold ground still wrapped in the blanket, he sat on a fallen log to catch his breath. The blanket fell away and Penny kicked her legs. Dennis watched as she rolled over and groaned and fidgeted. He was anxious that she didn't wake, so he gently wrapped her again and soothed her back into sleep. He didn't notice the small object that dropped on to the ground from her coat pocket.

Dennis started to walk more briskly now, taking care not to trip. A fall at this stage would be disastrous. Soon he was out in the open and on the downward slope towards his cottage only a couple of hundred metres away across clear, smooth snow. He almost tumbled into a deep drift on the way down, but reached the cottage, slightly out of breath, within a few minutes. He set Penny down on a rustic bench on the veranda whilst he fetched the key from its hiding place in the outhouse.

Inside the cottage his breath formed a fog in the freezing air and he spent several anxious minutes persuading the fuel in the wood-burning stove to light. Even when it was burning with a rich glow it took a while before any heat penetrated the simple room. In the meantime he placed Penny, still wrapped in the blanket, onto the wooden settle close to the fire. He went into the tiny kitchen to see what provisions were there. He always left some necessities here in case he needed to use the bolt-hole in an emergency. Tea and coffee, a little sugar, a few biscuits and tins of meat, milk, vegetables and fish lined the shelves in the small larder. Combined with the things he's brought from his apartment in a rucksack on his back, they would have enough for a day or two. He hoped Fritz remembered to buy bread as he had asked; then they'd have enough for a feast.

Eventually Fritz joined him. He glanced at the roaring fire in the stove, which had warmed the interior to a cosy glow.

'You'll have to put that out for a start,' he growled. 'You can see the smoke for miles around. None of the other cottages are occupied; they'll know you're in this one straight away.'

Dennis looked alarmed, then he realised the truth of what Fritz was saying.

'Blast! You're right. OK, I'll put it out, but we'll freeze if we have to be here for long.'

'Haven't you got more blankets here? We'll have to huddle together to keep warm and wait for them to turn up with the ransom. When did you say that would be?'

'Tomorrow; but not here. There's a place in the woods...' he paused, reluctant to give Fritz details. 'There are some blankets and things in the chest, but they may be damp, I haven't been here since the summer.'

'That'll do,' said Fritz and got up to rummage in the oak chest.

He spread blankets and a thick quilt over the floor, then wrapped himself in another rug and settled down, like a large woolly chrysalis, to sleep beside the extinguished embers of the fire. Fritz had checked outside and seen that the smoke had been dispersed by the crisp wind from the north. It had snowed again and covered their footprints, but it looked as if it would be stopping soon as the sky was clearing and weak sunshine beginning to appear.

Dennis watched Fritz for a while and then decided to wrap up and sleep himself. He felt incredibly tired. Penny was still asleep; until she woke he would try to rest. God, I hope she doesn't have a tantrum, I'm not sure I could cope with that. Or the drugs might have had a lasting effect on her, making her ill. What would he do then? This was when fear began to overwhelm him and acute discomfort robbed him of sleep as icy slivers of cold air forced its way between the floorboards.

His last transient thoughts were optimistic. I can make this thing work; we're safe, we have food for a few days. Soon we'll have the ransom and can give back the child. I'll go and cash it all in and can go back home a rich man. Everything will be fine.

Chapter Thirty

There were four in the big 1938 Mercedes. John sat in the front beside Hank; Isabel and Zelda spread out on the back seat with their furs around them. The car was built like a tank, it may even have been bullet proofed. Isabel supposed it must have belonged to a senior *Wehrmacht* officer before it was requisitioned by the Americans. Settling into the seat, wide enough for at least three people, she could feel the little Mauser and box of ammunition forming a hard mass in the pocket of her coat and moved it aside to make herself more comfortable.

Hank had arrived promptly at 7.30 wearing a greatcoat over his uniform and a non-regulation woollen hat. He helped Irma put the bags in the boot with the flasks and food she had supplied for the journey. They threw in a shovel in case they became stuck and had to dig the car out of a snowdrift. Several anonymous cartons containing the precious ransom were packed as well. The car's big tyres had been covered in cumbersome snow chains.

'We'll need those out in the country,' said John. 'The roads are cleared here, but the snow's going to be thick on the country roads.'

As it happened the roads had been cleared by snow-ploughs almost as far Bad Hartzburg; only a few kilometres from their destination. A fresh fall in the night meant that some snow covered the tarmac in a thin layer, but it was not nearly as bad as they had expected. Flakes fell gently, but visibility was good and Hank had no difficulty in negotiating their route. But everything changed once they passed Bad Hartzburg. Out in the deeper countryside the roads were still blanketed with snow and driving through it became a struggle. Snow poured more heavily from the sky; they were higher now, close to the mountains. At one point they had to get out and use the shovel to remove banks of snow and the whole group had to push to get the car moving again. The wheels spun noisily and the engine laboured.

'My God, this thing is heavy!' said Isabel as they struggled up the incline.

'Yes, they're very well made, these Mercs,' said John, grunting with the effort.

'Too bloody well made if you ask me.'

They soon resumed their journey, after a drink of hot coffee and a sandwich eaten in the car. They each breathed a sigh of relief when, after three hours on the road, the distinctive black and white architecture of the Hotel Schauser hove into view through gaps in the falling snow, like a ghost house appearing from a mist.

'Gee, I'm glad that's over,' said Zelda. 'I can't wait for stiff drink. Are you on, Isabel?'

'Gosh, yes,' she replied. 'I can't wait.'

They strode towards the hotel, bags in their hands, whilst John and Hank heaved in the rest of the luggage, including the ransom. Bill materialised in the porch. He wore his uniform; hadn't even loosened the collar, but stood as stiff as a guardsman, making no move to come forward and greet them.

'Bill!' shrieked Isabel. 'I'm so glad you're here.' She ran towards him, her fur boats slithering in the new-fallen snow.

'Hello, Isabel.' Bill regarded her coldly, making no attempt to steady her precarious progress. 'Come inside. Hurry up.' He made no move to help with the luggage, but strode back into the hallway.

Isabel followed and went to embrace him but he moved away; subtly turning out of her grasp.

'We'll talk in a minute, Isabel,' he said, making it clear that he wanted to wait until the others were out of earshot.

Herr Schauser fussed around them, allocating rooms and directing the servants to take the bags to their destinations. As usual he maintained a steady stream of dialogue.

'*Komm*,' he said, 'to the *Gastzimmer* - there are drinks for you there. *Komm, komm*.' He waggled his chubby hands and directed them to the smaller lounge where a log fire burned in the grate.

Before she could follow, Bill gripped Isabel's arm as if in a vice.

'Wait, Isabel, I need to talk to you,' he growled as he pulled her back into the hall, his gaze as stern as a schoolmaster about to reprimand a pupil. 'How could you let this happen? Why weren't you watching the child?'

Aghast at his obvious fury, Isabel was silent. This was not what she had expected. It was so unfair; it hadn't been her fault. She didn't feel she had to explain. As if she hadn't had enough trouble with that awful Major Goddard and his machine-gun questions. She was momentarily dumbfounded and then the words started to pour out of her as did the tears that streamed down her cheeks; it had all been too much. She took Bill through every detail from the moment that she stood on the steps of the Grunewald house saying goodbye to the ballet class, gasping the story out between sobs.

They were still standing in the middle of the hotel's hallway, like two prize-fighters circling each other before they strike the first blow. Rage still burnt in Bill's eyes and Isabel was sure he was not listening to what she was saying.

'It wasn't my fault. She just disappeared and we couldn't find her anywhere.'

'Of course it was your fault, you should have kept your eye on her.'

'I thought Prince had been run over.'

'I suppose you thought that was more important than our child?' sarcasm edged his voice in steel.

'No, of course not. But I had no reason to suppose she was in danger. She was there beside me.'

'You're saying she was miraculously spirited away?'

'I thought just that at first. But now we know that it was Dennis that took her.'

'Dennis Masters? Don't be ridiculous.' Disbelief and disdain rang in every syllable.

Isabel realised that Bill didn't know the rest of the story or Dennis's involvement in it.

'For goodness sake, Bill,' she said. 'Come and sit down

and I'll tell you the rest of it.' She drew Bill over to a sofa nearer the fire and made him sit. Drawing the ransom note from her coat pocket and handing it to him, she explained it all from the moment the nightmare began.

'We've got the ransom with us. John's been marvellous and got it all from the stores at HQ, or the pharmacy or something.'

'So that explains why we're here. I wondered why we had to meet in the Hartz mountains.' Bill still appeared angry, but the information obviously gave him pause for thought. He studied the note with care.

'I know. It seems weird. But I think he must have a hidey-hole somewhere near here; he couldn't very well keep Penny in the flat, could he? We'd have found him quickly, or that horrible Major Goddard would.'

'Dennis Masters. I can hardly believe it. I knew he was a moody bastard and hated us, but I didn't think he could be this vindictive. I wonder who else is involved.'

'Anya thinks it may be something to do with the Russians, but I don't believe that.'

'Anya! She knows about this too?' Bill's eyes narrowed.

'She has taken an interest, yes; so have John and Zelda, and Irma and Hank too. They've all been a tremendous help, Bill. You weren't around and I had to turn to someone. That's why they're here now. Zelda got Chuck to lend us the car and Hank to drive it. Zelda's here for moral support.'

'I suppose you think I should have been there to help you?'

'It would have been nice. It was very difficult for me when I couldn't even get in touch with you on the phone. But you weren't around, so that's that.'

'I'm here now,' said Bill. 'I brought some help too. I didn't know what we were up against. If it was the Russians I thought I might need some heavies to sort things out.'

'What do you mean?'

'There's a Special Forces Sergeant and a few squaddies in the annexe, armed to the teeth. I co-opted them in Hanover. It may be overkill against Dennis Masters.' He spat out the name with contempt.

'Goodness, how did you wangle that?' asked Isabel.

'I pulled rank,' Bill managed a wry grin. 'I think they were glad to come. They're itching for a bit of action, there's been nothing for them to do since the war ended.'

'I'm not so sure about the overkill,' said Isabel. 'I think he may have some help. There may be more people involved than we're aware of.'

John came into the hall. 'Come on, you two,' he said. 'Schauser's made some *Glühwein* that'll rot your socks. Come and drink it while it's still hot.'

Obediently the pair went to the lounge where they were handed goblets of steaming wine fragrant with spices.

John stood beside Isabel and spoke to her softly. 'Was he giving you a hard time?'

'Yes, a bit,' she replied. 'But I think it's all right now, thanks. I explained everything to him.'

'Shall I have a word with him?'

'No. He's calmed down a bit. He's brought a bunch of Special Forces men with him.'

'Really? Well, they may be a help. I hope they're not too trigger-happy. Drink that wine, Bella; it'll make you feel a whole lot better.'

Isabel smiled at him gratefully; he had been such a rock through all this. John turned away and went to talk to Bill. He was probably filling him in with the details, maybe he'd manage to explain it all and tell him it wasn't her fault.

Soon they were sitting down to one of Herr Schauser's rib-sticking meals, bacon and sausages with cabbage and potatoes, guaranteed to make you want to sleep for the rest of the afternoon.

Hank stayed with them for the meal; it seemed only fair after all the driving, they couldn't just put him in the annexe as if he were a servant.

After lunch John, Bill and the Special Forces men gathered on the snow-covered gravel outside the hotel.

'There are some summer cottages down by the lake, what the Russians would call dachas; little log cabins. We haven't been able to establish exactly who owns them, but I suspect one of them may belong to Masters. I think that's the most likely spot for him to have taken the child,' Bill said to the assembled men.

The soldiers wore winter combat gear, snow boots and helmets; all but John and Bill carried rifles. They bristled with ammunition and pockets bulged with hand grenades and other ordinance. John and Bill carried hand guns in holsters beneath their coats. Isabel stood in the porch watching them; she had never seen a group of fighting men in all their gear before.

'We're going on a quick reconnoitre through the forest,' said Bill, 'before it gets dark or starts to snow again. See if we can find anything. We won't be long.'

'Can't I come with you?' asked Isabel.

'No, of course not, this is a military operation,' said Bill. 'We can't take a woman along.'

'It couldn't do any harm, Bill,' said John. 'Isabel's been cooped up for days, driving herself mad with worry. Maybe this'll make her feel as if she's doing something constructive. It's only a reccy; we're not likely to see any action.'

'Oh please, Bill,' begged Isabel. 'I won't get in the way. If you found Penny or any sign of her, I'd want to be there, she'd need me.'

'All right then. If you must,' Bill gave in. 'Keep well back and out of the way if anything happens.'

'Thank you. I won't be a minute; I'll just get my coat and boots.' Isabel dashed back into the building.

Five minutes later the party strode off into the pines trees a short walk from the hotel. Although several inches of snow lay outside the forest, between the trees only a thin dusting lay on the ground. The thick canopy of branches held the snow above them like a thick tablecloth and only thin sprinkles drifted through the branches, like flour sifting through a sieve. In some clearings between the trees bushes, heaps of stones and rocky outcrops were garnished with a coating of white.

Occasionally the weight of the snow caused the branches to bend and release their burden in a noisy mini-avalanche. Sparse light glimmered between the branches and little sound could be heard. Even though sunset was a couple of hours away the darkness between the trees made it difficult to see ahead. Gentle rattles and soft footfall sounded from the soldiers, but generally their passage through the trees, over a thick carpet of pine needles, was silent as a peaceful walk in the English countryside.

The winter camouflage worn by the men was hardly suitable here because the white stood out clearly against the dark trees, the undergrowth and the forest floor. But as they were up against a single enemy, as far as they knew, this did not appear to bother them.

The party stole through the forest, the soldiers spread out in a line with Bill, John and Isabel bringing up the rear in a closer group. They walked for twenty minutes without seeing or hearing anything. At one point the Sergeant raised a hand for silence and to make everyone stop as he had heard something amongst the trees. Isabel's breath caught and she felt her heart beating faster; had they found something? But it was only a young deer foraging on the forest floor; the animal raised its head, even more terrified than Isabel and he leapt away into the undergrowth.

The forest floor appeared at first to be smooth and flat, thickly covered with fallen pine needles, but many obstacles stood in the way. The thick girder of a fallen tree trunk, a deep hole where a forest animal had dug a haven, sudden deep ditches where a stream from the mountains above, on its way to the lake, had dug a trench. One of the soldiers fell into one of these unexpected brooks, amidst colourful swearing and enough noise to alert anyone within a mile of their presence.

'Shut the fuck up,' snarled the Sergeant, 'or I'll have you on a charge.'

From then on they progressed more carefully, hardly daring to whisper in the iron cold stillness.

Isabel found it harder to keep up than she had expected. The beaver coat kept her warm but it also hampered her movements. It drifted and tangled around her ankles and several times she felt as if she might stumble and fall. How humiliating that would be in front of the men. She had promised she would not to be a nuisance. She swore under her breath as her ankle twisted around a root looping treacherously out of the carpet on the forest floor.

Weariness also began to overtake her. Perhaps she should have had a good rest back at the hotel instead of coming on this expedition. They were only trying to get the lie of the land, after all. They didn't think they would be doing anything. How far were they going to walk? Miles, or just as far as the lake, glimpses of which she could see in the distance? Doggedly she struggled to keep up with John and Bill, but even they were falling behind the soldiers, probably to accommodate her slower pace. John looked back over his shoulder.

'You OK, Isabel? You could wait here if you like. We're just looking around for now. Nothing's going to happen.'

'I'm all right, thank you, John. I want to stay with you, just in case.'

'I understand. But don't get too far behind; we don't want to lose you.'

'Just try to keep up, Isabel,' said Bill without looking back.

They trudged on for another few hundred metres. The glitter of the lake became clearer in the distance, weak sunshine reflecting on its surface now the snow had ceased to fall.

The Sergeant halted the men in mime and sent a pair of soldiers ahead to examine the shores of the lake more closely. They had a heavy pair of Zeiss binoculars with them. The remainder of the party took a brief rest. John and several of the soldiers lit cigarettes and Isabel watched the smoke drift up into the trees.

She felt as if she had found her second wind. Her annoyance at Bill's uncaring attitude spurred her on and now she felt eager to get ahead, to find Penny, rescue her and go home as quickly as possible. She wandered between the trees, always keeping the party in sight. There's not going to be any signs, she thought, I'm not likely to find anything. But then she did.

Her fur boots disturbed the surface of the forest floor. In her restless mooching she kicked at the pine needles and dead leaves, turning over the top layer as she went. She spotted something incongruous in the dark brown mess. Blue and white; a tiny thing that she recognised at once. Her heart started to pound and she picked it up. Excited, she ran back to where John and Bill were standing, holding the object in her outstretched hand.

'John, look! I've found something!'

'What is it?'

'It's a doll's house teapot. Blue and white china, just like a real one.'

'Anyone could have dropped that,' scoffed Bill.

'No. Penny had it. She took it from the doll's house at the hotel. She didn't know I knew about it, but she pinched it, she loved it so. It means she's been here, so we know we're on the right track; someone brought her through these woods and she dropped it.'

'She couldn't have dropped it on another occasion could she, Isabel?' asked John.

'No, we've never been this far into the woods before. Penny is afraid of the forest. She thinks it's full of witches waiting to carry her off, like Hansel and Gretel.' Isabel reflected for a moment. 'Of course that is what's happened to her. She must be terrified.' She turned to Bill, who was turning the tiny teapot over in his hand; Penny's precious talisman.

'Oh, please Bill, can't we just carry on and find her and take her home? I can't bear this much longer.'

'No, we're in the hands of the Sergeant now. He knows what to do for the best. We need to get a firmer idea of where Dennis is. We don't want to spook the bastard and send him running. He could take Penny somewhere even further away and we won't know where she is. Or he may just cut his losses and get rid of her,' he suggested grimly.

Isabel gasped in horror. 'No!' She stared towards the lake. Penny was down there somewhere, frightened and cold. She would never forgive Dennis for this.

The two soldiers sent ahead emerged into the clearing and reported to the sergeant.

'There's several cottages, cabins really, around the edge of the lake. The three nearest ones are close together on the north side, just down there. There's no sign of life; no smoke coming from the chimneys or light at the windows, so they may all be empty. The kidnapper could be in one of the houses further away of course, but the snow is deeper round there, because of the north winds, and there's no sign of a vehicle having been near any of 'em.'

'What about footprints?'

'Can't see any, Sarge. But there was more snow earlier today, so they would have been covered by now.'

'We know that they've been through this way,' said John.

He showed the Sergeant the tiny toy and explained how Penny had it in her possession. The Sergeant looked doubtful, but finally accepted it as evidence that the kidnapper has passed this way.

'Righto. You, Clarkson and Dee, stay here. I'll see you're relieved around midnight. Keep a close watch on those three cottages. Report back if there's any activity. We'll return to the hotel for and wait till morning.'

Leaving the two soldiers to their vigil, Bill, John and the rest of the party trudged back to the hotel. The going was more difficult now as they were moving uphill and the temperature had dropped.

By the time they reached Hotel Schauser Isabel was consumed with cold and weariness. In spite of thick gloves her fingers felt as if a swift tap would snap them off. She stretched her hands out towards the log fire in the entrance hall, keeping the big fur coat on until she felt warmer. When she eventually removed it, the metallic sound it made against the wooden arm of the settee reminded her that the Mauser was in the pocket.

Bill strode into the hotel after a chat with the Sergeant. His face glowed with cold, his nose and his cheeks florid. A dark frown creased his forehead.

'Come and stand by the fire, Bill,' suggested Isabel. 'You'll soon warm up.'

'I'm all right, thank you,' he said, but edged nearer to the blaze. 'You're cold, are you? Serves you right, I told you not to come.'

That's a bit spiteful, thought Isabel, but she didn't retort.

'Perhaps we can get a cup of tea, or some more of that delicious *Glühwein*. I'll go and ask Hilde, I'm sure she'll be glad to make some for us.' She started to move towards the bell-pull near the door.

Bill grabbed her arm. 'No, Isabel. Stay here. I need to talk to you. I haven't got to the bottom of this affair. You haven't explained how you managed to allow Dennis Masters, of all people, make off with our daughter.'

'I didn't "allow" him to do anything, Bill. He just did it. Out of greed, I suppose. He saw an opportunity to make something out of us and took it. I don't know. I can't read the man's mind. I never did like him and I'm sure he has no respect for me.'

'I don't suppose he has any reason to respect you.' Bill replied.

'What do you mean by that?'

'Well, he probably thinks of you as a flibbertigibbet with no thoughts in her head beyond clothes and dancing classes.'

'That's what you think of me, Bill. Why don't you just say it? You think I'm a waste of space and this is all my fault.'

'I must admit it crossed my mind. Now we've got a complicated situation on our hands with the Special Forces involved, searching through the forests for our child.' He was pacing up and down the hall now; his boots ringing a tattoo on the polished parquet.

'Well, I didn't ask for that, it was your idea to bring them. You said they were glad to come, needed something to do. I'm sure it's a fun day out for them, playing soldiers again.'

'Oh, shut up, Isabel. You don't know what you're talking about. Why don't you go and gossip with Zelda, that's all you're fit for.'

His rage had built to a crescendo and his face was even redder. He removed his greatcoat and flung it onto the sofa.

John had entered the front door a few moments before and stood nearby listening to this exchange. When Bill finished his tirade, he stepped forward.

'Steady on, Bill. Isabel's had a really bad time. She was devastated by what happened and this isn't helping.'

Bill turned towards his friend and snarled. 'It's really none of your business, is it, John? This is between Isabel and me. The silly bitch was careless and naturally she's had to suffer for it. What can you expect from someone like her?'

'You can't talk about her like that, Bill. It's totally unfair.' John moved to Isabel's side. He appeared shocked by the whole interchange and instinctively extended a hand towards Isabel. Bill ignored them both and strode towards the stairs which he took two steps at a time until he was out of sight.

Isabel's eyes filled with tears and she grabbed a handkerchief from her pocket. John silently took her hand and drew her into the small sitting room off the hall. He turned towards her and drew her into his arms.

'Come, darling, don't listen to him. He doesn't know what he's talking about.'

'But he does, John. I can be a bit silly sometimes and forgetful and vain. But I have always been so careful about Penny; looked after her and made sure she was safe. How can he be so cruel?'

Tears streamed and John softly brushed them away with his fingers and kissed her, gently at first and then with more urgency. Isabel slowly began to respond and her body, still trembling with grief, clung to him and her hands stroked his thick dark hair, his back, his shoulders, feeling his strength and his passion holding her safe.

After a lifetime of an embrace they drew apart, breathless.

'I love you, Isabel,' he said. You know that, don't you?'

'I think I guessed,' she smiled. 'You've been so good; so kind and patient.'

'But you, Bella, how do you feel?'

'Oh, John. I think I do love you. It's hard at the moment to know how I feel. Bill has been so beastly about this whole business; I hardly know how I feel about anything. I need time to think and I can't think about anything until Penny is back safely with me.'

'I understand. It's all been very difficult for you. We'll have to talk about this again though, when Penny is back. I'm not just going to let you go, you know.'

'John, I really don't think there can be anything between us, not really. I owe my loyalty to Bill. I waited all through the War for him; I can't just ditch him now, when things have become difficult. It wouldn't be fair. I owe him that much.'

They were seated on a low sofa, holding hands.

'Don't decide anything now, Bella. I will wait and abide by whatever you say.' He stood abruptly. 'But now you need to get some sleep.'

'I can't sleep in the same bed as him tonight, John. Not after what he said and... what we just did.'

'No, I understand that. I would suggest you came and shared my room, but...' he smiled ruefully, 'I suspect you wouldn't agree to that.'

'No, sorry, John.' Isabel smiled sadly. 'I'll ask Zelda if I can sleep with her. She won't mind. I'll say goodnight.' She stood and dropped a kiss on his head. 'Sleep well.' She went towards the door and turned back for a second, leaving John staring after her with such a look of love and longing on his face that she would never forget.

Zelda hovered on the edge of sleep when Isabel knocked on her door.

'Zelda, can I come in?' she stage-whispered through the thick door.

'Sure,' Zelda murmured.

Isabel entered the room and sat on the edge of the bed. Her friend opened one eye, looking at her blearily.

'Wassup?' she asked.

'I've had a terrible row with Bill. Can I sleep here tonight? I can't bear the idea of sleeping with him.'

'Sure thing, honey. I'll hunker over; there's plenty of room in this bed for the two of us.' Zelda closed her eye again and within seconds she was dozing off.

Isabel found her head was full of conflicting emotions: anger at Bill for his unreasonableness, fear for Penny and her wellbeing and another emotion, for John, sweeter and more joyful than she had felt for a long time.

She undressed and, in her slip, slid into the bed and gave herself up to exhaustion. Sleep, when it came, carried with it vivid dreams and, intruding into the chaos, the taste of John's lips on hers and the feelings of warmth and security she had in his arms.

Chapter Thirty-One

The next morning Zelda arranged for breakfast to be brought to their room, a luxury that Isabel had never experienced before.

'Room Service,' said Zelda. 'At least we Americans have contributed something to civilisation. It's wonderful, I think you'll admit.'

'Someone else must have thought of it before you, Zelda. I'm sure the Savoy will have been doing it for years.'

'Well, maybe. But it's great whoever invented it. So, tell me what happened last night before you invaded my room.'

Isabel took her friend through the row with Bill.

'How could he be so unkind to you, Isabel? I thought he was a gentleman. I may be reviewing my opinion of him. Wait till I tell Chuck about this.'

'Oh, don't, Zelda. He's probably right; I was careless, thinking of other things. But he didn't have to be so horrible about it.'

'What happened then?'

'Well, John took me into the little sitting room and ... comforted me, I suppose you'd say.'

Zelda looked thoughtful. 'Comforted you, you say. Well. That is interesting. Anything more I should know about?'

Isabel laughed shyly. 'No, Zelda. Nothing more, just comforting.'

'He's crazy about you, you know.'

'Yes, I'm beginning to realise that.'

'What are you going to do about it?'

Isabel gave her friend a playful cuff. 'Nothing. Certainly

nothing until Penny is safely home with me. But I will be thinking about it – a lot.'

'I'm sure you will, honey. Make sure you think about it carefully and make the right decisions.'

'Oh, do you have any ideas on the subject then?'

Zelda smiled enigmatically. 'Let's just say that I know what I would do.'

As she walked across the landing Isabel could hear the sound of Bill's voice barking orders downstairs so she slipped into their room to find a change of clothes and dressed for another cold day in the forest. She emerged in an outfit that included several layers of sweaters and a pair of trousers tucked into her boots. She left the beaver coat behind as it was so cumbersome the day before. She did, however, put the loaded pistol into her pocket. She walked down the stairs into the hall. Bill turned and surveyed her with a cold gaze.

'I hope you don't think you're coming with us,' he said.

'Of course I'm coming. For the same reasons as I gave you yesterday. I need to be there when we find Penny.'

'No. I forbid it. You'll only be in the way. There may be shooting, I don't want you to be a part of that. You may as well go back to bed.'

Daunted by his contemptuous tone, Isabel stayed silent although a multitude of words sprang into her mind. Fury at his prohibition rose and she had to use all her self-control not to strike out at him and vilify his stupidity and lack of compassion. She held her tongue and stood in the hall and watched as he marched to join the Sergeant and his platoon outside in the snow.

Several of the men bundled into a jeep and set off around the edge of the forest to approach the cottages from the southern edge of the lake. The rest, led by the Sergeant, marched into the forest in an apparently haphazard formation, their armament clinking gently and their boots striking chords on the hard ground and rocks where they protruded through the snow. Once they entered the wood all sound became muffled as they strode over the mossy pine-needle carpet. Bill, in his greatcoat and wearing his officer's cap at a stern angle, strode behind them.

John, hurrying out of the hotel, lingered for a moment beside Isabel.

'He won't let you come, I suppose.'

'No. But I don't think I'm going to take any notice of that. He can't keep me away from Penny.'

'You must do what you think best, darling. After all, you're not under orders, are you? I'll see you later.' He blew her a kiss as he disappeared into the trees behind the rest of the party.

Isabel waited for as long as she could bear and then, stealthily at first, she moved into the woods and followed the others, taking the same route as yesterday. The soldiers had still not established which cabin Dennis was in. There had been no sign of him or of Penny; not a footprint, not a wisp of smoke.

Perhaps we've made a mistake, thought Isabel, and he's not here at all. Perhaps Penny's not here, but somewhere else in the mountains, somewhere even more dangerous. But apparently there had been a report of a man carrying a child from someone in the village. A battered truck that didn't belong to anyone local was parked in a side road. Any unfamiliar vehicles were always noted and reported promptly as the inhabitants were still wary after the war when every strange car or truck could mean a Gestapo raid or unwelcome SS incursion.

Isabel made good progress through the trees. She found that without Bill telling her to hurry every few yards she could cover the now more familiar ground quickly. Pale sunshine sparkled through small gaps in the branches and the scent of the crushed pine needles beneath her feet filled the air. It was not as chill in here as in the open and she soon felt warm and thirsty. She wished she had brought something to drink. She could have used one of the flasks from the car and filled it with coffee. It was too late now. She walked on.

Isabel could hear the platoon in the distance. She must have narrowed the gap between them because they seemed nearer now and every now and then she caught a glimpse of one of the white camouflage suits through the trees. They kept their pace leisurely and measured.

Suddenly everything changed. A shot cracked through the still of the forest. Isabel stopped dead in shock. Someone was firing at the party moving through the trees.

'Shit! What was that?' The Sergeant yelled. 'Hold your fire!'

Another shot answered him. Other armed people stalked the woods.

'Injury here, Sarge.' One of the soldiers called.

Several more shots were fired and cries came from the forest ahead.

John and Bill had stopped moving and stood behind a pair of thick tree trunks. They looked around them, into the dense wood. Several men, dressed in civilian clothes and bent low, were dodging between the pines in the near distance. They carried rifles and handguns. One of them, a bulky man, well over six feet tall, seemed to be leading and urging them on, using an unfamiliar tongue. She moved closer to Bill and John, who were talking in whispers.

'Bugger!' said John. 'It's Lujic.'

'Who?' said Bill.'

'Lujic. Ruthless Serbian bastard. He's the *Grosschieber*, the boss, of the Black market ring I've been dealing with. He must have got wind of the ransom and wants to pinch it for himself.'

'How can that have happened? Have you been talking to someone about this?'

'Of course not, Bill. If I had my guess I'd say it was that devious bastard Fritz Keller. He can't keep his mouth shut and he's greedy as hell, likes to play one side against the other. You can be sure he's making a few bob out of this.'

Isabel crept closer to the men, but they didn't hear her. She stood quietly behind a tree keeping well out of range of where the shots had come. As long as they didn't circle round behind her, she was safe for now.

More shots sounded from nearby, it was impossible to tell whether they came from the guns of the Serbians or the British platoon. John and Bill remained out of range, allowing the soldiers to do their work. The sound of heavy men charging through the undergrowth reached Isabel. She was terrified to look at what was happening, but at the same time afraid to miss anything.

The big Serbian stormed into the clearing below where Bill stood. The man was pursued by two soldiers, shouting and challenging him to stop, but Lujic ploughed on, ignoring their cries and waving his rifle threateningly towards where Bill and John were concealed.

It looked as if Bill could bear inaction no longer and with a mighty leap he sprang from behind the tree with his revolver in his hand. The light from the morning sun outlined him in silhouette in an heroic tableau. He flung himself forward in the manner of a First World War warrior going over the trenches. A flash came from the Serbian's rifle and Bill, still in air-borne motion, twisted and fell to the ground, his face pressed against the forest floor.

'No!' Isabel dashed forward, falling to her knees beside him. She put her hands to his back and they came away covered in hot blood. She opened her mouth to scream and felt John's hands covering her face.

'Ssh, Isabel, not a sound. They'll all come down on us if you do.'

She brushed his hands away and whispered. 'Is he dead? Oh, John, say he's not dead.'

'No, Bella, there's a pulse. We'll get someone to take him to the hotel in a moment. Stay here; press something over the wound. There's something I must do.'

He crept around the thick trees sheltering them and, keeping under cover, slithered down the bank to where the Serbian had taken refuge behind a massive rock.

Silently John circled the man's position and came up behind him.

'Don't move, Lujic,' he growled, 'or you're dead.'

The big man whirled round, his rifle held like a club, and swung out at John. Repeatedly he tried to jab John with it; to batter him with his fists and his feet, but never managed to make contact. Finally John ducked and swivelled and with a huge leap kicked the rifle out of the man's hands. Lujic stood, his chest heaving and sweat pouring from his forehead.

'Not very fit, are you, old chap? Too much good living.'

Lujic snarled, unable to get any words out.

The sergeant and two of his men arrived and took the Serbian into custody. John turned away and joined Isabel where she kneeled on the ground beside Bill, who was beginning to stir. She had attempted to make Bill comfortable and turned him over and put a folded scarf behind his head and pressed a handkerchief to staunch the blood pouring from the wound. She looked up as John approached.

'That was amazing,' she said. 'Thank God they've got him. Where are all the others?'

'Two dead,' said John bluntly, 'and the rest have run off. It's not worth their while hanging around when there's nothing in it for them. Lujic's hardly going to be able to pay them their share from where he's going.'

'We've got to carry on, John. We've still got to find Penny.'

'I know. We'll stay here till someone comes for Bill, then we'll carry on with the platoon down to the lake and see what's happening in those cottages.'

After stretcher bearers had borne Bill off, they started through the forest again. Adrenalin was still coursing through Isabel's veins and she couldn't wait to get to the cottage and get this over with. Several of the soldiers were still with them and soon they were at the edge of the forest.

Isabel stood at the summit of the snow-covered slope looking down on the roofs of the three lakeside cottages. Penny is in one of those, she thought; we'll have her soon.

The soldiers began to slide down the incline in silence. Isabel was reminded of her nephew, Keith, last Christmas, whooping and hollering as he skimmed down the steep icy slope in the park. The paper facsimile of a Sioux war bonnet swayed on his head and a rubber tomahawk shook in his hand, ready to defeat the enemy ahead. These men were a lot quieter of course, not wishing to draw the attention of anyone in the little houses below.

Isabel fingered the Mauser in her jacket. The normally cold steel had warmed in the pocket. Earlier she had loaded the gun, filling the tiny magazine with the bullets. This had proved a fiddly job that could not have been done at speed. She wasn't sure what she was going to do with it, but if she had to she would not hesitate to use it. That bastard Dennis wasn't going to get away with this.

John came up behind her and placed an arm around her shoulders.

'Bill's all right,' he said. 'He took the shot in the shoulder. It'll be bloody painful, but he'll get over it.'

'Where is he?' Isabel looked back into the trees with detached disinterest as if Bill no longer had anything to do with her.

'The stretcher party came from the village. We've got a vehicle there. They'll take him back to Berlin I expect.'

That's fine, Isabel thought. One less thing to worry about. A niggle of guilt stirred at the back of her mind. It was her fault that Bill was injured; she had got him into this. But he didn't have to behave like a bloody hero. How ridiculous, going through five years of war without seeing a shot fired in anger and then getting shot all this time after the war was over.

Now it was time to focus on the activity around the buildings by the lake. The men had quietly circled each one and now the sergeant was yelling.

'Dennis Masters, if you're in there, come out immediately. We have you surrounded.'

He repeated these words several times with no visible results. Meanwhile John and Isabel slithered to the bottom of the slope. Dennis must have heard the shots in the forest, perhaps he has chosen to ignore them. It seemed an eternity before there was any response from the cottages. Eventually the door of the centre of the three buildings opened a couple of inches.

'Don't come any closer, I've got a gun.' Dennis's reedy voice came through the gap followed by a hand holding an old Browning pistol. The door opened further and he pushed Penny ahead of him through the widening gap, waving the weapon close to the child's head.

Isabel's gasped and started forward, but John held her back. Her heart leapt with mingled joy and fear. A rush of adrenalin filled her veins as Dennis stepped onto the veranda. He looked pale and pathetic, waving the old revolver like a Wild West villain, with his hand on Penny's shoulder. Rage filled every inch of her in a surging tide. No-one was going to stop her. She sprang forward like an avenging tigress; all restraint forgotten, all caution abandoned.

'Take your perishin' hands off of my kid, you soddin' bastard,' she screamed, gentility and diction forgotten. ''And her over here now.'

John vainly stretched out a hand to restrain her and watched in horror as she drew the Mauser from her pocket and aimed at Dennis's head. Without a thought, she pulled the trigger. A tiny pop echoed in the stillness. Not one of the soldiers surrounding the cottages moved; stunned into immobility. A sharp crack sounded as the shot hit the wooden lintel of the cabin's door.

Isabel squeezed the trigger again, as Bill had shown her. Once more the shot missed its target. Her third attempt, however, connected with Dennis's head. He swore and staggered back, releasing his grip on Penny.

'Fuck! You stupid bitch – you've shot me.' Copious gouts of blood appeared between his fingers as he swayed and fell heavily onto the veranda.

Penny had barely moved and looked around, bemused by these events. Her eyelids were heavy and she looked disorientated. John leapt forward and gathered her up into his arms and carried her to where Isabel stood.

The soldiers were finally galvanised into action from where they had halted, still as statues and as silent, completely dumbfounded by the unexpected turn of events. Two of them scooped Dennis up from the veranda and dragged him away through the snow with no respect for his injuries. His blood patterned the snow.

Isabel turned towards John, stunned by what she had done. He took the Mauser from her hand as she grabbed Penny from his grasp.

'Oh, darling, darling, are you all right? I was so frightened. He hasn't hurt you, has he?'

'Mummy – I'm very sleepy.' The child gazed at Isabel groggily, her eyes glazing and lids drooping. 'It's so lovely to see you, Mummy.' She promptly fell asleep on Isabel's shoulder.

John pulled them both into his arms and kissed Isabel lingeringly on the mouth. She responded joyfully and clung to him.

'You know that now everything's going to be fine, don't you? I love you, Bella,' he said.

She turned towards him and smiled.

'I know,' she said, knowing that there were many hurdles to surmount, but it would all work out in the end. As they walked away, close together, she knew she could look forward to the future with optimism and hope.

Epilogue

Gibraltar, 1952

I sit on our balcony overlooking the Mediterranean; a sublime sunset is ornamenting the sky with swathes of pink and purple light. The Rock of Gibraltar points majestically towards Africa and I can faintly make out the calls of the Barbary apes quarrelling in the distance. The scent of the honeysuckle reminds me of home. Our son, James is sleeping in the nursery and I can feel the tiny kicks and stirrings of the new baby within me, impatient to be born.

It is only now that I realise how naive I was in those days before the war, thinking that my life with Bill was the pinnacle of happiness. I was dazzled by a style of life that was so far away from what I was accustomed to. With John I now have an utterly different existence. Our life represents a miracle of contentment with love given and received in equal measure.

The aftermath of our adventure in the Hartz Mountains turned out to be relatively painless. I had expected much more trouble; inquisitions and courts. The shot I inflicted on Dennis, to my regret, was only a flesh wound even though it produced a satisfying amount of blood. I had proved to be a terrible shot, a shame really, as at the time I could happily have killed him.

I still have the little box of bullets, with just those three missing. John took the Mauser away and disposed of it – into the Havel, I imagine.

John led Penny and me away from the scene and back to the hotel. The Special Forces people cleaned everything up. I never heard any more about the shooting and worried for weeks afterwards about the possibility of being clapped in irons and carted off to a military prison. I didn't like to ask what had happened at the time, not wishing to draw attention to myself. It wasn't until much later that I found out that the Sergeant claimed that Dennis was shot by a stray bullet from one of his men.

Dennis was patched up and sent home to Cheltenham in disgrace. He raged about the disappearance of Fritz Keller, the black market man. Apparently Dennis raved about his antiques and treasures for ages, but he never found out what happened to them. It was decided, probably by Bill, that a prison sentence for the kidnap was unlikely to help anyone and, as Penny was unharmed, the incident was all swept under the bureaucratic carpet.

I was far too euphoric with having Penny back safely to worry about what had happened to Dennis. John became my rock and guided me through the minefield of explanations that followed our return to Berlin. We visited Bill in the military hospital and I think he realised immediately that things were over between us. His lack of support in his reaction to Penny's abduction had killed off any residual feeling I had for him. I no longer felt he deserved my loyalty. Once he realised our marriage was over he was resigned to the situation; even relieved.

'You must do what you wish. I'm sure Marriott will look after you,' he sneered in those cold tones.

He moved into the Moser and I remained in the apartment with Penny and Prince, and Irma still looking after us, until I was repatriated. Prince had to endure six months in quarantine, but I visited him every week in his prison and he came out unscathed and happy.

We lived with Mum and Dad in Wembley until John was able to join us and I followed him to his next posting in Singapore. Our initial cohabitation caused quite a stir amongst the ex-pat community until we were married, in 1949. Penny made an adorable bridesmaid.

Irma married her Hank and they now live on the outskirts of Chicago, near his parents. She writes to me regularly with snapshots of their wholesomely chubby baby boy. Zelda and Chuck also keep in touch. They are back in their rich life now he is retired from the army with a social whirl that I would find exhausting. I never heard what happened to Anya, I expect she found a new protector and carried on. John never saw her again.

Bill eventually re-married - a pretty, compliant girl who originated from a grand county family. His mother must have been overjoyed, once she got over the shock of the divorce. How happy she must have been to get rid of 'the cockney gal'.

Penny is now at a boarding school in England, a lovely place in the countryside. I miss her terribly, but it is best for her education, we move around so much. At least Bill visits her regularly and takes her out, and she comes to Gib for the holidays. She seemed to suffer no after-effects from her experience with Dennis. Most of it was wiped from her memory by the drugs he gave her to keep her asleep and she regarded it all as an adventure.

'Just like the Pied Piper of Hamlin,' she said. 'And I was rescued by the brave soldiers.'

John's work is still in covert operations, but now he works at the Embassy or High Commission, wherever we are posted, and he wears a suit. As before, I have no idea what he's doing most of the time. But I do know that whatever he is doing his family is his first priority and he will always return to me with abounding love and we will face whatever life brings – together.

Lightning Source UK Ltd.
Milton Keynes UK
UKOW04f1918300813

216259UK00001B/34/P

9 781782 996026